CONTEMPORARY AMERICAN FICTION

LOVING LITTLE EGYPT

Thomas McMahon is Gordon McKay Professor of Applied Mechanics and Professor of Biology at Harvard University, and the author of two previous novels, *Principles of American Nuclear Chemistry: A Novel* and *McKay's Bees*. He lives in Wellesley, Massachusetts, with his wife and two children.

LOVING LITTLE EGYPT

THOMAS McMAHON

PENGUIN BOOKS

PENGUIN BOOKS
Viking Penguin Inc., 40 West 23rd Street,
New York, New York 10010, U.S.A.
Penguin Books Ltd, 27 Wrights Lane, London W8 5TZ
(Publishing & Editorial) and Harmondsworth,
Middlesex, England (Distribution & Warehouse)
Penguin Books Australia Ltd, Ringwood,
Victoria, Australia
Penguin Books Canada Limited, 2801 John Street,
Markham, Ontario, Canada L3R 1B4
Penguin Books (N.Z.) Ltd, 182–190 Wairau Road,
Auckland 10, New Zealand

First published in the United States of America by
Viking Penguin Inc. 1987
Published in Penguin Books 1988

LIBRARY OF CONGRESS CATALOGING IN PUBLICATION DATA
McMahon, Thomas A., 1943–
Loving Little Egypt / Thomas McMahon.
p. cm. — (Contemporary American fiction)
I. Title. II. Series.
[PS3563.C3858L6 1988]
813'.54—dc19 87-18639
ISBN 0 14 00.9331 1 CIP

Printed in the United States of America by
R. R. Donnelley & Sons Company, Harrisonburg, Virginia
Set in Perpetua
Designed by Ann Gold

FOR CAROL

AUTHOR'S NOTE

There was a famous rumor, when I went to college, about horseplay with telephones. It was said that some of us were learning to do fabulous things with funny homemade boxes full of electronics. When it came time to write this novel, I read about the telephone miscreants of my own generation in old newspapers and magazines, and no source was more provocative than Ron Rosenbaum's article in *Esquire* (October 1971) titled "Secrets of the Little Blue Box." This book is about another time, and, of course, it is made up.

Most of the plot contrivances and many of the inventions I have attributed to Bell, Edison, and the others are made up, too. It is never a good idea to believe a made-up story as if it were the truth.

LOVING
LITTLE
EGYPT

———

CHAPTER 1

Finally, of course, Little Egypt made a great reputation for himself, and for a few weeks in the summer of 1922 everyone knew his name. The Hearst newspapers reported where he had been detected in various states—in Massachusetts, in Florida, in Michigan, in California. There was the suspicion, at last confirmed, that he was not one person but a whole network of people, most of them blind, all of them intent on causing the collapse of the telephone system of the United States. Because blind people ordinarily achieve little in the way of criminality, this was thought to be marvelous.

In those days, at the height of the glory, people drove their cars through Bucks Falls on Cape Breton Island and said, "What a funny little place, to be the home of a great saboteur."

Before he was a great saboteur he was a low-vision child, and before he took the name Little Egypt, he was Mourly Vold, the only son of Peter and Ilse.

From the moment of his birth, it had been apparent that there was something wrong with his eyes. He was an alert child, obviously intelligent, but he paid attention to objects only when they were brought within a few inches of his face. His hearing was normal, even particularly acute, but his vision was weak. In a rare display of candor and honesty, the doctors said they could do nothing for him.

By the end of his third year, it was clear that he possessed an intelligence considerably above normal. He could repeat stories and poems his mother had read to him months earlier. He could mimic the sounds of all the animals—chickens, ducks, goats, horses, dogs, cats, and geese. He could do arithmetic in his head. He could calculate the date Easter would fall upon next year, or the year after that, or many years into the future. Most remarkably, he could imitate absolutely faithfully the voices of all the adults who came within his presence.

More than once, his mother was duped by a shouted greeting, which she took to be her husband's announcement of his arrival, only to discover after a search that she was alone in the house with her little son.

"I thought I heard Daddy coming home," she would say to him when she found him, putting her arms around him and picking him up. "But it was only you, wasn't it?"

Ilse Vold loved her son and disliked being suspicious of him, but sometimes she wondered whether his weaksightedness might all be a ruse. Once in a while it crossed her mind that he might be so wicked as to be pretending it all. Frequently she observed him through a keyhole. Once, she even left the house, banging the front door, and stood on an inverted bucket to see him through the window of his room. On that day, he was playing on his bed with wooden toys. One of the toys fell from the bed and lay on the floor out of his reach. His thick eyeglasses covered half of his little face. The lenses exaggerated his eyes the way a fishbowl exaggerates the fish. She watched him reaching for his toy, patting the bedclothes with gentle touches in random directions, and felt a terrible love for him. Something about the way the light fell on his face and shoulders revealed a beauty in him which shocked her deeply.

As she watched him, she thought how strange it was that he was separate from her, when only so recently he had been inside of her. Then, also, he had been blind and yet canny. He had moved, and reached out with his arms and legs, and his intelligence had begun to stir. Now he was an individual on his own, and for some unfair reason, he was unable to see normally. At this moment, that seemed to be no reason to be less proud of him, to love him any less. She wondered what would become of him, but this question had no power to frighten her.

He grew up a solitary child, with few playmates. From Gillis MacGillivary, who was more than eighty years old, he learned to whistle, and he learned to smoke a pipe.

Old Gillis was then too weak in the fingers to get the pipe ready for smoking. The tobacco was Appleman's Twist. It had to be cut in narrow strips, and the strips had to lie across each other in the bowl like the sticks in a bird's nest. Old Gillis could no longer do this for himself, and yet he continued to have a need for tobacco.

"I don't suppose a boy like you uses tobacco."

"Sometimes," Mourly Vold told him.

"As long as you do, you can make yourself useful and get me a smoke."

He was sitting on the floor in Gillis MacGillivary's house, in front of the stove. There were drafts in this house strong enough to blow out a candle. The drafts came in through the cracked panes of glass in the windows, under the doors, and through chinks in the walls. Gillis MacGillivary tolerated the drafts. He spit in a tin pot. He had been a fisherman. He had narrowly missed death by drowning forty-seven times in his life. He had seen his two brothers and his father drowned. He believed in God, but he was not certain this had saved him, since his father and at least one of his brothers had believed in God also.

Mourly Vold took the pipe in his hand. It had a surprising weight, and the end of it was rough from having been bitten. The old man was missing teeth, but the few he had left had done their work. Mourly Vold bent over the pipe and peered into it, holding the bowl only a half-inch from his eye. The ashes from an earlier smoking lurked there, cold and damp. These residues were as bad-smelling and helpless as the old man himself. Following instructions, he scraped out the ash and cleaned the bowl with a penknife.

"Now cut the tobacco up small," Gillis told him. "There's a way to do it. I can't tell you how. I just found it out for myself. If you're going to do it at all, do it right. Otherwise, the smoke is no good."

Mourly Vold cut the pieces into the right size and arranged them in the bowl. He took his time, and he showed Gillis his work at every stage. He tamped the tobacco down with his finger. The only way to tell if it was right was to light the pipe, and so he did. He took the matches and lit the pipe. When it was going well, he passed it to the old man. This is how he learned to smoke when he was nine years old.

It was said afterward that Gillis MacGillivary had taught a little weak-eyed boy to smoke. MacGillivary asked a good question about that: "What does his being weak-eyed have to do with it?"

With few exceptions, Mourly Vold's friends were the old people of the town. In addition to Gillis MacGillivary, he visited Fermin Fraser and old Donald L. MacDonald. One of the conveniences of these old people was that they were stationary. He could be confident that he could find them when he wanted them.

There is an irony in the way tolerance skips a generation. Mourly Vold received little attention from adults of his parents' age. No one knew what he did with his time. His handicap seemed to make him invisible to most of the citizens of the town, just as they were all but invisible to him. He crept about the neighborhood in search of an education, and picked up what he could from old people.

He heard mainly accounts of life on isolated coastal farms. It became clear that there was always the danger, in such places, of evil charms. A family could keep several cows and get little or no milk from them because the cows of a neighbor down the road would be taking the milk. The neighbor family would be getting milk that wasn't their own. Usually the trouble would be that a woman had put a charm on the cows. She could do this in several ways, but one way was to go to each of the nearby farmhouses and borrow something in order to rob the land and its animals of their power. When a charm was suspected, it was not uncommon for the merchant to refuse to accept a woman's butter if she offered him more than her cows had a right to give. The difference was stolen, and it would be as wrong as taking a stolen horse to take stolen milk or butter.

Certain stories he heard Donald L. MacDonald tell raised questions in his mind about the nature of time.

"You were there, weren't you?" Donald L. MacDonald said once. He was talking with Fermin Fraser on a windy afternoon. Mourly Vold sat on the floor between their chairs. "I think you were there. The tree dropped right by his shoulder, and he never looked at it. He never turned, and he never stopped. He just kept walking down the road. Angus MacLeod."

"I remember that," said Fermin Fraser.

"He went on down the road toward Titusville. He should have dropped to his knees, but he acted like he never knew a sign had been given to him. We shouted to him, but he wouldn't look at us. That tree knocked his hat off, and he never picked it up. The clouds came apart and let a little puddle of light down on him. Really, it was just like a little puddle there. Shining, like. And it followed him until he was gone over the hill, into the next county."

"I was there," Fermin Fraser said. "His bald head was glowing."

"We went to his house to tell his wife, and she said, 'He's been here the whole morning.' And she opened the door and showed us. And there he was. This time he turned his face and looked at us."

"That's right," Fermin Fraser said. "That man lived another nineteen years, even though they say that when you see them split like that, they're already dead."

"I'm not going to say he was dead just then and I'm not going to say he was alive," Donald L. MacDonald said. "Nobody knows about these splits in time. You're going to see it happen a little differently, not the way it happened in the past or the way it's going to happen in the future. Now, we saw him walk out from under it, but in the past, years ago, it could have killed him. And we're only seeing it differently. Or it could be something from the future, that's come long before it's supposed to happen."

"I'll tell you something else," Fermin Fraser said. "My aunt Jane Morrison saw a man going around the barn. She told her mother, and her mother, my grandmother, went out to look, but he wasn't there. Later, a man came to town selling blacking for stoves and she married him. The first man was a forerunner. My grandmother says she suspected it then, but didn't say anything."

"That could have been," Donald L. MacDonald said. "The first man could have been coming toward the house to take her, and time could have split."

"It had to," Fermin Fraser said. "She was too young."

"That's what I mean," Donald L. MacDonald said. He was a heavy man. His chair cried out when he shifted his weight. "There was a reason why he couldn't come in then. The second time was a reoccurrence of the first time, except that he did come around the barn and he did come in."

In the year following Mourly Vold's birth, Albert Einstein wrestled with the problem of time. He was then technical expert third-class at the Federal Patent Office in Bern. He ached to become a professor of physics. This seemed unlikely, as he had written only five scientific papers. Two of these concerned his speculations about a universal molecular force. The other three aimed toward a dynamic basis for the laws of thermodynamics. All had fallen short of their lofty targets. Einstein was apparently undaunted by these failures. In the spring of 1905, he wrote a great shower of papers, one of which made garbage out of all classical doctrines of space and time.

The insight had eluded him for a year as he worked alone.

One fine day he had visited his friend M. Besso and begun to talk with him about his problems. He told Besso that he felt certain that the Maxwell-Lorentz equations in electrodynamics were true. If these equations were to hold in a moving frame of reference, then the velocity of light should be invariant. But this invariance of the velocity of light was not possible unless one ignored one of the most fundamental rules of mechanics, the rule of addition of velocities. Besso listened to all this patiently. He served Einstein a cup of tea. Einstein ignored his napkin and blotted his mouth with his fingers. Before long, he stopped talking and went away. The next day he called on Besso and said to him immediately, "Thank you. I've completely solved the problem."

What he had done was to tear up the idea that time is absolutely defined. He let there be as many times as there are reference frames. He required only that the laws of physics take the same form in all such frames, and that the velocity of light should be the same, whether the light is emitted by a moving body or one at rest. In his paper, he remarked in casual language that if a clock is taken on a journey around a closed path and brought back to its starting point, it appears to have lost time relative to clocks fixed at the starting point. In this way, preserving the most balanced judgments ever tendered about the nature of space and time, he explained what had always been a source of great wonder until then—how the past may visit the present.

CHAPTER 2

Mourly Vold's father owned a small steam launch, the *Kitten*. He ran it between Bucks Falls and Sydney, carrying grocer's supplies one way and furniture the other. Sometimes passengers rode with him from Sydney. In foul weather, the people waiting for these passengers climbed up into the bell tower of St. Mary's Church and looked out with spyglasses. They said that sometimes they saw the *Kitten*'s smokestack disappear when she sank into the troughs between the high waves.

When Peter Vold had owned the *Kitten* five years, without asking anyone's advice he dropped the insurance on her, and later people said this was what brought on the disaster. On a day when the snow was falling gently and evenly into the ocean, he left Sydney with a cargo of groceries and hardware for the mercantile store. There was no wind. The visibility was satisfactory, although the snow made the horizon indistinct. In addition to her cargo, the *Kitten* carried three passengers and six sea gulls. The gulls rode on top of the wheelhouse.

He allowed himself to be drawn into a conversation with Mrs. McPhee, a young widow. In Bucks Falls, Mrs. McPhee was considered dangerous because she wore no corset. He had never spoken with Mrs. McPhee before, nor was he likely to again, at least not on land, because of the risk of scandal. That made this trip something of a special opportunity.

Throughout the morning, as he stood in the wheelhouse, he could see Mrs. McPhee from various aspects. For a time, she stood beside a keg of pickles on the forward deck. The snow began to accumulate on her hat. When she turned her head,

Peter Vold could see her fair face contrasted against the water. Her eyes appeared to be the same green color as the water, but this may have been only a trick of reflections.

Peter Vold liked women and regarded himself as generally skillful in matters concerning women. When he was thinking of himself generously, he gave himself credit for being a patient and persistent womanizer. He put himself in the place of women in order to conquer them. He matched a softness in himself against their softness in order to win their friendship, to slide into their confidence. The trick was to have ambition toward them, but not to display it. Imagine his consternation, then, when he discovered that the sight of the snow melting on Mrs. McPhee's bare neck had thrilled his trousers into an odd shape.

Later, out on the ocean, he lashed the wheel and went out on deck to talk to her. Before long, they discovered that they were the same age, namely thirty-one years. Something about this simple fact seemed to let down a barrier between them. They fell into a conversation as pleasant and sincere as either of them had known in their lives. They spoke about their parents and their spouses, and told each other their most secret dreams and fears, and never noticed the peril descending upon them until the *Kitten* struck a rock off Cross Island.

"Now look what you've done!" Mrs. McPhee said in a shrill voice. Somehow this remark seemed unfair, and later Peter Vold had trouble forgiving her for it. The passengers ran back and forth on the little deck, making the stability of the boat more precarious than it would have been otherwise. The gulls found the rolling of their perches on the wheelhouse unsatisfactory and flew away. Trading on luck as much as skill, Peter Vold put the *Kitten* on the beach at Indian Bay. The tide happened to be falling, so that the captain and his passengers merely waited an hour before walking to shore, and never got their feet wet.

The next day, all the supplies for the mercantile store were taken out of her hold, but the *Kitten* herself stayed on the beach for the next two years. In all that time, Peter Vold occupied himself every day with searching for the money to salvage her.

Peter's wife Ilse was a tall woman with handsome legs and light-colored hair. She had blue eyes and white skin, and was widely regarded as a beauty. Her father owned interests in mines from Glace Bay to North Sydney. Here is how she came to marry beneath herself. One morning, shortly after her nineteenth birthday, she happened to be looking out of the window as she was eating breakfast. She was alone; she had long ago made the habit of eating late to avoid confronting her mother and father at the table. The manservant brought tea, a poached egg, a portion of smoked salmon, and a slice of fruit bread. The sun coming through the window fell on the heavy silver and warmed it. The knife and fork were already the temperature of Ilse's hand, but the spoon, in shadow, was still cold. This was one of the first warm mornings in May.

Outside, a ridiculous wagon was passing down the street. Behind the driver's seat, the bed had been removed and a twelve-foot-high lacquered cigar had been substituted. The cigar stood erect between the two rear wheels. Somewhat above the mid-point of its shaft, it was girded by a red-and-white cigar band, ornately painted with the name of the promoted product. The spokes of the wagon wheels were threaded through with lavender bunting, and the horse wore a gold crown. A young man with broad shoulders and a melancholy expression drove the wagon. He wore a straw hat blazing with reflected light. Ilse watched him clip-clop out of sight.

A little while later, he came back. She watched his horse walking, its head and hips swaying with the alternating victories of muscular and gravitational force which also control the swoops of a child in a swing. Giving no one any reason, least of all herself, she jumped up from the table, taking a number of sugar cubes, and went out to meet this young man who was making himself ridiculous and not even smiling about it. The giant cigar lurched as he reined his horse. Even when the wagon was stationary, the cigar continued to wag back and forth, because its weight and length were almost an equal match for its strength.

Ilse gave the sugar to the horse, and later she gave herself to the man as his wife, with absolute certainty that she could cheer him up. Her parents protested vehemently, and this added to her thrill. Despite many unsatisfactory performances on the part of her husband in the first year of their marriage, she continued to look for his good side, reasoning that any man her mother opposed so strongly couldn't be all bad.

She was surprised to discover that men and women like to make love in different ways, so that the act is never better than a compromise for either of them. At the beginning, they lived in rooms over a sweetshop. Peter Vold would leave before dawn each morning, to drive his cigar wagon to neighboring villages, where he visited shops and took orders for tobacco. By the time he returned for his noon meal, his blood had thickened. From the parlor, he would watch his young wife preparing lunch in the kitchen, and the sight of her shape—her long legs and her handsome breasts—would stimulate an ancient, reptilian center in his brain. In broad daylight, with the sun flowing through the kitchen windows, he would drop his trousers and present his compliments.

And for Ilse, of course, the timing was utterly wrong. She did not see it as convenient to be taking off her clothes in the kitchen in the middle of preparing food. Why did it all have to be so urgent? Before her marriage, she had assumed that men enjoyed the same fantasies that women did. An hour of intimate conversation in subtle light, followed by an hour of caresses, and then, step by step, an ascent, like the climbing of a staircase. This was what she imagined her husband would want, too, but instead he chose to push her against the kitchen sink, among the broken eggshells and fish heads, to copulate standing up.

When Peter bought the *Kitten*, they went to live in Bucks

Falls. They rented a pretty little house near the tombstone-cutting works. Here, horse feces left behind the heavy wagons blew in the street in dry weather. The same material became a slippery paste in the wet. All around her were the superstitious country people who had come to work in the tombstone factory. They were friendly and good-natured, but they believed in spells applied to animals and would wash their cow's head with money in the tub if they felt someone had put the evil eye on her.

When Ilse became pregnant, she was amazed to find how much trouble it was. She had been led to believe that morning sickness would be nothing more than a faint alteration of appetite, but instead it left her rolling and weeping on the bed most of the day. Her husband could not be persuaded to understand the sensitivity of her breasts. He accused her of acting cold toward him, and she found it convenient to let the accusation stand.

"Men are mostly only good for the one thing," said Mary MacDonald, her neighbor. "After they've done it, they only take up room in the house." But, although Mary MacDonald said this, Ilse noticed that she behaved more sentimentally toward her husband than these words would imply. For example, when she repainted the walls of her bedroom, she painted around the place where her husband's head customarily touched the wall, preserving his faint spot as a remembrance of him in case he should die.

As matters would have it, it was not Mary MacDonald's husband, but Ilse's, who died.

Peter Vold was driving a Ford truck above the town on the Pottsville Road. He was delivering coal to the houses on his route. On a turning overlooking Indian Bay, he stopped the truck by the side of the road and stepped out. Behind him, the forested hills climbed up toward Mount Baldy, ten miles distant. Below, the slopes of pine trees ended on the gravel of the bay. From where he stood, he could see the *Kitten* half submerged in the shallow water. Only her wheelhouse, her smokestack, and part of her stern showed above the water. The tide was high, and just turning. The sea was calm. It was winter.

A month before, he had hired Homer Johnson to help him salvage his boat. They had run both of Johnson's three-inch steam pumps, and never pumped her out. Johnson's winch never moved her. The sea worms had taken her bottom away. At last he had to admit that she was finished.

Now he was driving a coal truck up and down the hills, but wherever he had a view of the ocean, on any of the hundred or so overlooks on his route, he would stop and examine the remains of his boat from a new angle.

The seat springs of the truck had broken through the upholstery, exposing a wicked bar which Henry Ford had meant to keep covered with horsehair, but which was now bare. Shortly after Peter Vold resumed his route, the truck struck an outcropping of rock in the road, sending him flying up into the air. When he came down, the edge of the naked seat bar jabbed into his tailbone.

It was as if a hot straw had been introduced into his large intestine. He stopped the truck and lay in a patch of frozen ferns until he caught his breath. Above him, the air was clear and hawks were turning. He noticed that the feathers at the ends of their wings were curled up. Some of them came low enough to let him hear the aerodynamic noise of their flight. The sound was like the wind blowing past a taut clothesline. One of the hawks came low and dared to make eye contact. He threw a stone at it to send it off.

Two weeks later, when the bump on his tailbone turned to cancer, he went to Dr. Ingraham. No one was sure whether Dr. Ingraham was a real doctor, and there seemed to be no way of finding out. Even so, there was no choice, because Dr. Ingraham was the only medical man in that part of the province who would treat a cancer.

Dr. Ingraham operated his practice from his house, a large stone building near the center of the town. He was a big man, with wide shoulders and strong arms. He wore his white hair cropped short. On his nose sat a pair of stylish rimless spectacles. In his waiting room there was a parrot in a bamboo cage.

Dr. Ingraham located the cancer by listening with his stethoscope. He explained that cancers beat in synchrony with the heart. He drew an illustration on his blackboard, showing how a cancer has roots, in this case roots extending into the shoulders and the back teeth. He cautioned against making abrupt movements which could break one of the roots. A broken root would allow the cancer to go straight to the lungs. He made a particular point of forbidding sex.

The doctor brought out a poison poultice of oatcakes and sheep's urine. He told Peter Vold that the cancer would be drawn out if the poison poultice were used conscientiously. He showed him a cancer pickled in a jar of alcohol. With its filamentous roots, it looked like a sea creature. Dr. Ingraham made him strictly promise to examine the poultice for anything which looked like that, and so he did, but nothing ever appeared. Within five months, Ilse Vold was a widow.

CHAPTER 3

By the time he was seventeen, Mourly Vold had reached his full height, which was just above six feet. He was very thin, and somehow this made his posture bad. He continued to wear thick spectacles, but now, when he needed it, he attached a short tube to one of the lenses. Within the tube was an auxiliary lens. He had fashioned this arrangement for himself using the parts from a pair of opera glasses. Through the use of this double-lens system, he could read a book.

His double-lens system gave him the appearance of a jeweler, or a watchmaker. To see him, you would have the impression that he had ruined his vision in a lifetime of watch repairing.

These were the first few months following the Eighteenth Amendment and the Volstead Act, when Demon Rum was finally dead. In the United States, you were not supposed to sell anything with more alcohol in it than a half of a percent, and people said that this made even sauerkraut illegal. In New York, a heavy little man named Isadore Einstein knocked on the door of a speakeasy. He said he wanted a drink. The proprietor asked him who he was. "I'm a Prohibition agent," he said. "I just got hired." This was judged to be so charming that he was admitted and sold a drink, and immediately he issued the proprietor a summons. In the next five months he issued 137 summonses at ninety-seven establishments, following essentially the same procedure each time.

All over North America and off the coasts, rum running depended on large and powerful internal combustion engines. The mother ships, the schooners, would lie off the coast outside the territorial limit where the revenue boats couldn't interfere with them. The schooners would be loaded with Demerara rum. At night, or in bad weather, the small boats would come out, and with their big engines they would send up rooster tails and leave the revenue boats behind. Most of this work was done by honest fishermen. They risked their necks and took their livelihoods from the mother boats the way their grandfathers had risked their necks and taken their livelihoods from whales.

There was rum everywhere—in Glace Bay, in Sydney, in Mabou, and even in Bucks Falls. It seemed that everyone had a part to play in the rum trade. Boys no older than Mourly Vold went with their fathers and uncles to meet the dories. It was said that the dories rowed up Salmon Brook to a place above Bracken's Point, and that the kegs were carried from there farther up the brook to a cache in the woods. They wore boots and walked in the water to keep from leaving tracks. In the winter, they went in there with a snow tractor somebody had made from a Model T Ford. Its rear wheels drove a set of improvised tractor treads and its front wheels had been replaced by skis.

In New York, the bootleggers were young men of Mediterranean ancestry, but on Cape Breton Island everyone was involved, even cripples and mine widows. The RCMP found cases of rum under coal stoves, in sheep-dips, and in flour barrels. In Malcom MacLeod's house, the rum was kept in the clothes boiler. Even the housebound were bootleggers, and for many of them, liquor funny business was the only way they had to earn a little money.

There were still milling frolics as in the old days. As many as twenty people would come into a house to do the work and take part in the singing. They would sit down at the milling board and take up the homespun soaked in warm water and oatmeal, and they would pound it on the board to the tune of the song and pass it on to the next person. When it was time to eat, they would be served their baked beans, oatcakes, and tea right on the milling board. Then they would go back to it again, singing and pounding once more. But who could look at this scene of tradition and community without remembering that John Alex MacAskill, who could hear a song of twenty verses and then sing it back to you perfectly, also owned a four-hundred-horsepower speedboat? Who could forget that Thomas Shaw, sitting fourth from the end of the table, burned up a hundred gallons of gasoline a week in the engine of his big Packard? That was a car that didn't have any seats at all. Even the driver's seat had been removed to make room for the cases of whiskey.

The beginning of Prohibition occurred during Mourly Vold's years at the School for the Blind in North Sydney. His mother had been forced to place him here after the teacher in the little Bucks Falls school refused to have him in her class any longer. His sight was too limited, she said, to allow him to progress successfully with her. It was decided, when he was twelve years old, that he must go to a special school where he could be in the care of teachers trained to teach the feeble-sighted.

In that year, Mourly Vold and his mother rode the steam ferry *Anne Braddock* to Sydney. This was a vessel not much larger than the *Kitten* had been, and the sights and mood about the boat, the chipped paint on the wheelhouse, the gull droppings on the decks, the smell of fish and sheep at the stern and vomit at the bow, reminded Ilse of her husband's dear old boat. He had come from farm people, not sea people—the perfect evidence of that was his ability to swim, and his enjoyment of swimming in the ocean. No fisherman of the time could swim. Her husband had never been accepted among the seafarers. He had not wanted to be accepted. He had been a private man, and the boat had been his private place.

Ilse and her son were charity passengers aboard the *Anne Braddock*. Dan Alan MacDougal was the captain. He would not take Ilse's money, nor would he take the money of any other poor widow. But she was not his guest; she was a charity passenger, and somehow he made this clear to her without saying it.

They took the train to North Sydney and walked the remaining mile, past the steel plant. The smell of coal burning was in the wind. The streets were flowing with a black mud. The gulls turning above the smokestacks flew on blackened wings.

When Ilse saw the School for the Blind, she turned around and led her son away. "This is not the place for us," she said. But her eyes filled with tears, because of the shock of the ugliness of the place, and because she did not know what to do next.

They walked to a restaurant, where Ilse ordered fish cakes and tea for both of them. She went to the ladies' room and wept for twenty minutes before washing her face and returning to the table.

"Darling," she said. "I'm taking you home. I'll teach you myself."

As soon as she said this, she burst out in tears again, because she realized it was impossible. If she knew how to teach him, then why hadn't she taught him before now? She had tried and failed hundreds of times to help him with his lessons. It had never worked. He was not a stupid child—no, in fact, he was quite the opposite. What he wanted to learn, he seemed to be able to discover by himself, effortlessly. But he was not a good student; he was not even a marginal student—and why? Certainly, his sight was poor, and this was part of the explanation. What else was involved, Ilse could not be sure. She could be certain of only two things. One was that this was the only school for two hundred miles where the staff was prepared to accept her son's handicap. The other was that if she brought him home, the prospects for his future looked very bad indeed.

She thought of her son grown into a man, and knowing nothing, and holding a beggar's cup.

They returned to the school, and Ilse met the headmaster, who treated her courteously. She and her son accompanied the headmaster on a tour of the classrooms and dormitories. She saw the little blind boys and girls clinging together as they walked in the corridors. Their voices were as bright as the peal of bells. Of course, she said to herself, of course. The ugliness of the steel mill and the dirty town may be outside, but they never see it, even if they should happen to look through a window right at it. Inside these walls, they have each other, and that is what we all need, more than anything, the touch of people like ourselves, the company of our own kind.

When it was time to leave, she embraced her son and left face powder in his hair. "I don't believe it," she said. "It doesn't seem fair. When you were first born, I thought I'd have your company forever. Never mind. I'm talking too much. It's time for me to leave. Let me hear from you when you think of it. Don't wear underwear with holes in it. Don't let people spell your name wrong. Remember Daddy in your prayers."

And with this, she kissed him and left him there.

The School for the Blind occupied a set of brick buildings which had once been used as a madhouse. Its windows were covered with iron grilles. In the spring, when the sashes of these windows were opened, the blind children could hear distant foghorns. Blind children are often insomniacs, because they have lost the regulation of the light as well as its comfort. Throughout the night, children would wake up and speak, asking the time, asking whether it was morning. Some of them were afraid of the dark, even though they could not see it.

Mourly Vold made his reputation by answering the teachers back in their own voices. For this he earned stern reprimands. Finally, many of them were frightened to ask him a question or speak to him at all. He could answer them in a voice so accurately theirs that it might have come from their own thoughts. More than once, he was disciplined for this. He would not learn that stealing a person's voice is an unnatural crime. The more perfect the mimicry, the more threatening it is. He would not understand that taking a person's speech, his exact tones and modulations, is worse than breaking into his house and taking his money.

The lashings were a small price for the fame. There was not a student in the school, male or female, who didn't know about Mourly Vold's exploits. It was said that he had discovered the keys to the master's spirits cabinet by jumping down from a table and listening for the clink of the keys as they rattled together in their hiding place under a rug. It was said that he had eaten a caterpillar at the Class Day picnic, placing it on his plate and using a fork to cut it up. Finally, it was said that he had stolen a telephone.

This last was not true. He had only stolen parts from a telephone, and made the rest of it himself. He had wound the induction coil using a pencil for a mandrel. He had adapted a magneto from the ignition set of a Ford car. The hookswitch was made from a hairpin. Only the transmitter and receiver were parts from an actual telephone.

He mounted all the parts on a wooden cigar box. One night, he climbed the telephone pole in the schoolyard, carrying with him an armload of iron wire. At the top of the pole, he discovered himself helpless. The moon vanished behind a cloud, and with so little light he could see next to nothing. He found the wires by listening for them—the wind made them reveal themselves. They struggled when he touched them. Terrible forces pulled on them. It was as if every human being in the world were on the other end of the wires, pulling them out of his hands. The wind sent mechanical shocks flying up and down their length. Then the sky cleared for a moment, and with the moonlight so strong he could see well enough to complete his splices.

At the conclusion of his work, he descended to the ground and sat under the pole for several hours before he felt strong enough to stand up. At his back, the pole vibrated. It was like a stick poking into a fast stream. Although his palms were flat on the ground, he still felt the tension of the high wires in his hands. It was a feeling he would never forget.

When the rogue telephone was finished, Mourly Vold tested it. At this time, he still knew very little about the telephone networks. What he knew about telephone instruments he had learned by taking apart the instrument in the master's office and reassembling it. When his own instrument refused to work the first time he tried it, he removed the magneto coils and placed them closer to the rotor. It still wouldn't work. He suspected that his hairpin hookswitch might be making a poor connection. He scraped it clean with his pocket knife. Still nothing. He paid another secret visit to the master's office, and this time checked every part of his homemade telephone against the original. He could find nothing out of place in his own instrument. As he was returning the master's telephone to its case, he noticed a wire leading from the induction coil. He took it between his fingers and followed it down the wall, across the room to its termination on a cold-water pipe. What could be the purpose of this wire?

The following day, he connected a similar wire to his own telephone. When he turned the magneto crank, an operator answered.

"I don't want to call anyone just now," he said to her. "I just want to ask a question. I want to know why there has to be a wire connecting the telephone to a water pipe."

There was a long silence from the other end. Finally the operator said, "Where are you calling from? What's your number?"

"I don't see what that has to do with anything," Mourly Vold told her.

"I have to know your number if I'm to report something wrong with your telephone."

"There's nothing wrong with my telephone," he said. "It's just a question. I only asked you a question."

More silence. "Who is this speaking?" she asked.

Mourly Vold broke the connection. He saw in a moment that he must never reveal himself like that again. In the future he must make his own discoveries in his own way. He must take up a new identity inside the telephone and never again appear in his own voice. He must conceal his origins, and work invisibly.

Another of the elements of Mourly Vold's fame within the school was his truancy. According to the legend, he formed the habit of letting himself out of the school's grounds not less than once a week to creep into North Sydney and mingle with the normally-sighted. He did this to avoid certain classes he considered disagreeable, and to expand his knowledge of the world.

The place he investigated most often was the Bickledome, an amusement arcade on Welliver Street, near the coal company yards. This establishment featured cheap pies, unusual French magazines, and a wall lined with Edison Kinetoscopes.

Although moving-picture theaters were now well established and one could see Pearl White tied to the railroad tracks, or asleep in a boat drifting toward the falls, or crying for help from the window of a burning building, there was still a clientele for the Edison Kinetoscope, with its opportunity for private viewing of more specialized materials. The kinetoscopes at the Bickledome offered, for a five-cent fee, brief views of a cockfight, a Mexican knife duel, a lynching, and a scalping. There was also a strip called *Heap Fun Laundry* and another called *Fred Ott's Sneeze*.

The kinetoscope instruments were contained in rosewood cases which sat on the floor. They were as tall as a man's chest. Mourly Vold found that by clipping his homemade double-lens system to his spectacles and pushing it down into the eyepiece of the kinetoscope, a queer and happy optical accident allowed him to see the scene. The image flickering in front of his eye appeared to him clearer than anything he had ever seen in real life, since it happened to be confined to that narrow arc of his vision free from pathology. It was peculiar and delightful to be able to see a whole building and several people at once, with none of them distorted or eclipsed by areas of white or gray, as normally occurred in his view outside the kinetoscope. After making this discovery, he watched the antics of the cops and the Chinamen around the Heap Fun Laundry dozens of times. The cockfight, the knife fight, and the lynching were far less interesting to him, although they were popular with the other patrons of the establishment.

One of the machines was perpetually out of order when Mourly Vold visited the Bickledome. Finally, on his fifth visit, he was surprised to find that it had been repaired and returned to service. On depositing his coin, he was greeted with the view of a girl not many years older than himself. She was dressed in a low-cut halter, sheer pantaloons, and veils. Her midriff was bare. She wore jewels and coins in her hair. As the light behind her flickered, she did a snake dance. With her feet fixed to the floor, she moved her abdomen in sly heaves, all the while pulling her veils through the air. In the strange light of this miniature world, the veils looked like translucent flying creatures. At other times, when she moved her arms up or down, the veils trailed behind and took on the appearance of membranous wings.

The title on the machine said that the dancer's name was Little Egypt.

No information survives that could allow us to know today just which Little Egypt Mourly Vold saw in the Bickledome. It could have been Catherine Devine or Joyce Jessel or Mavis O'Conner, since all these lovely ladies made hootchy-kootch peep shows for Edison in his West Orange studio at one time or another. How Edison and kootch dancing came together is a story worth a brief note. Edison had been offered a fat contract to put kinetoscopes in the World's Columbian Exposition at Chicago in 1893. Owing to his distraction with other projects, only a single machine ever appeared at the fair, and that one showed *Fred Ott's Sneeze* to but a few people before breaking down permanently. On his own to see the sights, Edison wandered into the Midway Plaisance, where he observed a performance of Little Egypt and Her Dancers, a troupe of heavy Syrians brought to America by the promoter Abe Fish particularly for the fair. These ladies were *awalem* dancers, specialists who performed at Syrian weddings for the serious purpose of instructing newlyweds in sexual peacefulness. What had been educational in Syria was celebrated as lewd in Chicago. Edison was impressed by the huge crowds at the Plaisance. He wrote a note to his kinetoscope associate Charles Burns: "Let the Sneeze go soak & get us Little Egipt [*sic*] or better a White Woman for Same." The rest is history, and by the time Mourly Vold witnessed this performance in the Bickledome, over ten million men had seen the same or similar dances through peepshow machines all over the world.

During his years at the school, Mourly Vold shared his room with a young man named William Humberhill, blind since birth. Humberhill was soft, wide, very talkative and sweet-tempered. For a reason he never explained, he was fond of the work of the cartoonist C. Briggs. He kept a large envelope stuffed with the newspaper cartoons of C. Briggs and often asked Mourly Vold to read them to him.

"Do the one about Buck Engledorf," he was always saying.

Mourly Vold would then describe the picture. He would begin with the boys and girls seated in a circle, obviously at a birthday party. "They are playing Post Office. There is a boy with his hands folded on his knee and a girl with light-colored hair. Next to them are two boys smirking and grinning, and one of them is saying to the other, 'Oh-ho, Buck gonta kiss the gir-hirls!' Next to them are three girls with a picture book open in their laps, ignoring what is going on. Then there's a boy saying, 'Oh, Buck! Give her one fer me—' "

"Hurry up and get to the good part," Humberhill would say.

"Over on the right side of the room a door is open. In the doorway a tall girl is standing. She's wearing a white dress with dots on it. There's a dark sash tied around her waist. Her left hand is resting on the doorknob. I can just see a tiny bit of her undergarment below the hem of her dress. A big boy with protruding front teeth is walking toward the door. He has freckles on his cheeks and a cowlick on the back of his head. The girl is smiling. She's saying, 'A letter for Buck Engledorf.'"

When Mourly Vold was finished, there was a silence for a few moments. Humberhill lay back on his bed. He had a rounded, pink face which was otherwise handsome except for a few adolescent blemishes. "Oh, God," he said. "Tell me more about the girl. Can you really see her pants?"

"As I said, just a little bit. There's only a little white showing under her dress. Nothing very exciting."

"Maybe not to you," Humberhill said. "You look at that stuff all day long. I don't even know what you're doing in here if you can see that well."

"I can only see things close up," Mourly Vold told him. "And even then, only in a little window right in front of me. Everything else has blurs and stains over it."

"Still," Humberhill said, "you can see that picture, can't you? Tell me more about her."

"She has one bow on the top of her head and another two bows behind, at the back. Around her neck she has a little locket or something on a chain. She's fairly skinny—and I'd say she's at least as tall as Buck Engledorf, maybe a little taller. The sleeves of her dress have puffs."

"Is she pretty?"

"I don't know," Mourly Vold told him. "She's just an ordinary girl. Maybe she's pretty. She's smiling, and that makes her look better than she would otherwise. But it's only a cartoon, after all. I don't think the man who drew her was trying to make her look beautiful."

Humberhill rolled onto his side. "You tell it differently from my mother and sisters," he said. "It's the same picture, but you make everything sound different."

He turned his head toward the wall. "Sometimes when this happens to me, I feel like biting somebody," he said. "How can two people look at the same picture and tell me different stories about it? My mother says that seeing is like hearing with your eyes, but it can't be like that, because when I hear things I understand them perfectly. If I could see for just one minute, I'd want to see that picture, because none of you are telling me what's really there."

CHAPTER 4

No one doubted any longer that things were changing, but the changes were not clearly toward the social and moral improvement which had been predicted. The soldiers and sailors had been home from Europe almost three years now, and still the only literature that interested them was a pseudo-military girlie magazine called *Captain Billy's Whiz Bang*. In White Plains, a physician witnessed a performance of a new dance called the shimmy. He remarked to his companion that a presentation like that, if it had taken place in a medical office, would have earned the young woman a week in a straitjacket.

Most remarkably of all, the mother ships waiting outside New York harbor had turned on their lights.

It was a sight no one who saw it will ever forget. From Long Beach, from Jones Beach, from West Gilgo Beach one could look out and see them, their lights making a luminous line on the horizon, like the glow of a city. Passengers aboard the *France*, bound for Southampton and Le Havre, steaming along the south shore of Long Island saw them plainly, schooners and steamships mainly of British and French registry. They were floating warehouses, and the lights were on to advertise their location and attract customers. The launches coming out at night were painted gray, and nothing lighted them but the glowing gases from their exhaust stacks as they planed over the water toward the territorial limit.

The nation drank its bootleg rum with Coca-Cola. In Atlanta, the secret formula for the vital ingredient of Coca-Cola was still mixed by hand, following exactly the procedures established by the inventor, Dr. Pemberton. The laboratory where this was done was entered through an iron door with a combination lock. Only two people knew the combination; only they were allowed into the room. When packets containing the secret seed kernels, oils, coca leaves, and cola nuts arrived in Atlanta, these two men brought them into the laboratory immediately and locked the door. The room was lined with steel and had no windows. The first thing they did was to remove and destroy all labels and scratch off all identifying marks from the bottles and cans. Thereafter, the only identification of an ingredient was its position on the shelf. Taking up the identical graduates and scales used by the inventor thirty-five years earlier, the two men measured and mixed the various oils and leaves. The formula was not allowed to be written down. All the knowledge was in the possession of these two. Their identities were kept secret, even from each other, to protect both the formula and their lives.

Such secrecy! Such integrity! The result was a product so pure that it was possible to confuse it with an ideal, and many people did. The bottles, with their shapes like maidens, had followed the doughboys to the front. In the slough of the trenches, amid the poison gas, the blood, and the carrion-eating rats, they were comforted by the belief that they were fighting for the dear, good things, including Coke.

After the war, even so pure and pleasant a thing as Coca-Cola was used in a fraudulent way by an increasingly reckless society. It was mixed with bathtub gin to make gin rickeys. It was mixed with rum and consumed by flappers from their boyfriends' flasks. There were even uses found for Coca-Cola which did not involve drinking it. Motorists discovered that Coca-Cola would loosen rusty lug nuts on automobile wheels. Young women used it as a spermicidal douche. For these reasons and others, people considered it wise to carry Coca-Cola in automobiles, and it became widely available at gasoline stations.

Barely a month after he first used his rogue telephone,

Mourly Vold established contact with students at the Perkins Institution for the Blind near Boston and the Rockingham Industrial School in Toronto. A network of illegal telephones was beginning to spring up under his guidance. He and his associates in fraud exchanged homebuilt telephone parts by mail. The instructions were printed in Braille. Inside the telephone circuits, they lived under pseudonyms; he now called himself Little Egypt. In his imagination, he whirled like a bright dervish through the wires, invisible in his many voices. He saw himself as master of a confined world. Like the Little Egypt of the kinetoscope, he lived in a piece of machinery, and he lived there brilliantly.

He had discovered how to use his telephone as a scientific instrument, a sharp-tipped probe to investigate the organization of the telephone networks. Once he had directed himself out of the local exchange, he could send himself wherever he wanted to go by speaking to the operators in their own language.

He made contact with the traffic service engineers, the route managers, the local office technicians. Sometimes he appeared in disguise, representing himself as a lineman or a local office electrician in need of information. He found the technical people of the telephone system willing to talk with him, whoever he was. They answered his questions and explained things to him. Nothing was kept secret. They gave him codes and signaling addresses. They explained the operation of Strowager switches, and demonstrated how battery-ground pulsing could be used to select a path through a trunk without the intervention of an operator. They showed him the difference between high-low and wet-dry signaling methods, and explained how each was used.

With the benefit of these tutorials, the organization of the telephone system grew clearer in his mind's eye. They had constructed it with an open path, a paved highway even, for an invader. He saw himself standing on this highway with nothing in his way. He could race up and down as much as he liked, and he could bring his friends in to enjoy the freedom, too.

Why had they taken so few precautions against him? They had presumed that no one would ever be interested.

He knew at every moment what was going on in a line, how every click and pop changed its status. He knew when he was in a local office, a toll center, a primary center, a regional center. He ran up the networks the way a squirrel runs through the branches of a tree. He jumped from one crazy place to another, and never stayed long enough for his weight to be detected.

In the evenings, he sometimes called the party line. This was a number in a maintenance utility trunk he had discovered months earlier; now it had a certain fame. He had uncovered an echo within a set of relays which made it possible for everyone who called this line to hear everyone else. On a typical evening, he found them reading a book.

"Shut up!" a soprano voice said. "I came to a good part. Everybody shut up and listen to this!"

"Watch out who you tell to shut up," another voice said.

"Squire Dickey unbuttoned her blouse. By the light of the fire, he saw that her nipples were standing up."

"I'm standing up, myself," a voice said. "If you know what I mean."

"Shut up!" three or four other voices said.

"He caressed her stomach in a broad circular motion. 'Don't you remember?' he said. 'I used to do this for you when you were a wee girl, when you had an ache.' 'I have an ache now,' she said."

A chorus of cries and groans.

"Oh, God," a voice said. "I wish some bitch would say that to me. I'd take care of her."

"That's pretty big talk," another voice said, "for somebody whose best friend is his own hand."

Somewhere in the background, a voice asked if Little Egypt were present. When it was known that he was on the line, the usual noise was supposed to cease.

"Can't you bastards shut up for one minute?" said an outraged voice. "Somebody wants to talk to Little Egypt."

"He isn't even here."

"Yes he is. I heard him pulse up to us a minute ago."

"That doesn't mean he's still here."

A Gramophone playing in the background was turned off. Gradually the line fell silent. The clicks and hums of the circuits were the only sounds.

"Why don't you ask him if he's here?" someone said.

"Are you here?"

For a moment he remained silent. He could stay invisible as long as he wished, or he could show himself. Sometimes he revealed himself only partially, in a series of vocal noises, including railroad whistles, cornet riffs, and organ tones. These could be substitutes for speech, if he wanted them to be—he gave them mostly as reprimands. This evening he chose to appear in his own voice.

"What can I do for you?" he asked.

"I crashed coming out of the director system in a central office," someone said to him.

"Where in the director?"

"I think I was in the register-sender."

"You think. I can't do anything for you if you think you were somewhere. You have to know where you were."

"I was in the register-sender. I heard the reeds taking the pulses."

"Did it take all the digits?"

"It stopped halfway through. On the last one, I heard three reeds go down."

"That's your problem," Little Egypt said. "Only two of those reeds are supposed to be down at a time. Take it slower when you're pulsing, especially when you think it might be old equipment. Just work the hookswitch with your finger and listen to what you're doing in the receiver. I told you that before."

"I didn't want to know, before," the voice said.

For this insolence, Little Egypt let him have a barrage of animal sounds, mostly donkeys and geese, at a punishing level of sound power. Then a railroad bell, then a church bell, then a small explosion. "Please stay on for overtime charges," said an operator's voice. Then a delay. "That will be one dollar and eighty-five cents." Then the sound of coins being deposited: six quarters, three dimes, and a nickel. Then an outrageous farting noise, followed by a diminuendo of rattles and clicks, and Little Egypt disappeared from the line.

CHAPTER 5

These were the months of passionate discovery! He learned what he needed to know to enter the networks at odd places, close the doors behind him, and tunnel recklessly here and there. This was wonderful! He moved at blazing speed, and covered his tracks as he went. Sometimes he deliberately went into a number 1 crossbar office, slipped into the line-link frame, and pulsed at the message timer until it noticed him. Then he caused it to run backward, or forward, or any direction he chose, merely by sending it tip pulses of the correct polarity. How delightful, to be so small, and quick, and intelligent! How fantastic, to have the entire telephone company by the gonads, on the basis of a few clear-minded discoveries!

In teaching his disciples telephone chicanery, Little Egypt taught them to put aside their sightlessness and replace it with a special kind of vision, a power to travel without effort or danger. For some of them, particularly the ones with other handicaps, this was nothing less than coming to life. They had discovered in the telephone a society of equals. They spent every waking moment on the telephone, relaying messages and other traffic, getting together on the party line, and teaching, always teaching. A new person would always know of someone else, someone whose life might be changed if he were only given the opportunity. This was how the knowledge propagated, through the evangelism of friends.

He stressed the fundamentals. They had to learn, first and foremost, how to make their voices sound like the voices of operators and switchmen. They had to know the operator's job;

they had to keep an image of her panel station in their minds. They had to know what to ask her to do, and how to convince her to do it. And once she had let them in, once she had made the patches that exposed the long-lines switching relays, he taught them how to send the tip and ring pulses that would let them jump about on their own.

Part of this teaching involved letting them listen, for days, if necessary, to the voices of the central office operators and route managers at their work. Then he made them practice talking like that. The voice had to have a quality that was bored, authoritative, and impatient. It had to have a perfect command of telephone jargon. It had to be bitchy, but never shrewish. Until a new voice knew what it was doing, he never let it loose on the networks.

Furthermore, Little Egypt had improved his equipment. He had substituted a telegraph key for the hookswitch in the instrument, and this enabled him to increase both the speed and accuracy of his outpulsing. He had discovered a way to install a muting switch, and had proven that this device would prevent the central office timing equipment from knowing that an incoming call had been answered. Finally and most significantly, he was working on a method for making connections to telephone wires without having to climb a pole.

This method depended on two physical principles, the principle of electromagnetic induction and the principle of the bullwhip. In his imagination, he saw himself standing under a telephone wire. Fastened at his belt was a monstrous coiled bullwhip of the type used by western film heroes for removing guns from the hands of their adversaries. He would take this bullwhip from his side and crack it over his head, sending the vicious tendril straight up, where it would wrap itself many times about the wire. Inside the bullwhip would be a braided copper wire which would detect pulsations of current in the telephone wire by electromagnetic induction.

And what a marvelous improvement this would be! The

rogue telephone and its operator would then be mobile, and would no longer have to depend on a permanent connection. One could walk under a pole, crack the whip, and be operating in the circuits within seconds. The coils of the whip would squeeze the line and choke the intelligence out of it. Later, a tug of the whip would bring it down, leaving no more evidence of the intrusion than a faint bruise around the wire. If this could be made to work, it would guarantee that telephone experimenters would never be caught with their equipment connected to the lines. This was certainly a worthy objective.

Furthermore, there was every reason to expect that it would work. Little Egypt had read James E. Parsons's *Experiments in Electricity a Boy Can Do*. In this book, Parsons laid bare all sorts of potentially dangerous information. He explained how a compass needle can be driven out of its mind by a simple dry-cell battery and a few loops of wire. He gave an account of how a blob of mercury continues to beat rhythmically, like a vertebrate heart, when allowed to touch a nail while bathed in a suitable salt solution. But the experiment which drew Little Egypt's attention most keenly, the one he saw as propitious, concerned the electrical behavior of two loops of wire in close proximity. Parsons said that when a fluctuating current flowed in one of these wires, a fluctuating current of the identical pitch could be detected in the second wire, even though no physical connection existed between the two. Something carried the energy through the open space, but Parsons didn't say what it was.

"Have you ever noticed how different we are?" Humberhill said to him once, when he was deep in Parsons's book. "Even if I had as much sight as you, we'd be different. You're always thinking about something. Always mulling something over in your mind. You might as well not be here, for all the talking you do. Am I right? Nobody could say you were exactly gabby. I'm not like that. I need to talk to people."

Following the instructions in the book, Little Egypt made

a galvanometer from a magnet, a coil of wire wound on a pencil, and a needle. With this instrument as a detector, he verified Parsons's claims. He proved for himself that under some circumstances a moving magnet can cause the same effects as a fluctuating current in a primary circuit. Furthermore, he discovered a fact that Parsons never mentioned, that winding more turns in the secondary circuit gave a greater inductive response when a magnet was moved past.

He now had all the experience he judged necessary to cheat the telephone company inductively. In a critical set of experiments, he wound an antenna around the telephone line leading into the school office and attempted to eavesdrop on conversations when he knew the telephone was in use. The result was nothing at all. He tried another time, using more turns of wire and an improved method of making connections to his receiver. Still nothing. He tried again and again, but no combination among the many variables proved successful.

Humberhill persuaded him to forget the telephone for an afternoon and come with him to the petting place. This was a new social institution at the school, an invention made by Humberhill himself. Each afternoon, between the hours of three-thirty and five, after classes were finished but before the sound of the dinner bell, boys and girls would meet for sexual adventures on a landing at the top of the northwest staircase, in a dark turn just before it disappeared into the attic. Here, on the square brick floor, six feet on a side, Humberhill had arranged pillows and coverlets for his guests. Often, as many as ten couples were in this small space at one time, which meant that they sat and lay upon each other as frequently as they reposed on the Roman beds that Humberhill had put out for them. On the afternoon Humberhill invited his roommate, he also arranged for Beatrice McBride to be there. Beatrice was a large girl with generous breasts and hips. Like Humberhill, she had no sight at all.

"I want to try petting," Beatrice said, "but I don't want to pet with just anybody. I want to pet with Buzz Hollohan."

"He isn't here," somebody said. "He's practicing with the wrestling team."

"Then I'm not going to do it," Beatrice said. "I'm not going to let just anybody kiss me and put their hand inside my blouse. I don't think that would be fun."

"But it *is* fun," Mary Rory said. "If they do it right. It isn't fun if they grab or pull, but it's fun if they do it right."

"Who did you get for me?" Beatrice wanted to know.

"They got you Mourly Vold," Alice Maddocks said. "I felt his scrawny arm."

"Great," Beatrice said. "That's just great."

"Relax and enjoy yourselves, my dears," Humberhill said. "As the man says, it's all the same in the dark."

When Little Egypt returned to his work, it grew clear to him that he must somehow go beyond a Parsonsian knowledge of electromagnetic theory if he were to make any further progress. *Experiments in Electricity a Boy Can Do* had led him this far, but there was no information in the book which would allow him to calculate how many turns of wire of what size would be required to strangle the telephone company without their knowledge; nor was it even stated anywhere whether one dared hope that such a thing could be accomplished. He consulted the school library, but found nothing among either its Braille or print volumes which approached even Parsons in sophistication.

After considering his alternatives for several days, he announced his decision to Humberhill.

"I'm going to leave," he said. "I'm going to Baddeck, to see if I can get Professor Bell to teach me electricity."

Humberhill greeted this revelation with silence. After many minutes, he asked, "Why would you want to do that? You already know about it."

"I want to know more."

Humberhill refused to understand this. He raised a great fuss, and argued that his friend would not be permitted to leave voluntarily. He would have to run away, and after that, he might get lost and starve to death. But even Humberhill saw shortly that although these perils quite realistically threatened himself and other totally blind students, Mourly Vold had enough sight to make his way through the world outside the school gates. Appreciating this, he changed his line of attack.

"If you leave," he said, "we'll never be able to keep the party line going. Sooner or later it will break down and none of us will be able to fix it. Then we'll be right back where we were before, and I'll have nobody to talk to but Froggy and James P. Bishop, and you know how I hate those little bastards. Now that I know what else there is, I just don't think I could go back to that."

"I'll be calling in," Mourly Vold reassured him. "I'll still be around to fix things. I just won't be here."

And as a parting gift, he made for Humberhill one of the most difficult projects described in Parsons's little book, a machine for separating and storing electric charge. It operated on the same principle as a comb rubbing against a cat, except the cat in this case was replaced by a squirrel's pelt and the comb gave its place to a continuous ribbon of silk. A hand crank from an ice-cream freezer caused the belt to move, carrying electric charge to a tin cup which served as the accumulator. Turning the crank for a few minutes charged the cup sufficiently so that a respectable spark could be drawn from it to the tip of one's finger.

Humberhill had friends everywhere—in the boys' section, in the girls' section, among all the years. He was as easy with human beings as Mourly Vold was with machines. After his friend was gone, Humberhill thought about him a great deal. He was intensely proud of Mourly Vold, and in many ways in awe of him, but for all the study he gave to Mourly Vold in his recollections, he had to admit that he did not understand beans about him.

At last, he had to conclude that it was Mourly Vold's sight that made him chilly, if that's what he was. His friend was a mystery in many ways, but there were two facts about him that were absolutely true, and these seemed to be connected. One fact was that Mourly Vold could see better than any student in the school, although certainly not as well as people with normal sight. He could find his way through corridors and classrooms without touching the walls, he could recognize people, and he could read a book. His eyes, then, had most of their natural power. The other fact about him was that he was aloof, removed, and withdrawn in the very way that sighted people are. They see what they wish to see, and keep it to themselves. They never ask what's there—they merely look at it and they know all about it. They use their eyes as tools—even as weapons. And the power of their eyes somehow takes away from their other animal senses.

Take his friend's afternoon at the petting place, for example. Mourly Vold was a red-blooded young stud, was he not? He had a root growing between his legs like the rest of us, did he not? So, then, why had he done badly? He had gotten something from Beatrice, to be sure, but merely to have gotten "something" in a situation like that was like signing up for a riding lesson, putting one foot in the stirrup, and then declining to get on the horse. Yes, there was a coldness there, a reluctance, like the one Humberhill had met in the so-called volunteers who came from the outside as readers. The girls among these pretended to have concern for the poor blind boys, but they would scream to high heaven if you put your hand on their knee. They had no fun in them at all, and no sense of how to treat people.

On second thought, Humberhill decided, it was not as bad as all that. Mourly Vold is more nearly one of us than one of them, he said to himself. The proof of that, if any is needed, is the way he has been generous with his discoveries. He could have given the party line to sighted people, and used it to help him get on in the sighted world. Instead, he gave it to us— and, for some of us, it has made all the difference.

So Humberhill took the charge machine with him as he made his rounds and visited his friends. But he also enjoyed using it privately, to create a most extraordinary effect. A needle or pin was placed on top of the cup, and the handle was cranked to bring up a high charge. Humberhill would then lean close, and he could feel on his cheek or on the back of his hand a subtle but deliberate breeze issuing from the point of the pin. Children who had some sight said that the point of the pin would be glowing at these times. Mourly Vold had told him the effect was called "electric wind."

CHAPTER 6

Twenty miles west of the School for the Blind, Alexander Graham Bell was living in a large house facing the great Bras d'Or Lakes. This house was heated by ten fireplaces in addition to the large one in the main hall. It was built to resemble a French château. There were several round towers, each topped by a cone roof. The main roof was cut through in many places by stone chimneys and dormers, and a wide porch faced the water. Inside were great long runs of ash and cherry paneling. The house stood on a sloping point, surrounded by wild grass. Peculiar varieties of sheep could be seen in pastures all around the house.

Bell had become interested in sheep breeding. He was attempting to create a strain of sheep in which the ewes had extra nipples. He was interested in the observation that ewes with more than the usual two nipples often gave birth to more than the usual one lamb. He reasoned also that the extra nipples could be used to nourish extra lambs. An elaborate system was being used to keep track of the genealogy of his flocks. The sheep's ears were punched according to a code. Samples of their wool were taken and tested in a machine of Bell's design. A young man standing in the pens wrote down the number of times a ram penetrated a ewe. Every time it happened, his trousers tightened. The ram gripped the ewe, using his front legs like arms. From the way they jittered about in the pen, they might as well have been treading water. The ram appeared to be trying to save himself by climbing on her back. Eventually the ewe stood still and opened her mouth. They both panted like fire dogs.

Bell was at this time in his seventy-fourth year. The circumstances of his life were comfortable and agreeable. It had been nearly fifty years since he had invented the telephone. In all this time he had been free to pursue an independent life devoted to invention, public service, and leisure enjoyed with his family. He belonged to the Philosophical Society of Washington, the Washington Academy of Sciences, the Anthropological Society of Washington, and was a Fellow of the American Association for the Advancement of Sciences.

One summer evening years in the past, Bell and his guests, Samuel P. Langley and Simon Newcomb, had had a terrible argument about the righting ability of cats. It had started in the living room of Bell's house after dinner. Bell and Langley were talking about animal reflexes, as part of their continuing speculations about the future of manned flight. Sitting in a heavily stuffed chair facing an open porch, Bell had said that he thought a nation might defend itself against hostile aircraft by blowing them out of the sky with giant fans. An engine and a propeller could be mounted on a tower, and the draft thus created could be aimed at the approaching enemy. He noted that flying machines had to be made so light that they could be driven out of control by a stiff breeze. He went on to speculate that the limitation on control might well be in the reflexes of the pilot, so that no improvement in the machines could ever allow them to be operated safely in turbulent air.

Langley and Newcomb countered that a cat, dropped on its back, is able to right itself before it strikes the ground. Bell replied that he had heard this said, but he did not believe it since the cat would have nothing to push on as it was falling. With nothing to push on, it could not possibly rotate itself in space. Langley presented an argument in which the tail was used as an inertial paddle. He made use of physical reasoning which Bell could not follow.

Finally the argument was put to an experimental test. One of Bell's grandchildren was sent to the barn to round up cats. Oil lamps were brought to the porch, and mattresses were placed on the ground ten feet beneath the porch railings. Dogs ran in circles, barking, as the cats flew through the air. After the cats struck the mattresses, they ran in random directions and couldn't be recaptured. The children enjoyed the game more than the adults. They screamed with excitement as the cats dropped through the dark air into the illuminated space above the mattresses, where observers checked to see how they landed. Some of the children were scratched launching cats, but it was such a pleasure to be throwing cats around without being reprimanded for it that they forgot their wounds. In the end, Bell had to admit that a cat can right itself in midair.

Long before this famous argument, in the year that Charles J. Guiteau had shot President Garfield, Bell had offered his services to the president's physicians, who had not been able to find the bullet. As Garfield lay near death, Bell experimented with techniques for finding metal in the body. He placed an electric light, along with a bullet, in the mouth of an assistant, and observed that the bullet cast a shadow on the man's cheek. He proposed that President Garfield should swallow an even more powerful electric light bulb connected to a source of electricity through wires leading from the mouth. The physicians protested that the president was too feeble to swallow weak tea, let alone a light bulb. Bell went back to his laboratory and returned two days later with a modified version of the Hughes induction balance. By this time, President Garfield had fallen into a state of septic delirium. None of his physicians had taken the trouble to wash their hands before probing his wounds, with the consequence that extensive infections now inflamed his body.

Bell set up the induction balance by the president's bed. He put an earphone to his ear and asked for silence. Slowly he moved the coil over the surface of the body. A newspaperman standing among the onlookers misinterpreted what he was seeing—later he wrote that Bell had been listening for the bullet with a telephone. In the course of seven hours' work, Bell located not one bullet but twelve. The bullets were arranged in a rectangular pattern over the president's thorax and abdomen. Bell drew a little circle on the skin around the location of each bullet, using a grease pencil. The physicians were dumbfounded, since they knew only one shot had been fired.

After the president's death, a Yale physics student wrote a story for the campus newspaper speculating that the rectangular pattern sensed by the induction balance had been due to the steel springs in the president's bed.

James Garfield died from the infections introduced by his physicians' fingers, not from the bullet wound, but this fact was unknown at the time and Bell blamed himself heavily. He fell into a depression which lasted several years. His inventions of that period took on a manic quality. He coiled a length of wire around his head. A similar wire was coiled around the head of an assistant. Experiments were conducted on electroinductive thought transference. He suspected that Thomas Edison might be using this principle to steal his ideas, but he was never able to prove this. He was fascinated by the photoelectric properties of the metal selenium, and thought it might be possible to implant selenium in the eyes of the blind to make them see. He recklessly applied the current from a spinning magneto directly to his own eardrums. He published a paper in a technical journal in which he maintained that a man could save himself from slipping into madness by bouncing on a patented jumping platform suspended on springs. In this paper, he advocated the placement of jumping platforms in madhouses on an experimental basis to see if the basic causes of mental disease could be reversed. He worked on devices to be used on lifeboats utilizing microscopic quantities of selenium for condensing drinking water from fog.

Through this difficult period, his wife, Mabel, supported

him and encouraged him to come out of his thoughts. She tracked him by the smell of his cigar, often into the attic. Others could depend on their ears to know where he was, but Mabel couldn't hear him because scarlet fever had left her deaf from the age of five. She loved everything about her husband—his originality, his kindness, even his great size.

She accompanied him on exploring trips by foot and by boat along the East Coast of the United States. They sailed into Bar Harbor aboard the yawl *Flora G. Benthic* and walked along the carriage roads. At Jordan Pond, they sat on salmon-colored granite rocks and looked up at Mount Sargent. They ate simple food from a basket and watched lens-shaped clouds shadowing the top of the mountain. They talked about their children— their dead infant sons and their live, grown girls. Mabel read her husband's lips. She held his hand and walked beside him in the woods. The carriage roads were paved with gravel and graded to climb in smooth curves around the mountains. Where the roads passed over streams, they were carried by elegant pink stone bridges. Italian laborers had built these bridges to resemble similar ones on the high paths above Udine. Bell enjoyed walking, and let his wife far into his confidence when he held her hand in the woods.

"Don't you think it's peculiar," he said, "that I'm becoming more and more famous for the telephone, and more and more ignored for everything else I do? Even my so-called friends think I happened on it by accident, and since then I've contributed little else of value."

"How do you know what they think?"

"I know."

"I don't believe you do," Mabel said. Her speech still had some of the distortions of the deaf voice. "You don't know what they think because you've fallen out of the habit of being with people."

This was true. Bell worked alone through the night. His best hours for concentration, he told everyone, were between midnight and four in the morning. He said that new ideas only came to him between these hours, and when they did, they were like recollections of things forgotten. Sometimes he put on his hat and coat at 2:00 A.M. and walked ten miles, the way a mourner will do when he is trying to recall the sight of a beloved face. After a brief sleep, he would bathe, breakfast, read a newspaper, and then return to bed until late afternoon.

In the maple groves, Mabel made him see that this was shutting people out. Too much solitude, she said, is risky. It is an opiate. It can promise to refresh a person, and end by destroying him.

Bell looked into his wife's face and was filled with astonishment. If anyone else had said this to him, he would not have taken it seriously. Coming from Mabel, it struck him sharply. He stared at his wife as if he were regarding her for the first time. In speaking of solitude, Mabel would know what she was talking about. Perfect solitude was the private territory of the deaf. Mabel had lifted herself out of it only by making the effort a climber makes when ascending a rope. Every day, she rescued herself afresh. She had become a master speech reader, and once wrote a celebrated and useful journal article on that subject. Here was a lady full of generosity and goodwill, but even so, she could not stand to be in the company of other deaf people. Instead, she preferred the naïve faces of the hearing. When a deaf person came into the room, she averted her eyes. How selfish this was! How meanspirited! And yet, she had to do this, because such a shock, such a flash of electricity would result if she let that person catch her eye! The deaf and dumb. Ha! If the word *dumb* had any meaning, then its opposite should describe the deaf, who can speak to each other across a crowded room with their eyes. Mabel was particularly uncomfortable meeting a teacher of the deaf. Such a person would know she was an impostor among the hearing from her first words. And this was so unfair! Because of her enormous effort, because of her courage, because of her intelligence, Mabel had made her handicap almost invisible. Many people met her several times without knowing she was deaf. As Bell gazed into the face of his thin and still beautiful wife, he struggled to understand what she was telling him.

He resolved to change his ways, and, on the family's return to Washington that fall, he authorized Mabel to arrange several grand parties. His guest list included the scientific men Charles Walcott, Amos Berry, Samuel Scudder, and Albert Michelson. Many years earlier, Bell had provided Michelson with the funds he needed to measure the speed of the earth relative to the ether. The results of these experiments shook physics. Michelson had shown that the movement of the earth has no effect on the velocity of light in either direction near the earth's surface. A young physicist named Albert Einstein was at this moment full of dreamy speculations in which he depended on Michelson's results to propose that the speed of light is fixed, but the rate at which time passes is conditional.

At one of these evenings, when Michelson was present, Bell played the piano and sang folk songs from his native Scotland. Later, he dropped a scone on the oriental rug, jam side down.

"There's an interesting thing," he said to Michelson, who was at the time talking with Amos Berry. "Why do you suppose it always lands with the jam side down?"

It was during the same evening that he made the acquaintance of the physicist Samuel Pierpont Langley. Bell was already aware of Langley's interest in manned flight. At that time, the press was giving almost daily attention to Langley's experiments with model gliders launched from balloons. Bell himself had made flying toys, following the designs of the Frenchman Alphonse Pénaud.

He told Langley about an observation he had made concerning the lifting power of ice. He happened, he said, to have been walking in Nova Scotia during the winter. By accident, he broke through the ice covering a puddle. When he held a piece of this ice up to the sun, he noticed a translucent fog around it, a fog which was colder than the surrounding air, and which therefore descended away from the sheet of ice, forming a barely visible jet streaming downward. Now, he asked Langley, would it not be true that if the ice caused the air to move downward, this implied that there would be an equal and opposite thrust on the ice upward? While Langley pondered his answer, Bell went on to elaborate his invention. Thin sheets of ice, he said, could be cut from ponds using special saws. These sheets would then be mounted on a flying machine in lightweight racks like the ones used for making toast in an oven. The machine would take off straight up using its ice thrusters, and by the time the ice had melted, it would have reached a high altitude. Then it would glide back to earth using conventional wings, exactly as Langley's models did.

Langley thought this idea was preposterous, and said so. It is to the credit of both men that they did not fall into a quarrel over this matter or any other in the course of their long friendship.

At Langley's invitation, Bell was present for the first trial of Langley's steam-powered model airplane. It was to be catapulted from Langley's houseboat on the Potomac. Bell hired a boy to row him out on the river fifty yards from shore. The water was dead flat. The sky above was overcast, and therefore nothing on the shore had any color. As preparations were being made for the flight, the steam leaking from the catapult made Langley's houseboat look and sound like a crab cannery. Bell wore a large box camera around his neck. Even at this time in his life he was heavy. The buttons on his waistcoat were placed under a punishing tension. Since Bell sat in the stern, the bow of the little boat rose out of the water.

Then, with a rush of steam, the model flying machine lifted from the deck of the houseboat and climbed upward at a steep angle. It was borne by two sets of wings, each with a span of nearly twenty feet, one fore and one aft. The propeller flashed as it spun. The machine sounded like a flying locomotive. It flew directly over Bell's head and then turned inland. The boy at the oars didn't bother to look up. Bell squirmed in his seat and aimed the camera. The picture he took then still exists— it shows the model in flight high above the hills and trees of the Quantico shoreline.

CHAPTER 7

In 1921, the year Mourly Vold discovered the interior of the telephone, a letter came to Alexander Graham Bell in Baddeck from the Honorable G.H.A. Rivera, Minister of Commerce of the Argentine Republic. The letter was printed on heavy rag paper, almost a bleached cardboard. Hand-painted insignia crowded the heading, and the letter had affixed to it the Minister's seal. It invited Bell to be present at the opening ceremonies of a new hydroelectric station at Córdoba several months later.

In these days, electrification and the telephone were arriving in more than a hundred new cities and towns per month on the American continent. Sometimes they came in together on the same poles. In previous decades, the railroads and the telegraph had been built by a few men of pluck and determination who had speculated small fortunes to reap grand ones. Now, quite suddenly, everyone was a speculator, and even the most fainthearted bellhop was buying shares in electrification projects in Lima and street railways in São Paulo. Everyone was making big money in faraway places. Out of sheer high spirits, a twenty-three-year-old electrification tycoon named Robert ("Bobby") Brinkstone of Princeton drop-kicked a football out of a ten-story window across Wall Street to Knox ("Rusty") Simpson of Harvard, who was waiting on the opposite sidewalk. The football was painted to look like an electric light bulb.

The letter arrived as Bell was concluding a set of experiments testing the aerodynamic properties of ice. With the assistance of a technician, he had built a lightweight bamboo structure containing slots along its length. Into these slots were fitted planes of ice only one-half of an inch thick, cut from a local pond. Once loaded, the machine was placed on an elaborate spring scale to measure the vertical thrust. The results were as disappointing as Langley had predicted many years earlier.

It had occurred to Bell that the temperature of the air might have a large effect on the outcome of his experiments. He made calculations in his notebooks which showed that the ice thrusters might derive substantial benefit by being operated in the summer, rather than in the winter. An elaborate icehouse was built according to his directions, and ice sheets were taken from the pond and preserved until mid-June. Then he tried the experiment again, on the mildest day of the spring.

His grandchildren, who happened to be visiting him, joined in the activities of taking the sheets out of the icehouse. Everyone wore bathing costumes and enjoyed the cold straw underfoot. The daredevil motorcyclist and aviator Glenn Curtiss arrived from Hammondsport, New York, to participate. The children cheered as Bell and Curtiss carried the first ice sheet out into the brilliant sunshine. It was so flawless, so transparent that the eye could only barely establish its margins against the blue sky. Curtiss went first—a dark, muscular fellow in shirtsleeves, wearing a straw boater. Bell followed him, his bare chest pressed against the ice, his white hair lifting and falling with each heavy step. Dogs ran about barking through the tall grass, apparently not looking where they were going. Through the clear rectangle of ice, one was afforded a slightly rippled view of the pasture sloping slowly downward, a red barn abutted by a stand of white pine, and below that, the water.

When all the ice sheets were installed in the flying machine, Bell made measurements of the thrust, again using the spring scale. With great elation, he observed that the weight of the machine was falling. He encouraged Curtiss to get in and take the controls, as the thrust was now building up. Curtiss thought there was plenty of time. Annoyed, Bell went back to the spring scale. His face was very red from the heat and excitement.

Presently he came to Curtiss and urged him again to take command of the machine, as the movement of the scale showed it would soon be airborne. Curtiss replied that if the weight were falling, it was only because of the melting of the ice. He was correct, of course—by this time, most of the ice panels were completely gone. The children had caught some of the ice water in cups and bowls and were pouring it on each other's heads. Mabel used the last fragments of the ice to make lemonade, and served it on the porch.

Under ordinary circumstances, Bell would have declined an invitation such as the one Rivera had sent. There had been a time, earlier in his life, when he had been interested in travel, but now he preferred to stay at home. There was so much that needed his attention here! The multinippled sheep had grown into a giant population, and needed a large staff for their maintenance. He had recently begun work on a theory explaining the gravitational force in mechanistic terms, and was now having an intense correspondence with Niels Bohr about his ideas. He thought that certain moods were caused by the gravitational fluctuations produced by nearby structures. From his bedroom window, he could see the barn next to the house, and he could feel its pull. A calculation he had made in his notebooks showed that if the barn were to be taken down, the gravitational field in his bedroom would be restored to a magnitude and direction near its equilibrium value. He speculated that if this were done, he might be relieved of the lurches and sudden awakenings which now plagued his sleep.

Mabel convinced him to accept the invitation. She suggested that a period of rest and reflection away from his experiments might benefit him more than he could guess. She recounted other times in the past when he had been troubled by one impasse or another in his scientific work, and when the answer had come to him during a journey. He saw that once again she was right, and treasured her more than ever for her knowledge and love of him. He wrote a letter saying he would come, and they drove together to the town to post it. While they were there, they saw Mack Swain and Gloria Swanson in the Edison film *Atlantic City Romance*. Mabel read the players' lips, and whispered to her husband what they were actually saying, which was not what was shown in the titles. She did this for all but the love scenes, where their actual dialog left her deeply shocked.

As circumstances would have it, the lake steamer bearing Mourly Vold arrived in Baddeck the morning after the Bells left for South America. This was the *City of North Sydney*, a stout vessel ninety-seven feet in length with a single large smokestack protruding between the four lifeboats cradled on her top deck. In addition to the passengers, fifteen sheep wandered about the decks and enjoyed the views. In the hold were three hundred bales of hay, seven tons of coal for the boiler, and two hundred bags of cement.

On learning that the sheep were bound for Baddeck and that they were the property of the great and esteemed summer resident Alexander Graham Bell, Mourly Vold began a conversation with the man obviously in charge of them. This man introduced himself as Donald G. Morrison. In some ways, he resembled Mourly Vold. He was slight and wore thick spectacles. On his feet were large rubber boots, almost laughably oversized. Age or perhaps some infirmity caused him to walk well stooped over. He moved very slowly about the decks, herding the sheep into a pen at the bow of the boat. Mourly Vold heard him wheezing each time he passed. When the last sheep was closed in the pen, Donald G. Morrison sat down and lit his pipe. Mourly Vold took out his pipe and joined him in a smoke.

"When I was a young fellow," Donald G. Morrison said, "I never saw the light on a working day for ten years. The day after Christmas, the year I turned fifteen, I went down. Every day after that, except Sundays, until I was twenty-five. My father worked down there too, until he passed away. I lost my father

December the fifth, eighteen eighty-nine. That was the big explosion, when they had all the deaths. Aw, that was terrible. Some of them blown to pieces, so we never knew who they were. They tried to put them together again in the parish hall, so the women could find their men. Identify them. But there was no way to get the right pieces together. I was in there, but I was down deeper, with the horses. This was when they had horses in the mines. I heard it, but I thought it was only a shot. I walked out through the smoke and the firedamp. I had the horse by the tail. She brought me out. Firedamp killed most of them. Would have killed me, but I just held that horse's tail and kept my breath in. Aw, those shafts had all kinds of gas in them, always did. Company didn't care. They just wanted the coal, fast as they could get it."

Mourly Vold asked about Bell.

Donald G. Morrison smoked his pipe for a while before answering. "Since you asked me," he began, "I'll have to say I wouldn't give you a nickel for him. He's as vague and silly as they come. But she's all right. In fact, she's a fine woman. Not like most of your rich. They make pets of their money. But she won't do that; she'll spend it when it needs to be spent. And she knows her animals." Donald G. Morrison crossed his legs. This exaggerated the contrast between his thin shanks and his enormous boots. "She's deaf, you know, but she isn't deaf and dumb. She can understand you, if she can see your face. She goes by the lips. And she can talk, in her own way. Some say they can't understand her, but I can. Most of them think the world of her. I know I do."

Mourly Vold now revealed that his purpose in coming to Baddeck was to call on the Bells. He said that he was interested in electricity, and hoped to engage Professor Bell in discussions about the electrical arts.

"Then you come along with me," Donald G. Morrison said. "I'm taking the sheep there anyway. Might as well take you."

The *City of North Sydney* tied up at the dock in Baddeck shortly after noon. As this was only a brief stop, she kept up her head of steam. The air was calm; the water lay in an absolutely level plane. Donald G. Morrison drove a Ford truck onto the dock and loaded the sheep into the back of it. Now the sun was hot. The only cloud in the sky was the black plume issuing from the steamer's funnel, and it provided nothing in the way of shade. Because of the sun and the still water, there was a white glare in every direction.

When the sheep were secure in the back, Donald G. Morrison shuffled to the front of the truck and cranked the engine. Mourly Vold climbed in, and soon they were driving out of the town. They passed over a set of railroad tracks, then followed these tracks for some distance.

"On a day like this, you're going to get a sun kink," Donald G. Morrison observed. He pointed his pipe at the tracks.

"What?"

"Sun kink. A rail is straight, just straight and nothing wrong with it, and then all of a sudden it jumps out to the side. If a train comes over it then, boy, it's a derailment for sure. You have to go in there and change that rail before any trains can go over it, or that train is going in the woods. You know what I mean? You can't take a train over a sun kink. Somebody's going to get killed."

Some moments went by as they climbed a hill in low gear. "You worked on a train?" Mourly Vold asked in a pleasant manner.

"Of course I did," Donald G. Morrison said. "Of course I did. I wasn't allowed back into the mine. Mother wouldn't let me. She said she had lost her husband and she had lost two of her sons, and she wasn't going to lose anyone else. I was ready to go back down, because the pay was the best you could get at that time. But Mother said no, and I wouldn't go against her. That's when I started on the M&B, on April the seventh, eighteen ninety. Brakeman. I was always a brakeman. And I took home five dollars and four cents a week. I always wanted to ask them what the four cents was for, but I never had the guts."

The road climbed and fell as it crossed a series of low hills. Toward the north were well-kept fields; at the south, the briny expanse of the Bras d'Or Lakes. Larks flushed up from the sides of the road as the truck passed, and one of them struck the windshield, but flew on unhurt. The shoreline continued northeastward, turning past Boularderie Island, until somewhere in the distance this water became continuous with the Atlantic Ocean.

"It was a good job, but I guess you'd say it was dangerous," Donald G. Morrison was saying. "Aw, those old fellers worked for their money, and they took chances. Lost fingers, all of them. You couldn't make up trains without losing fingers in the couplers, especially in the winter. And don't forget, this was long before they had any tie plates to keep the rails from spreading. You come through with one of those heavy locomotives, what they call a Pacific-type locomotive, and in a weak place, she'd spread the rails and come off. Then the pipes would break and the crew would get scalded. Cooked. Take the dead men out, put her back on the rails, and send her off. We had one engine, we called her the *Mrs. Florence Deagle* because every other time you'd look at her, she'd be on her back. But I guess you don't think that's funny, because you never knew Florence Deagle. She owned the rooming house. This is where you get off."

Mourly Vold opened the door and stepped out of the truck. "Don't forget your bag," Donald G. Morrison said. Mourly Vold reached into the cab and moved his hand over the seat, searching for his threadbare carpetbag. Eventually he found it on the floor, near the shift lever.

"You don't see well, do you?" Donald G. Morrison asked.

"No."

"I thought not." Donald G. Morrison put the truck in gear. "I have to go," he said. "When you're through here, come up to the barn. That's where I'll be working. Just stay on this road. It's where the road ends, about half a mile."

When the truck was gone, Mourly Vold found himself standing before the front steps of a large house. He could make out very little of the house beyond its obvious bulk. At one side of the steps a flower garden began. Azaleas represented themselves in his vision as a blurred mass of pink and red. There were other scents and colors behind these—rhododendrons, larkspur, and irises. The air, which had been motionless all morning, was just now beginning to stir. He heard it tentatively producing breath sounds in the boughs of the pines rising up at his back.

At this moment, an aircraft engine started on the lake. A series of backfires, a ratcheting fall in the note, then a sustained roar. Shortly afterward, another engine started. These were the two enormous three-hundred-and-fifty-horsepower liquid-cooled Liberty engines sent by the U.S. Navy two years earlier. Each one swung a four-bladed aerial propeller with curved leading edges. The craft bearing these engines was now moving. As it turned, and the plane of the blades shifted, the quality of the sound changed from a resonant throbbing to a rattling, like the shaking together of sheets of paper. The sound reflected from the front of the house and came to Mourly Vold's ears from two clearly different angles. It was as if the movement of the seaplane, or whatever it was, were imitated by an identical movement of an image seaplane within the house. The quality of the sound changed again, and then slowly dropped as the craft moved away. The engines were abruptly throttled, allowed to idle for a moment, and then fell silent together. Mourly Vold never saw the thing that made this noise, nor could he have hoped to do so even if it had been in plain view, because the lake and its details lay well out of his range. In that direction, he could perceive only a harsh and indistinct brilliance.

The maid who answered the door told Mourly Vold that the Bells were not at home, nor would they be back at home for two months. They had left that morning for New York, on their way to South America. When Mourly Vold gave this information to Donald G. Morrison, he said, "That's typical. He never said a word to me."

Donald G. Morrison was even more surprised when Mourly Vold informed him that he planned to wait in Baddeck until the Bells returned. "As long as you're going to wait, you can stay right here with us," Donald G. Morrison said. "You can help me with the carding. I'll teach you the multinippled sheep business. He still thinks there's something to it, but I wouldn't hold my breath waiting to get rich on it if I were you."

In New York, the Bells boarded the *Athenia* and sailed for Buenos Aires. There was a warm drizzle as they left New York harbor. Rain falling through the heavy smoke of the four giant stacks reached the deck in dark droplets. One still saw sailing vessels in the harbor, their holds heavy with coal. The canvas of these vessels was blackened by the smoke of passing steamships.

Outside the territorial limit, the mother ships waited listlessly. The Coast Guard cutters steamed around them, waiting for a false move. As the *Athenia* glided through Rum Row, drunken sailors came up on the decks of the mother ships. It appeared that these men no longer cared what they did. Some of them waved and shouted; others exposed themselves. A man with a red beard wearing no clothes at all urinated from a high deck into the ocean far below. The arc of his pee followed a mathematical shape known as a parabola.

The *Athenia*, at this time of her life, resembled a steampowered swan. From any view, she was white and splendid, the pride of the line. Gulls followed this ship out of the harbor and stayed with her for miles at sea because she was so beautiful they could not take their eyes off her. She started this passage with twelve thousand pounds of prime beef, eighteen hundred pounds of truffled pâté, six thousand pounds of brioche, five thousand two hundred pounds of live lobsters, and a wedding cake. The wedding cake was for Mr. and Mrs. Claude Elmos-Durrier, who had just been married in a tethered balloon above Battery Park.

Bell explored the ship and was surprised by its loveliness and attention to detail. At one end of the smoking room was a Tudor fireplace. One could obtain service in this room sitting before the fire in a heavy leather chair almost like the one he had in his study at home. Dark carved woods in this room reflected the firelight. He opened one of the glass-fronted bookshelves and discovered there one of Joseph Henry's works on magnetism. Delighted, he replaced the book on the shelf with the spine pointing inward, so that no one else would be attracted to it before he could return at some later time to read it. He found the swimming pool and admired its Roman pillars and its decks of Italian tiles. In the grand salon was a piano of unusually large size, contained in its own semicircular niche a step above the sprung dance floor. Everywhere were green plants and even trees of modest size. He was particularly intrigued to find that there were telephones in all the staterooms.

At the end of his exploration, he stepped outside on the promenade deck. It was night. The *Athenia* had outdistanced the rain and was now steaming in calm seas under overcast skies. The air lifting up and flowing over this deck had fog in it. This seemed to be not a natural fog but one the ship had created by her disturbing motion.

An enormous distance ahead on this deck, almost out of sight, the lights from a set of windows reached into the fog and pointed toward Europe. Bell walked toward these lights, following the gleaming tracks of tar between the decking planks. Under his feet, several thousand people were eating, reading, cooking, stoking, talking, walking, and fornicating, but he was absolutely alone on the subtly curved roof of this mechanism, one of the largest machines that ever moved. A flag rattled over his head, but it was invisible in the streaming protofog. As he drew closer, he saw that the lights were coming from the florist's shop, with its stores of orchids, ferns, and roses. He bought a spray of daisies and took them to Mabel, who was resting in their cabin two decks below.

Meanwhile, with the Bells away, Mourly Vold worked with Donald G. Morrison on various sheep projects. Each day began with a breakfast of oatmeal porridge eaten by lamplight before dawn. The work was physically demanding—digging postholes for fences, shoveling manure, repairing the many farm buildings. In the first weeks, Mourly Vold was exhausted by noon each day. Once, working in the direct sun digging stones out of a field, he collapsed and had to rest several hours in the shade of a tree until his strength returned.

Donald G. Morrison brought him a pitcher of lemonade. They sat in the shade of the tree together and drank it.

"We're going to have to call you 'Old Horizontal,' " Donald G. Morrison said, "if you do much more of that. Yes, indeed. Old Horizontal."

"I feel better now," Mourly Vold said. "I can go back to work."

"Not so fast, not so fast," Donald G. Morrison said. He lit his pipe. "That rock will still be there five minutes from now." He leaned back on the dry grass, resting on his elbows. A large fly droned out of the pine woods and flew down the hill.

"We'll feed you up, rest you up, work you up," Donald G. Morrison said, "and before you know it, we'll have you strong. Maybe you'll even forget what you're running from."

"I'm not running from anything," Mourly Vold said.

Donald G. Morrison looked at him for a moment without speaking. "No?" he said, at last. "That's good. Then your people know where you are?"

"The only people I have is my mother."

"She know where you are?"

"Not exactly," Mourly Vold said. "I was planning to write to her."

"You were planning to write, but I never give you any time, is that it?"

Mourly Vold didn't answer.

"Listen to me," Donald G. Morrison said. "Tonight, after supper, you take the pen in your hand and see if you can remember how to write. I don't know what this world is coming to. They don't make boys like they used to. This one falls down on the job, and he won't tell his mother where he is."

That evening, Mourly Vold did write to his mother, but then two weeks went by, and he received no reply. He decided to return home for a few days to be sure that she was well. He took the steam ferry *Nora MacDowell* to Bucks Falls exactly one month after arriving in Baddeck.

When he reached his mother's house, he found it locked and silent. Deciding that she might be out on an errand, he sat on the front porch to wait. An hour passed, and then two. At last, he went next door and asked Mrs. Whittin if she knew where his mother was.

"She lives up to the Murches' now," he was told. "Paid companion. She's a paid companion to that old Mrs. Murch. Very rich people, don't you know. The father was a mine operator. He's gone now. And they say that the son wants to marry her. This is what I hear. I don't know what the truth of it is."

Mourly Vold received directions from Mrs. Whittin and began the long walk to the house of the Murches, which was several miles from the town dock. The road rose continuously as he walked. He left the tombstone factory and its marble dust behind. Pretty farms stretched out in all directions on both sides of the road, and the fragrance of the hay in the fields made the journey pleasant.

He reached the house of the Murches in midafternoon and knocked at the door. A maid appeared.

"I would like to speak with my mother, Mrs. Vold," he said.

The maid seemed quite surprised. "Please wait here," she told him.

Before long, Ilse came to the door. She was dressed in a very youthful frock. A generous décolletage was provided at the top. Her hair was arranged in curls that fell forward toward her eyes, and she was wearing rouge and lipstick. As this was so unlike her customary appearance at home, Mourly Vold hardly recognized her.

"Darling," she said, embracing him. "You tracked me down. How wonderful. But what are you doing here? I thought you were in school."

She did not take him into the house, but instead led him around to the garden, where there were lawn chairs on the grass and a swing hanging from the bough of an oak.

Mourly Vold explained to her how he had left the school to apprentice himself to Alexander Graham Bell for the study of the electrical arts. He also mentioned that he had been working, for the past month, with the sheep on Bell's farm.

"Ah, yes," his mother said. She took out her handkerchief, touched it with her tongue, and rubbed his neck. "You brought some of the farm with you," she said.

They sat in the lawn chairs. The trees at the edge of the garden were making long shadows. Somewhere in a distant field, a tractor was working; it could be heard but not seen.

"Maryellen was surprised to see you," his mother began. She waited a moment before speaking again. "They're all going to be surprised to see you, because I haven't told them about you yet."

Mourly Vold looked at his mother with a question in his face, but said nothing.

"I've been here three months," she said. "The work is quite pleasant. My only real duties are to read to an older woman and to look nice—both of those things were explained to me at the beginning. This is a job I know how to do, because the house and the circumstances here are quite close to the ones in which I grew up. My own family were more like the Murches than you would believe."

She took a comb out of her own hair and combed her son's hair.

"I know," she said. "The look on your face says you wonder what I'm doing here. Is that right?"

"Yes," Mourly Vold said. "I expected to find you at home."

"You expected to find me at home. Well, I'm here," she said, replacing the comb in her hair, "and I expect I'll be here for some time to come. Now let's go in. I want you to meet everyone."

Ilse had been right about the Murches. They were indeed surprised to discover she had an adolescent son. All of them said so several times, leaving room for the interpretation that they felt they had been deceived. Ilse ignored the innuendo. She readied a room for her son to sleep in, since no one in the household would order a maid to do it. She put fresh sheets on his bed, and she arranged flowers from the garden in a vase and placed it on his bureau.

"You're absolutely enormous," Mrs. Murch said to Mourly Vold. "If someone had come to me this morning and said that Ilse was old enough to have a child your size, I would have called that person a liar. I have always thought of her as not more than a child herself."

In addition to Mrs. Murch, Mourly Vold was introduced to the Murches' unmarried daughter, a severe woman of about forty, and the staff of the house, including the housekeeper, two maids, the cook, and the gardener. Toward evening, the Murches' son arrived home.

His reaction to Mourly Vold was the most extreme of anyone's in his family. When he heard that this person who stood before him—who, in fact, towered over him—was Ilse's son, his expression darkened and he excused himself from the room. Ilse followed him up the stairs, and they were not seen again until dinner, although the son's voice could be heard shouting behind a closed door. In order to move out of the center of the conflict, and because no one else seemed to wish to speak to him, Mourly Vold helped the cook scrape carrots for dinner.

At the meal, Mrs. Murch talked constantly. "Bernice told me that the MacKenzie boy took his father's truck, the one with the snowplow on the front, and pushed what's left of the MacIvor cottage into the sea. It's only by the grace of Our Savior that he didn't kill them both, because that's what he intended to do. They weren't in the cottage at the time."

"Who wasn't in the cottage?" the old-maid daughter asked.

"Jane MacArdle and her gentleman friend. I don't know his name. You know who that is, Daniel. The one who's been living in the MacIvor cottage. Although, I don't know how he could actually be living there. That place hasn't had a roof or any walls on one side since the fire. They only go there to do their business, so they tell me. And the MacKenzie boy thought she was all his, until someone gave him the news. Anyhow, the truck is a mess. The snowplow is all pushed in at the front. Please pass the potatoes here, young man."

In this way, she uncovered the fact of Mourly Vold's poor sight, and put it on display for everyone to see. In the dim light of the dinner table, he was practically blind. The conversation hushed as he reached out in front of his place, groping carefully to the left and to the right, feeling for the dish which might contain the potatoes. No one spoke. Every eye was upon him, except those of his mother, which were wet with tears of deep feeling.

The following day, Mourly Vold worked beside his mother in the flower garden. He dug holes for her as she transplanted roses.

"It's wonderful to have your help," she said. "You seem so much bigger and stronger than when you went to the school."

"Don't thank the school for making me strong," Mourly Vold said. "I never did a thing there. None of them do. They all sit around like fat white cutworms."

He dug a few more shovelfuls.

"And besides," he continued, "I didn't *go* to the school. You *took* me."

Shortly afterward, Mourly Vold returned to the kitchen to fill a pail with water. He ran straight into Mrs. Murch.

"Stop a moment," she said. "I have something to say to you. I must apologize for us, for the way the house is, and the dinner table. It isn't set up to be convenient for a blind person. We didn't know you were coming, of course, and we certainly didn't know you'd be blind, or half blind, or whatever you are."

Mourly Vold gave her no reply.

"Tell me, did you get a disease?"

"Pardon me?" he asked.

"Did you get a disease in your eyes?"

"No," he answered.

"Then you've always been this way, from birth?"

"Yes," Mourly Vold said. "I've always been this way."

"How much of this is in your family?" Mrs. Murch wanted to know. "How many other people in Ilse's family have things wrong with them?"

"What do you mean?"

"I mean, is there anyone else who was born blind, or deaf, or crazy? I think I have a right to know. She's a pretty little thing, and bright as paint. We all love her, don't you doubt that. But I need to have some answers before she takes one step farther into this family. Now, what do you say?"

"There is no one that I know of who was born deaf or crazy," Mourly Vold answered.

"Of course, I'll ask her myself," Mrs. Murch said. "And I'll make a few outside inquiries. She never said a thing about you, after all. There's no telling what else she might be covering up."

In the morning, Mourly Vold and his mother sat together in the lawn chairs again before he departed.

"They're rude, of course they're rude," Ilse said, while holding her son's hands. "I don't ask you to love them for it. I don't ask you to love them at all, just to understand them and perhaps forgive them. They haven't been on their best behavior while you were here. It all has to do with me, not with you.

"I wonder how much I should explain to you. I came here to be Mrs. Murch's companion; I told you that. I needed the job. It was either that or go back to work in the tombstone factory. But I wasn't here very long before they took me in, more or less, to their family. And I enjoyed it, I admit that. I enjoyed returning to my own class, after all this time. I see their faults, and I don't admire them for the way they are, but everyone feels more comfortable with their own type.

"I didn't tell them much about myself, except that I had been married and my husband had died. They're wonderful at making things up; I let them make up things to believe about me. And, after a while, Daniel began talking about marriage."

When she said this, Mourly Vold removed his hands from his mother's grasp.

"Darling," she said. "Don't be like that. You're the only person I love, and that will always be so."

He stood up. "I'm going home," he told her. "Are you coming?"

"No, my dear," she said. "I'm not ready to come home now. There's nothing there for me any longer. You should go back to school. That would be best for you."

"I'll do what I like. I'm old enough to decide."

"Yes, darling," she said. "You *are* old enough. We both are."

And with that, she kissed him one last time. He walked off down the road, and never looked back.

■ ■

As the *Athenia* drew closer to the equator, the mood aboard the ship became more relaxed. In the latitudes of calm winds, the ocean lay flat, day and night. Bell, who suffered in any hot weather, sat in the shade of the lifeboats during the day and stood at the railings in the evening. From the open doors leading to the salons and smoking rooms he heard the orchestra playing a Gaiety light opera. At other times, a jazz band could be heard at work on "Dardanella," or "Pittsburgh Patty," or "I'll Say She Does." Through these doors, he could see down the grand staircase to the dancers fox-trotting below.

At dinner each evening, electric fans stirred the air over the white lace tablecloths. As this was not an American ship, there was no Prohibition. Many people drank not only the ship's wines but rare bottles from their own private stocks. The night the ship crossed the equator, Neptune held court at an entertainment which included public bathing in large copper tubs.

On a beautiful Sunday afternoon, the *Athenia* left the ocean and entered the mouth of the Río de la Plata. Here the river is so wide that for many miles there is no land in sight, although its yellow color and the many species of land birds flying above it differentiate the river water from the ocean. They passed a dredge working on the shipping channel. The mud it was bringing up was the color of egg yolk.

The Bells stopped to rest in Buenos Aires for a day before continuing their journey into the interior. They took rooms at the Majestic Hotel, widely acclaimed as the finest in South America, on the Avenida de Mayo. This building had a glass-roofed courtyard beginning on the third floor, then five stories of balconies, capped by a roof garden in which every species of native citrus could be found. The rooms were large, with particularly high ceilings. Above the clock tower was a gilt metal sun, which caught the light of the atmosphere and reflected it into the street, so that this sun appeared to glow even in overcast weather.

They found Buenos Aires pretentiously rich, even rudely so. All the wealth just then booming out of the interior, all the money from beef and grain and sheep, seemed to have been dropped here the way the Río de la Plata dropped its silt, in a choking heap. There appeared to be more automobiles than people; expensive touring cars lined the streets. Walking along the Avenida Alvear, a street of one outrageous mansion after another, they noticed on close inspection that the marble blocks and the carved stone with floral decorations were all stucco imitations, all false.

The next morning, they boarded a train of the Central Argentine Railway to Rosario. The stock pens and slaughter-houses of Buenos Aires fell out of sight quickly and were replaced by the pampas, a dead-level vista of wheatland in all directions, without a single tree or other prominence showing on the horizon. At noon, they sat down to luncheon in the dining car, and Mabel remarked that the lamps with their little red shades on all the tables were identical to the ones on the French dining cars between Paris and Nice. Through the afternoon, the tracks stretched on without a turn. Out the window, one occasionally saw a zinc-plated windmill pumping water. Bell recognized these as of American manufacture. After dusk, giant fireflies could be seen orbiting above the wheat.

They spent the night in a flimsy hotel in Rosario on the muddy Paraná River. The walls and roof of this building were fashioned of the same stucco that had been made to look so pretty in the hands of the Italian craftsmen in Buenos Aires, but resembled nothing more than horse manure plastered by hand against the crude walls here. The mistress of the estab-lishment, also its cook, was a short, stout, gray-haired woman of Portuguese ancestry. She could be seen through a door open into the kitchen preparing the meal. The beef was boiled in a vast pot, then emptied into a tin dish. Everyone at the table was expected to carve as much as he wanted and then pass the dish along. A roast, which was served at the same meal, was treated similarly. At the conclusion of the meal, the proprietress loaded some twenty pounds of meat into a wheelbarrow and took it to an open rubbish heap behind the building, where the dogs made short work of it.

Bell, never an easy sleeper, found it impossible to shut his eyes that evening. His usual habit when insomnia claimed him was to go for a long walk, but when he opened the door, several large dogs raced toward him with such clear intentions of murder that he quickly closed it again. He tried reading; he had brought with him volume one of James Clerk Maxwell's *Treatise on Electricity and Magnetism*, but this went as badly for him as it had every other time he had tried to read it because his comprehension was so poor of the mathematics it used.

At 3:00 A.M. he sat on the bed beside Mabel. Even though the curtains at the window were drawn, the moonlight outside was so strong that his wife's face was illuminated brightly. Her features were still delicate, even beautiful after all this time. In spite of disappointments, in spite of the deaths of her infant sons, in spite of the isolation of her deafness, in spite of the failed promise of her husband to do anything more with his life after his one achievement, she had found a way to be a happy woman.

There was very little different about her now, he thought, from when he had first seen her. She had come to him, about a month before her sixteenth birthday, as a private speech student. He had only recently taken up his duties as professor in the new Boston University School of Oratory. To supplement his salary, he took in the stammerers and speech defectives of the rich of New England—the Aldriches of Rhode Island and the Brookses and Hubbards of Massachusetts. Mabel had been a Hubbard. At fifteen, she had traveled widely in Europe and could read and write German, French, and Italian, but could not speak any language well enough to be understood. Already a skillful speech reader, she knew what people were saying to her, but she often declined to answer them, because they looked so shocked when they heard her voice.

What a satisfaction it had been to teach Mabel! As she leapt ahead in one triumph after another, he shared her pleasure. After a year of instruction, she reported that people now did not know she was deaf until she told them. Some of the fear of new people, which had been such an incapacitating part of her childhood and younger life, was now dropping away.

He recalled the day when he realized he was in love with her. There had been a great winter storm, and Boston had been buried in snow. The monuments in the Old Granary Burying Ground beneath his third-floor windows lay concealed in a long drift with a ridge on its back as thin as the fin of a fish. He had been lying in bed, reading a scientific book, when Mabel came knocking at his door. There she was, demanding her lesson, blizzard or no blizzard. She had walked all the way from her family's house in Cambridge, propelling herself through waist-high drifts, enduring stinging snow blowing in her face, removing all obstacles from her path.

Even now, he benefited from her willpower, but he also suffered from it. In the morning, she could be fierce in her determination to get him out of bed. She would use tears, threats, the promise of food, the denial of food, even physical blows to get him to put his feet on the floor. Sometimes this bullying began in a playful way, but she was so serious about it that it rarely ended that way. "I often wonder," she said once, "what our lives would be like if you held a regular job, like other men. Then you wouldn't be able to lie in bed for half the day. Then I would never have to scold you."

Suddenly he wanted to wake Mabel up and ask her a hundred questions. Why did you say that? What's so virtuous about holding a regular job? Or, for that matter, getting up in the morning?

He considered what job he might have done throughout his life if he had not been an inventor. Well before he met Mabel, he had been interested in the problems of the deaf. He recalled a visit to an orphanage in New York where a large proportion of the children were deaf or blind. The Sisters had established a window at the side of the building that was always left open. The unwanted babies that had formerly been victims of infanticide could now be left by their destitute mothers in this window, to be brought up by the nuns. He remembered playing with the children—some of them had been calm enough for games. He made his pocket watch walk along a table and jump into his hand. The watch would spring open when the children pressed his nose and close when they pulled his beard.

Some of the deaf children were unmanageable. He remembered one little girl in particular, a beautiful child who tore at her clothes and heaved about on the floor in frustration when someone misunderstood her monstrous speech. He might have spent his life helping such children. In such an occupation, he might have labored from early morning to late evening, and taken the satisfaction of their progress to bed with him each night.

Instead, he struggled with his own defective ideas. Like the children, these ideas were born blind or deaf, but they could not be helped as simply. The children needed only a patient man with ordinary sight and hearing to help them advance. His ideas for inventions needed a man of extraordinary senses to guide them, senses that he did not possess. Over and over again his imagination took him into scientific fields where he had no competence. At the moment he had projects under way in sheep genetics, although he knew no biology; in the use of Roentgen rays introduced into the body for treating deep cancers, although he knew no medicine; and in the mathematical theory of gravitation, although he knew little mathematics. He knew that both the best and the worst scientists in history had been like this, reckless in the way they spent their energies in all directions. It was terrible to know this and yet not to know whether he was one of the best or one of the worst.

He lowered his head to the pillow and listened to Mabel's breath running in and out of her lungs. The wind moved the curtains at the window. For a moment, the moon was revealed, then the gauze closed over it again.

The following morning, on the train to Córdoba, they saw gauchos heating their branding irons in open fires. The fires were made from the bones of dead cattle because there were no trees to give any fuel. A man sitting next to them told them about the swarms of locusts which came down from Brazil. When a cloud of them passed in the air, they dimmed the sun so dramatically that the light had the quality of late evening. They learned that when the locusts alighted, the entire populace turned out with all their animals to crush the insects beneath their feet.

In Córdoba, they met their host, General G.H.A. Rivera, Commerce Minister of the Argentine Republic. He was a short, solid man with many lines in his face, and he wore a uniform heavy with medals. He chain-smoked a series of brutal little cigars known as PimPims.

General Rivera spoke enthusiastically of the future of his country. He said that the farmland of the vast Paraná Valley was richer than any in Ohio. He spoke about the Transandine Railway and its fantastic tunnel through the mountains, which he said was the longest of its kind in the world. He took them to the new hydroelectric station and showed them the massive turbines and dynamos which would soon be supplying electric power for the whole central region of the country. He said that this equipment had been built by the General Electric Company, and was of the same design as that in service at Niagara Falls. He let them look down into the immense hydraulic tunnel and explained the details of its construction, only recently finished. There were birds down there, flying up from the darkness. He knew the horsepower and dimensions of every piece of equipment. It was amazing that such a sleepy-looking person knew all those facts.

At the dedication ceremonies that evening, General Rivera thanked Professor and Mrs. Bell for coming such a great distance, and praised Bell for his invention of the electric light.

CHAPTER **8**

Meanwhile, Thomas A. Edison, the real inventor of the electric light, was sitting in a chair on a lawn in West Orange, New Jersey. The chair was built of two-inch cedar timbers with the bark left on. Edison was wearing a soiled linen suit. A cigar was in his left hand; a book was in his right. The wide brim of a straw boater shaded his face, but the oblique rays of the sun reached his collar and illuminated it with a queer intensity. Edison's heavy face included a number of sags, and the shadows beneath these appeared perfectly black and cold against the potato color of his skin. His generous abdomen pushed forward, stretching his linen trousers and making a prominence that now and then captured a falling ash from his cigar.

The book in his hand was Dr. Lulu Hunt Peters's best seller, *Diet and Health with Key to the Calories*. Behind Edison's chair, a subtly curved lawn stretched a hundred yards to Glenmont, his enormous residence. This was a château of the 1870s period typical of the buildings erected by oil money, steel money, pork money, and railroad money in Pittsburgh, Chicago, and the suburbs north of New York. Its eight-gabled roof boxed the compass. Awnings ten feet wide stretched over huge windows, some of them glazed with stained glass. There seemed to be no particular architectural style, as if none were required. There was a porte cochere and a broad vestibule; there was a roof deck with a white railing; there were several large living rooms, each with a chandelier protecting a central glass globe.

Something was moving in Edison's peripheral vision. He

turned his head slightly and saw that it was a wasp. The insect flew up and for a moment was out of sight, then returned to exactly the same place he had first noticed it. The air was so clear that the wasp's shadow could be seen on the leaves of a bush near Edison's shoulder. The shadow and the insect fused as the wasp landed on a tiny leaf. Edison put Dr. Lulu Hunt Peters down on the grass. Slowly he rose to his feet and faced the bush. Then, in one powerful motion, he leapt forward and kicked his right foot high above his head, planting his shoe precisely under the leaf where the wasp was resting. When the bush stopped shaking, there was no sign of the wasp anywhere. It could have gone up to the moon.

Forty years earlier, following the ballyhoo attending his invention of the phonograph, Edison announced that he was feeling weary and ill. He would take a trip, he said, to the West. The Union Pacific provided him with a special car built by George Pullman. Its interior was paneled in cherry wood, and the hardware was nickel-plated. A chemical laboratory was set up for Edison's use during the journey. He permitted correspondents from the New York press to ride with him. As the train rattled across the level emptiness of the Midwest, he heard himself talking about a new invention.

The French were then the great illuminators. As part of the Paris Exposition, a long tract of the Avenue de l'Opéra had been lighted by Jablochkoff arc lamps. Fine, Edison said. But this was not where the real money was. The real money was in putting lights in people's houses. An arc lamp couldn't be used in a house; it was far too bright, and noisy besides. What you wanted to do was somehow make a quiet little light that people could read by. It would work just like a gas lamp, except that you wouldn't have to ignite it with a match. You could simply throw a switch. All the electricity would come from one dynamo station located in the middle of the town, and a method would have to be found for measuring the quantity of electricity and charging for it. The entire thing would be developed as a system. The dynamos, the distribution wires, the meters, and the lamps would all have to be ready at the same time.

The correspondents who heard him say this thought it was preposterous, but they were under orders from their editors to regard Edison's ravings as news. How long, they asked him, would it take him to do such a thing? "Six weeks," he told them.

In Des Moines, the correspondents ran to the Western Union office to file their stories. By the time the train reached Denver, newspapers throughout the country carried accounts of Edison's plans on their front pages. Wall Street was already reacting; the stocks of the gasworks were plummeting. An urgent telegram from Edison's patent attorney advised him that a group of bankers from the houses of Vanderbilt and Morgan had formed a syndicate to promote his electric light invention. Edison himself took over the telegraph key to signal his reply. "Tell the old crooks this time it will cost them something," he said.

As the train climbed the Rocky Mountains, Edison insisted on being allowed to ride on the cowcatcher of the locomotive. He was given a small velvet cushion to sit on.

The views were spectacular. In front of him, the fir and aspen extended up the mountain grades in serene patches. The train moved slowly enough for birds to keep up with it, and they did. He could see raspberries growing by the side of the tracks. Blasts of steam released from the drive cylinders at the end of each power stroke blew the raspberry bushes sideways. The steam blasts simulated the sound of a series of rocket firings, and these harsh shocks echoed among the canyons. When Edison looked back at the train curving downward, he had a startling sensation of height.

Coming down the other side, he held the cowcatcher with both hands and screamed.

In Grand Junction, in Salt Lake City, in Reno, in Sacramento, Edison obliged the press with discussions about electric lighting. Each time he spoke to them, the story grew more elaborate. He said he had obtained the secret of a practical electric light by following a path entirely different from that of any other inventor. He said when the secret was revealed, everyone would wonder why they never thought of it. He promised that one machine would supply the power for thousands of lights. The correspondents fired off one question after another, and Edison gave them all the sunniest answers.

By the time he returned to his laboratory in New Jersey, it was clear to everyone but Edison that this time his big mouth had really gotten him into trouble. When his own six-week deadline for revealing the invention had come and gone, the newspaper stories about Edison began to get nasty. Scientists in both America and England were asked to comment about Edison's plan to produce an incandescent light. The gist of their remarks was that it was impossible, and Edison would know that if he had even the slightest understanding of electrical science. In London, Lord Kelvin said something very beautifully sarcastic to the *Times*. Edison apparently missed the sarcasm. He snipped the story out and pasted it in his scrapbook.

It was true, of course, that he was in something of a jam, since he had told the world that he had an invention, whereas in fact he had only an ambition. Also, he had accepted a fair amount of money from his financial syndicate, and if they had not invested in an invention, then what had they invested in? Clearly, something tangible was needed, and quickly. The laboratory at Menlo Park was put on a continuous shift. Machinists and glassblowers were expected to eat and sleep at their benches. Edison himself didn't come home for two-week periods, although, at the time, his house was only a few hundred yards from the laboratory. Whenever he did return home, his habit was to drag himself up the stairs without addressing his wife or children and to lie down on the bed, still wearing his soiled and greasy clothing.

His laboratory notebooks reveal some of what went on

during this period. In one place, he says, "Shitt! Glass busted by Böhm!" In another he says, "Vegetable Matter and Other Life By-Products. Tried carbonized filaments of red oak bark, cornstalks, pea creepers. No Damn Good. Tomorrow we do hairs from the scalp, armpit, and crotch. Male vs. Female? Getting female crotch hairs tricky."

Before he was finished, Edison tried some six thousand materials, including filaments from wild grasses, horse's hooves, jackass hides, hog's bristles, and a strip cut from his own (not very clean) linen handkerchief. He sent agents to South America, Asia, and India to find and bring back specimens of exotic vegetable matter. Members of the press traveled with these agents and reported their adventures. A man named William Cowley climbed into the Haleakala Crater on the island of Maui and brought back a rare silversword plant. Another Edison agent, Willis Farmer, risked death in a snake-infested river in New Guinea to pick a stem from a water plant known locally as "pig's pizzle." After one of Farmer's assistants drowned, the papers picked up the story and sensationalized it. They implied that the assistant had been strangled by a giant snake. In cartoons, Edison was represented as a wizard with a conical hat. The public was left with the impression that Edison had sent these minions out to bring back owl's tongues. Most people forgot that he was overdue on his promise to invent the light bulb.

In the end, Edison rescued himself with a piece of ordinary paper. When he finally made his announcement and the mobs came to Menlo Park to see what the world would look like in the future, they were shown an entire square mile illuminated by more than a hundred electric lights, and inside each one was a carbonized filament made from a piece of paper. On New Year's Eve, Edison arranged for a dozen special trains to come from New York to bring the spectators and take them home.

Edison's special guest that night, arriving from New York with her entourage in a private train, was the French tragedienne Sarah Bernhardt. The Divine Sarah was then on one of her many money-making tours of the United States. In Booth's Theatre, she packed them in with her exquisite performances of *La Dame aux Camélias*. Commodore Vanderbilt was in his private box for every performance, weeping piteously into a large white handkerchief. At the stage door, a young girl threw herself under Bernhardt's carriage and refused to move unless the great actress agreed to join her mother and herself for tea.

Bernhardt walked through the illuminated grounds at Menlo Park on Edison's arm. She spoke no English, and Edison spoke no French. He seemed to be captivated by her, and blushed conspicuously. The great Madame Sarah looked like a young girl this night, wearing a white suede jacket, high-heeled shooting boots, and a hibiscus blossom pinned in her hair. Edison showed her automatic writing machines, an electric arrow to be shot from a crossbow, and a device for magnetizing apples in order that they could be twisted off the tree all at once, by remote control. The incomparable Bernhardt, herself an innovator and in some ways a magician, smiled and applauded, but it was obvious she did not understand. Desperate to communicate, Edison tried the only foreign language he knew, which turned out to be pig latin. Bernhardt could barely hear him. The crowds and their noise were fantastic. At one point, overcome by weariness, Bernhardt collapsed, but Edison caught her before she hit the ground. He used his big belly as a kind of shelf to hold her up until she regained consciousness.

The gaslight companies infiltrated the crowd with saboteurs, but Edison and his men were ready for them. When Gilbert Rathbone, an agent for Baltimore Gas and Ice, attempted to short out the entire system using a thick piece of wire he had hidden in his clothes, he managed to do no more damage than to blow a safety fuse Edison's engineers had installed earlier. The man was apprehended by Edison's agents and brought to him, whereupon Edison delivered the would-be saboteur a swift boot in the rear.

Newspapers around the world reported the story of how

he had outwitted the saboteur. They paid Edison elaborate homage for his electric light. But they failed to give any account of an equally important Edison invention which stood before them that very night, an invention which would change forever the way new ideas would be manufactured and given to the world. This invention was Menlo Park itself, the first industrial laboratory.

The Bells returned from Argentina several days before they were expected. They had canceled a planned visit in Washington to come directly home. Bell was so weary from the trip and so disappointed by General Rivera's asinine mistake in inviting him at all that he took to his bed and wouldn't get up for two days. Mabel indulged him this extra rest, provided that he would work in bed on his correspondence at least two hours a day. A week went by and still Bell was seen outside the house only rarely during the daylight hours. Each night, he walked many miles alone on the hill roads.

It was during this period that Mabel befriended Mourly Vold. The day following the Bells' return, Donald G. Morrison brought Mourly Vold to the main house. Under the old man's tutelage, Mourly Vold had by this time become an experienced animal husbandman, and had been given modest responsibilities for the flock. In addition to his duties in the carding room, he was now the chief caretaker of the lambs.

One should keep in mind that by this time, Mabel was the owner and primary supervisor of the sheep. Two years earlier, in a moment of disappointment and frustration, Bell had ordered all the sheep to be taken away and sold. Knowing that her husband had a great deal of sentiment tied up in his sheep-breeding experiments and that he would soon regret what he had done, Mabel discovered where the sheep had been taken and had brought them back. As she had expected, Bell was moved to tears by the sight of them coming back in the trucks. But after that, he showed only a desultory interest in them. He went and looked at them in the pastures from time to time, but he showed little of the enthusiasm of the early years of the project, when his habit had been to lead his family up the hill to observe them every day.

In Mabel's company, Mourly Vold went looking for lost lambs. It became plain after they had done this for a day or two that her handicap would have been more of a limitation than his if either of them had tried to do the job alone. The lambs revealed themselves by their sounds first. Typically, Mourly Vold and Mabel would be standing in a high, fenceless pasture, its tall grass moving in waves under the sea breeze. There would be no animals in sight, and Mabel would have turned her back, ready to leave this pasture to walk still higher into the copses of inland forest, but that would be when Mourly Vold would hear something, perhaps a sound as faint as that made when an animal hidden in the grass takes a single step. Then they would find the lamb, led by combined senses—his hearing, her sight—that together were truly extraordinary.

When they made these trips together, Mabel would pack a lunch. Shortly after noon, they would stop and find the shade of a tree. Mourly Vold would then eat what was offered to him: chicken dumplings, corn bread, cherry pie, apples, and tea.

Mabel was delighted to see him eat. In feeding him, she was also taming him. As he gnawed on her corn bread, he became less wild. She was deliberately seeking something from him. She approached him the way she would approach a lamb that she planned to lift in her arms.

"What do you suppose they think of us," she asked, "when we catch them?"

"They don't mind," Mourly Vold said. "It's a game for them. They don't lead very serious lives."

Mabel was pleased by his intelligence, his judgment, and his understanding of how to be good company to old people. They talked easily together. He answered her questions about his home and his mother. He surprised her with his knowledge of the sheep experiments. He had mastered even the complicated coding system which Bell had invented to keep track of the genealogy of each animal. He matched his steps to hers when they walked together, and opened the gate for her each time they met a fence. He made it absolutely clear that he enjoyed her companionship.

But she wished for more than this. She wished that she could catch his eye. This seemed impossible. When they spoke together, he sometimes turned his face in her direction, but his eyes never precisely touched hers. The thickness of his lenses imbued his eyes with such distortions that eye contact in the usual sense was made bizarre. The magnification was the unsettling thing. His pupils appeared as large as those of a cat in the dark. These eyes of his, which seemed large enough to see everything in the world at once, were, in fact, almost dysfunctional. They did not even agree with each other, but frequently looked in different directions. In a disturbing way Mabel did not understand, the lack of a clear contact with his eyes made it difficult for her sometimes to read his speech.

"He certainly is the most remarkable young man," she reported to her husband. "The thing I find so exceptional about him is his thoughtfulness. He really talks to me, and he gives me the feeling that what I'm saying matters to him. Young people can't usually do that, or at least they don't."

"Maybe he isn't young," Bell said.

"Oh, yes he is. He's eighteen. But, in many ways, he's more grown up than some adults."

"No low blows, please, darling," Bell said.

"That wasn't meant to be a mean remark," Mabel said. "I'm just telling you about him. He really came to see you, after all. I think you might be able to come out of your mood soon and talk with the boy. He's been waiting all this time."

CHAPTER 9

Bell awoke shortly after midnight and sat upright in bed. He had been having a dream in which he was watching two women, nude, bathing in the water beside his houseboat. He could not recall who the women were. Because he couldn't return to sleep, he walked out of the house in the middle of the night, wearing an old silk robe over his pajamas. He descended the front steps and shuffled through the dewy grass. His bedroom slippers left long, lens-shaped tracks, making the grass appear slick where he had disturbed it.

He was on his way to the houseboat, walking under a bright moon. The sky was open from the eastern to the western horizon, without a cloud. At his back, the hills climbed up toward the thin mats of forest and the blank inland marshes beyond. Before him, at the foot of the long slope, the great Bras d'Or glittered, deep and cold as the heart of a city whore.

He boarded the houseboat by the slender gangplank and went forward to the breakfast deck, which was kept under canvas in the summer. He sat in his usual deck chair, but even before the weight left his feet, he remembered who they were, the two women bathing among the reflections of light and the darker wave troughs, in the water off the stern of the boat. He saw them suddenly out of the corner of his eye, but when he looked again, they were gone.

Not now, perhaps, but twenty years earlier, they had been there, and he had seen them by accident. The two women were Helen Keller and Anne Sullivan. They were living a life of heroism together, and Bell had been a famous part of their story.

At a time in his life when his own girls were becoming young women, Bell had met this young Helen, and had found her as delightful as people had said she was. Looking at her soft and beautiful face, all humanity appeared gorgeous to him, and for this reason: because she was without sight or hearing, Helen was perfectly and permanently guileless, so that her intelligence could never be deluded by appearances. Instead, she wanted to know what the human brain always wants to know when it is perfectly new. What is the world like around me? Why is water wet? What is the wind? Why do men long for women and women for men? Bell recognized these as the questions of the scientist, and it moved him profoundly to discover that Helen's interior, and therefore perhaps every human interior, if it could only be left unspoiled, was passionately involved with science.

First at the Perkins Institution for the Blind and then at Radcliffe, she opened like a flower, fueled by an intellectual energy that seemed strong enough to light a whole civilization. Bell spoke to her as her other teachers did, by spelling into her palm. She took his arm and they walked together through Cambridge. Once, they stood under a lilac by the banks of the Charles where it curls toward Mount Auburn Street. It began to rain. Bell took Helen's hand and placed it on a slender branch. He explained that the vibrations were caused by raindrops striking the leaves. He put her hand close to a puddle and let her feel the tiny fountains that reach up after every splash. He explained to her the mechanism of a piano, and later that evening found one in the common room of her dormitory. She felt its voice by touching the lid as Bell played. Someone had told her that diseases could be spread by kissing and she asked Dr. Bell about this. He told her what he knew, which was not much. If it came to him as a surprise that she could ask such questions without embarrassment, then he surprised himself even more by his own lack of embarrassment in giving the answers, vague as they were.

Helen and her teacher were invited to travel with the Bells

as members of their family. She enjoyed and even exploited the confidentiality her mode of communication with Bell allowed. She would spell outrageous things into Bell's hand, no matter what other company was present. "I'm bored," she said once, at a family party. "I want us to walk outdoors together." Bell's daughters, about the same age as Helen, resented the continuous attention she received from their father.

She was often with them during the summer in Baddeck. When Bell began his experiments with tetrahedral kites, she worked by his side. She helped him sew the fabric on the bamboo planes. There is a famous photograph of them together in the sheep pasture to the west of the house. She is holding his arm. It is not clear which of them has the kite string, which rises up into the gray sky. Anne Sullivan stands at some distance from them, her hands clasped over her hat, her extraordinary bosoms sticking out to leeward.

But then came that fortnight of miserably hot weather, so unusual in Nova Scotia. With the air motionless, the kite experiments came to a halt. Bell always felt the heat terribly; it had been his lack of tolerance for hot weather that had brought them from Washington to Baddeck in the first place. He retired indoors, and spent most of each day sleeping. For several days, no one saw him at all. Then one morning, at the beginning of the second week of the heat wave, he left his bed and went down to the houseboat, hoping that a breeze might be stirring over the water. As was his habit on the houseboat, he took off all his clothes. He lay prone on a chaise longue under the canvas awning of the breakfast deck. Presently he heard the voices of the young women, Helen and Anne. They stepped between the two giant black spruces that served as a mooring for the houseboat. Believing themselves alone, they had come to bathe.

They took off their hats and shoes, and rolled down their stockings. Anne Sullivan was faster at this than Helen. She unfastened the buttons of her dress at her back, one by one.

She brushed her long hair forward over her shoulder as she did this. In one amazingly skillful pull, employing an arcing motion as strong as the one a dog uses to shake the life out of a rat, she flicked her dress over her head. She folded it neatly and stowed it beside her hat on the grass. Next, she unfastened her undergarments and took them off: cambric underskirt, silk slip, corset cover, corset, and brassiere. When she was finished, she turned toward the sun and lingered for a moment, rubbing her alarmingly luxuriant bush.

In the next moment, both were in the water, laughing and splashing. They had forgotten that they were participants in a miracle. They were behaving like ordinary young animals. Bell pleaded with himself to give them back their privacy, but no matter what terrible names he called himself, he could not make himself look away. He had long admired Helen's beautiful face; now he saw in the rest of her body an even more striking and innocent loveliness. Her companion, she of the enormous breasts, rolled over in the water and floated on her back, leaving Bell with a set of mental snapshots that were to stay with him for the rest of his life.

Even now, as he sat on the deck in the darkness, he thought he could hear the sucking sounds of Anne Sullivan's limbs moving against the water. His own actual treachery was so long finished, why did these recollections remain? Because, Bell knew, a man, any man, is no better than a wild animal, and the maleness in him will take advantage of anything, even his own memory.

And so now, Bell could recall every detail of the scene: Helen's back, and her thin shoulders, and the white curve of her arms as she stood waist-deep in the water. Anne Sullivan's sprawl, with every orifice above the waterline open and pointing up. The morning glitter surrounding them both, making it almost impossible to look at them. But there was this one detail, and he could never be sure of it, one way or the other, however often he thought of it. At that last moment, had Anne Sullivan opened her eyes and seen him there?

■ ■

The following afternoon, Bell left the house during daylight hours for the first time since returning from South America. Although the weather was warm, he dressed in the same salt-and-pepper wool coat and knickerbockers he customarily wore on his walks at night. The knickerbockers were held up by heavy elastic braces. A bow tie was fastened at his neck. He wore a wool cap on his large head. He paused at the foot of the wide front steps descending from the porch and bent down to tie his shoe. When he straightened up again, his face was scarlet. Slowly his cheeks regained their normal color.

He walked down the hill toward the lower sheep buildings. The weather had been fair all morning, but now clouds were growing together in larger groups and their bottoms were beginning to show pale gray colors here and there. Their groupings seemed to have in them an order that one could make out, with sufficient attention. There was a structure in them like the structure of waves on water, a spacing between the lines of clouds that was similar to the spacing between the crests of ocean waves. Bell noted this and considered both the similarities and the differences. The timing was, of course, a major difference. Clouds require much more time for their flowing movements than do ocean waves. He had once invented a mechanical apparatus for extracting power from ocean waves, using a float and a ratchet. It now occurred to him that a kite might take the place of the float in a similar piece of equipment designed to extract the wave energy from passing clouds.

When he reached the main sheep building, there appeared to be no one around. Wasps circled the goldenrod growing by the door and flew away. Sheep could be heard muttering their harmless jargon in a nearby pen. Bell noticed a ladder leaning up against the building. The sight of it irritated him. It should not have been left there. It could be knocked over by accident and cause an injury. He took the ladder down and put it away in the tool shed.

Inside the sheep building, he encountered an unfamiliar object. It was a metallic ball hanging from a wire. The wire entered the building through a hole in the roof. The ball had been fashioned from two tin drinking cups joined together at their lips, their handles removed. He drew closer and examined it. The workmanship was of very high quality. The seam where the cups joined together had been soldered and filed smooth, and the entire surface had been highly polished.

Bell reached out to touch the sphere. Crack! A miniature lightning bolt jumped between his fingers and the surface of the sphere. He withdrew his hand and took a step backward. What a surprise! The tip of one finger ached as if it had been bitten by a meadow vole. What had happened?

Just then he heard a voice from the roof. "Has someone taken the ladder away?"

Outside again, Bell saw a young man clinging to the roof. He was holding the clay tiles with one hand and feeling along the edge of the roof with the other.

"Just a minute, just a minute!" Bell cried, and he quickly brought the ladder back from the toolhouse. With obvious effort, Bell climbed part of the way up the ladder. "I'm here," he said. "This way."

Mourly Vold crawled over the roof toward Bell's voice. With Bell's assistance, he placed his foot on one of the rungs and began to descend.

"That's the stuff," Bell said. "I'm right here below you." And so on. But most of the advice and encouragement Bell contributed now was not necessary. The only really helpful thing he had done was to put the ladder back.

When they were standing on the ground again, and facing one another, Bell said, "What the devil is going on? I got a nasty shock from that thing in there. What is it?" He was breathing hard from the exertion of climbing the ladder.

"It's an accumulator," Mourly Vold told him.

"I know that, I know that," Bell said. "But what's charging it?"

"The atmosphere," Mourly Vold replied.

He explained how his device worked. A glass insulator on a pole fixed to the roof held a steel needle pointing straight up. A wire connected the needle to the accumulator ball. There was nothing more than this. The motive engine responsible for charging the accumulator was the natural electric field present in the atmosphere. This grew stronger with the passage of charged clouds overhead. As the needle on the roof gave up electric charge into the air, charge of the opposite sign accumulated on the steel ball below.

They walked into the sheep house. Mourly Vold picked up a pitchfork and wrapped a wire around one of its tines. The other end of the wire was fastened to a cold-water pipe. He waved the pitchfork through the air near the accumulator ball and a bright purple flash reached out to strike it.

Bell wanted to try it.

"Hold the pitchfork by the wooden handle and you won't get bitten," Mourly Vold told him. "And move it quickly past the accumulator. You get a bigger flash the faster you move it."

Bell satisfied himself that this was the case. "I wonder why that is?" he said.

Now Mourly Vold grounded the accumulator by holding the pitchfork against it. He placed a steel sewing needle on the top of the accumulator ball and removed the pitchfork. Before long, when he judged that the effect he was looking for might have developed, he held out the palm of his hand in the direction of the needle. "Feel this," he said.

Bell held out his hand in the same place. "It feels like a breeze," he said. "There's a wind."

"It's the electric wind," Mourly Vold told him.

This is how Mourly Vold revealed to Bell his discovery of a simple method by which both the lightning and wind of thunderstorms may be brought to earth, even brought indoors, in a pleasantly miniaturized form. Such a thing is marvelous enough by itself, no? But Bell recognized that he was seeing more than this. He was seeing lightning and wind which were to come in the future. For at this moment, the clouds above were not yet thunderstorms. This afternoon there had been as yet no wind, no lightning, and no rain, although it was plain that all these would arrive soon.

Bell sat down on a bench and put on his spectacles. He took a tablet of paper from his pocket and began drawing on it. Because his hand shook, the drawings were composed of trembling lines.

"Look at this," he said when he was finished. "Your device can be made into a thunderstorm detector. In the primary circuit, we leave everything as you have it. But then we put another accumulator ball here, separated from the first one by a gap. The second ball goes to ground through a coil, and we use the changing flux through the coil to ring a bell."

As the light was poor and Bell's scratchings were faint, Mourly Vold had no hope of comprehending Bell's diagram. Nevertheless, he visualized Bell's circuit clearly in his imagination, and was delighted. Not only had Bell understood his experiment, but he had also found an application for it, all within the space of minutes. "That might work," he said to Bell. "If it did, you could adjust the sensitivity by making the gap larger or smaller. Faraway storms would need a smaller gap."

"Precisely so," Bell said. "Precisely so."

Many people have wondered, in the long years since these events took place, exactly how and when the collaboration between Little Egypt and Alexander Graham Bell began. The truth is that it began in a simple building devoted to sheep research, as we have just seen. But this is not the preposterous thing. The preposterous thing is that they should have been able to work together at all, given the gulfs in age and scientific temperament that separated them.

The matter of scientific temperament is, of course, most important, and here they were not at all alike. Bell was an inventor first and last, and although he was a patron of scientific men, although he undertook researches that he characterized as scientific, his training, judgment, and intuition in scientific matters were poorly developed. Mourly Vold, as we already know, had genuine and extraordinary scientific talents. This fundamental difference might have become a source of conflict between two men of comparable age and experience attempting to work together. It may be that the one difference between them, namely their vastly different ages, compensated for the other. Mourly Vold was never so proud of his scientific talent that he had no time to listen to an old person.

Within a few hours, they had fabricated the secondary circuit Bell had sketched. They did this work in Bell's laboratory in the main house. In the middle of the afternoon, Mabel joined them there for tea. During the meal, Bell talked with great animation about the project, but still managed to eat a dozen shortbread biscuits. When they were ready for a trial of the circuit, Mabel went with them to the sheep building.

The sky had now become quite dark. In the west, the bottoms of the clouds had the appearance of women's breasts, soft and pendulous. There was a far-off thunderclap, just a single one.

The moment Bell connected his coil, the warning clapper began to strike each time a spark jumped across the gap between the accumulator spheres. Mourly Vold's prediction was quickly proven correct: the instrument could be made far more sensitive by diminishing the gap. To their surprise, they found that a lightning stroke in the clouds above almost always produced a simultaneous discharge in their instrument, an arc of unusual color and intensity between the accumulator spheres. After one of these lightning-initiated flashes, the instrument remained quiet for a substantial period before resuming its activity. Mourly Vold remarked that this was evidence that lightning strokes caused major changes in the electric field near the surface of the earth, a fact he had not found mentioned in his reading.

"And what *have* you been reading?" Bell asked him. "I have Joseph Henry's collected papers in my library, and I enjoy looking at them, although the mathematics in them leaves me without a clue. I also have James Clerk Maxwell's two volumes. Whenever he draws a picture, I generally understand that, but not much else. You seem to know a lot about electricity. What books do you read?"

Mourly Vold admitted with some embarrassment that he had as yet read only one book, Parsons's book.

"Parsons's book?" Bell inquired.

"Yes," he said. "This one." He brought out his copy, now very much worn and ragged, of *Experiments in Electricity a Boy Can Do*. Bell opened the book and began turning through its pages.

"This is a perfectly beautiful little machine you've made together," Mabel said. "I see why you both like it so much. It gets its power from the sky and imitates so nicely what's going on up there. But I *have* been wondering about the practical part, although I agree that there's no reason why everything has to have a practical purpose. I just wondered, why would the average person need to have a bell ring to tell him a thunderstorm was coming? Couldn't he just look out and see it up there?"

On Bell's insistence, that evening, Mourly Vold moved his few belongings into a bedroom of the main house. Mabel and Bell personally put fresh linen on the bed and brought out an exquisite handmade quilt for his use. Later, he joined them for dinner. They dined on onion soup, fresh salmon in a white wine sauce, young asparagus, lobster claws, and champagne. Bell drank his soup through a glass straw. For dessert, there were strawberries and cream.

Throughout dinner and afterward, Bell kept up a steady stream of stories and reminiscences. He told about the steamer trip on Lake Huron he had taken, long before his marriage. He and George Coats had traveled through the mining districts. They had bought the skins of rare foxes from trappers. At night, they had slept in flimsy wooden hotels with loaded six-guns under their pillows.

Bell had an extensive collection of magic-lantern slides, and he brought these out after dinner. The pictures he projected on the wall showed himself and Mabel in the midst of journeys through Mexico, Europe, and North Africa. Standing in front of Notre Dame, he was wearing a Palm Beach suit with a gray pinstripe almost invisible against a black background. With Mabel by the Albert Memorial, he was dressed in a suit of dark manipulated serge, including a two-button coat, slit in back, and peg-top pants with cuff bottoms. Mabel wore a dress of cotton rice cloth in a pattern of small roses with elbow-length set-in sleeves. He showed slides of their daughters growing up, getting married, having families of their own. He gave an extensive narration about each picture before moving on to the next. Somehow he had forgotten that Mourly Vold's sight was poor, and that a magic-lantern show would therefore be an inappropriate entertainment.

Later, in the bedroom, he told his wife how happy he was to have this very intelligent young man living with them. It was almost as if one of their two little sons had come back to life.

"Yes," Mabel said. "He's wonderful, and I agree it will be easy to love him. But you haven't counted the years correctly. Both of our little sons would be near the age of forty today. This young man could be one of their sons, not ours. He almost came to us too late."

CHAPTER 10

Now, as the summer was ending, the Bells took Mourly Vold into their lives completely. When the harvest came from the vegetable garden, Bell began a series of experiments investigating how various vegetables might be dehydrated and stored. With help from Mourly Vold and Mabel, he took sweet corn, beans, and summer squash into his laboratory. The products of his researches were generally inedible, but these failures had no effect on his mood. In his care, the corn hardened to the consistency of gravel and the beans became stiffened twigs, but still he seemed to be delighted with life. He said that the fresh vegetables from the garden tasted all the more wonderful to him now that he knew how fragile their succulence was.

The three of them often walked together in the late morning, before lunch. They visited the cabin the Bells had built years earlier by a mountain lake. They rowed together on the Bras d'Or when the weather was calm. Bell lingered at the oars and watched through the clear water as crabs walked under them on the bottom.

They made the habit of taking their lunch on the old houseboat. They ate in the shade of the black spruce trees, listening to popular songs played on an Edison machine.... "Smiles," "Bouncy Boy," "I Love You Sunday." After lunch they would listen to Caruso on the same machine, and frequently Bell would sing along with the choruses. In foggy weather, when the surface of the water lay absolutely flat and the moisture-laden air paradoxically seemed clearer to the passage of sounds than it normally is, Mourly Vold could hear the reflections of Bell's deep voice coming back from Bone Island.

It was about this time, as the hardwoods began showing first yellow and then red leaves toward their tops, that Mourly Vold reestablished his connections with the telephone underground. They were very glad to have him back.

"I think we have some real problems," Humberhill told him. "The party line is showing signs of decrepitude. For the past two weeks, people have been having trouble getting into it. Sometimes it takes five or ten tries. I was wondering when you were going to show up. Not a moment too soon, if you ask me. Where the hell are you?"

Mourly Vold explained his present circumstances.

"That's wonderful," Humberhill said. "You must be happy as a pig in shit. Now, the question is, what are you going to do for us? Our fun is threatened here."

Two hours later, Mourly Vold spoke to his friend again. "I've checked into it," he said. "That circuit is on its way out. I spoke to a local office electrician and he looked it up for me. All the equipment in that office is being replaced with some fancy new system. That circuit we're living in will go out of existence eight days from now."

"Jesus Christ!" Humberhill said. "What are we going to do about *that*? I don't want to go out of existence!"

"Take it easy," Mourly Vold told him. "We'll just have to find another place. It should be possible. You can help."

Now a great united action began among the telephone experimenters with Little Egypt in command. Sighted or blind, the most experienced, the most ingenious, the most careful of them formed the front ranks, the scouts who went out on the wires across the country, searching for a new site for the party line. Following Little Egypt's instructions, they probed first at verification trunks, particularly the older ones found in some of the smaller central offices. Like a dentist with his pick, each one was looking for defects—not the enormous defects which would have been noticed and scheduled for repair already, but tiny defects of just the right type to permit some creative vandalism. They took on the voices of local operators, intertrunk switchers, and line supervisors. Little Egypt had taught them to imitate the people of the phone company so well that not a single real employee ever guessed that this supervisory switchman or line-crew chief who kept calling with work to be done was really a round-shouldered sightless student at a school for the blind in Toronto or Pennsylvania. Day after day, they galloped across the country, through local offices and intertoll centers, poking at the switch train as they went.

The party line became a desperate celebration. At peak times, hundreds of people were present in the line at once, laughing and singing and shouting to be heard. At other times, typically in the early morning hours, Little Egypt presided over precisely conducted meetings with his lieutenants. But everyone's thoughts were on the clock, and how it measured the time until the line would fall dead. It was like having knowledge of the exact time of the end of the world.

"There are now one hundred hours, thirty-eight minutes, and twenty seconds remaining," said a soprano voice known as the Syracuse Stallion. His voice was like the chirp of a robin. "I've got a beautiful old pocket watch here that came down to me from my great-great-grandfather."

"Aw, he wasn't so great-great," Humberhill told him.

The telephone company operators who came in were always cautious at the beginning, but usually it didn't take them long to warm up.

"The strangest part of all this," said Bertha from Toledo, "is what it feels like to be listening in and not worrying. We're never supposed to stay on the line, but sometimes, of course, you do. You'd go crazy if you didn't listen in once in a while. I'm convinced of that. The opportunity's there in front of you all the time. And once you've done it a couple of times, it's hard to stop yourself. I really think most of the operators stay on the job so that they can do it. It isn't the pay, that's for sure. Oh, I've heard some things, I'll tell you. And I nearly lost my job over it. But this takes the cake. I love it."

"We love you, too, Bertha!" This was the Syracuse Stallion.

"I have to go now. My supervisor just walked in."

"Come back when you can," somebody said.

Each night, Little Egypt worked without rest at the head of the team of scouts. Several times over the next few days they almost succeeded in establishing a new party line in some remote part of the networks. Once, in a small central office in New Brunswick, one of the scouts found what he thought was a shorted codelreed relay in the register-sender. But when Little Egypt investigated it personally, he found it operating normally. Another time, they thought they had the assistance of a switch-man in Shreveport to construct a suitable malfunction for them to live in, but when the time came for him to make good his promise, he wouldn't do it.

Time was running out, and still a new home for the party line had not been found. Humberhill began to despair.

"I know what's going to happen," he said. "This circuit is going to drop dead and we'll never get it going again. That will be the end of a very nice time in my life."

"Don't feel sorry for yourself yet," Little Egypt told him. "I'm working on something big."

And indeed he was. Faced with the failure of all his knowl-edge to provide a new open line, he had been forced to dig deeper into the organization of the networks. In a set of daring moves, he approached the line-link frame that held the party line from alternative directions. He tried coming in through the trunk-link frame and through the junctor grouping frames. This was familiar territory, and he knew it well, or at least he thought he did. He listened carefully for the reflections of the crossbar-switch transients. He could feel the individual select and hold magnets going down. Through the marker, through the incoming register, through the register link. And then nothing. Nothing! He found himself perched on the edge of a void.

The silence here was the silence of a winter forest. Every so often he could hear an isolated click like the sound of a twig snapping under the weight of snow. He was lost and alone. Somehow he had fallen through into an unfamiliar plane.

Then he noticed it. Very far off, very faintly in the distance, he heard a regular beat of relay clicks. Bap, ba-bip; bap, ba-bip. He recognized it as the powerful left-foot cruising rhythm of "Sad Eyes," done by Binky Bishop's Famous Canadian Cavaliers. Without giving much thought to what he was doing, he mimicked the rhythm by clicking his tongue on the roof of his mouth.

Immediately, the clicks disappeared and a faint purring took their place. He experimented with other percussive rhythms. After each one, the background purring was interrupted for an instant and then reestablished. Now it dawned on him what was happening.

Important discoveries are made so rarely that we have little information about any part of the process. The discoverer always mentions chance when asked how he did it. He was wandering, and came upon the insight, the idea, the realization by accident. But everyone wanders occasionally, without finding anything at all. In fact, ordinary wandering is generally unproductive. There must be a kind of alert wandering which results in discovery. It is absolutely necessary to work this way in order to find anything new, but the techniques for doing it can't be learned in any school. It was alert wandering which paid off for Little Egypt now.

Several hours later, he spoke with Humberhill again. "Listen to this," he said. "The new equipment they're putting in talks to itself with dance rhythms. It can be controlled by tapping to it in patterns it recognizes. I've already learned some of the code that matches up the beats and the numbers."

"That's great," Humberhill said. "So what?"

"Keep your mouth shut and listen," Little Egypt told him. "This opens up a whole new territory for us. It means we don't have to talk to switchmen and operators anymore to get where we want to go. Now we can talk directly to their machinery. Don't you understand? Among other things, it means we can create a party line in the network behind any telephone number. I've already proven that. A moment ago, I established a new party line in your number. Here, I'll demonstrate."

Humberhill heard the line go silent for a moment. He heard a purring sound, then a series of clicks and taps.

"I'm back again." Little Egypt's voice had an echo. "I'm coming at you from two directions now. I'm using two different class-five offices, one in Montreal and one in Boston. How does it sound?"

"You sound like you have your head inside a milk can," Humberhill said.

More clicks, followed by a series of sharp pops.

When Little Egypt's voice returned this time, it was chopped with echoes and quite distorted. "Here I am again," he said. "I'm sending my voice to you from eight different directions. One of me is coming from Tennessee, and the others are coming from Montreal, Boston, Philadelphia, Chicago, Toronto, Bangor, and Saint John's."

"Why would you want to do that?" Humberhill asked him.

"Wait a moment," he said, in his fuzzy multiple voices. "I'll be right back." More clicks and pops, with noises in the background that resembled animal cries. "I'm here again. Now, to answer your question, I did that to show what we've got here. You are now sitting in a party line that can be reached from anywhere in North America with no record made of the call and no toll fee. There is this new automatic equipment they're just putting into regional offices everywhere, and I've got it by the gonads. As things stand today, only operators in regional offices have access to this equipment, but I found out that they're planning to put this stuff in everywhere, so that someday anybody will be able to make a call anywhere in the world without ever talking to an operator. What this means to you right now is that we can re-create the party line at any time in any place, and we'll never again have to worry about being displaced or discovered."

"That's wonderful!" Humberhill said. "It's more than we need, even, and you found it just in time. I congratulate you! I kiss you on both cheeks!"

Returning the salute, Little Egypt let loose with a withering barrage of animal grunts and squeals, dishes falling to the floor, glass breaking, ashcans clattering in the street, and finally a train wreck, complete with boiler explosion.

"I have to go now," he said, when this was all over.

"Wait a minute," Humberhill said. "You haven't told me what I have to do yet."

"That's right," Little Egypt said, "I haven't," and he disappeared.

He returned to the networks, and in the next twenty-four hours he made one major discovery after another. His first discovery, and perhaps the most important one, was that the sounds which operated the new switching circuits were composed of two separate rhythms each. One of the rhythms balanced the other, like a melody and its counterpoint. Each contained its own intelligence, its own contribution to the routing information. A conversation he overheard between traffic service engineers revealed that the secret rhythms he was hearing were created by pieces of machinery known as Z-trunks. He learned to reproduce the clattering beats of the Z-trunks, idiom by idiom. With clicks of his tongue, he practiced capturing the Z-trunk machinery and putting it to work in his service. Hour by hour, he improved his mastery. He hurried about, and flung open door after door. Behind each door, a hissing Z-trunk stretched beyond the horizon, awaiting instructions. A Z-trunk could be captured in only one particular way. Otherwise, it would rise up and strike back, throwing him out of its way, sending him spinning into space. With the correct commands, it became tame, and carried him on its back at amazing speeds. In this way, each Z-trunk functioned as a separate watchful animal, protecting its own domain. But each one was as stupid as the last, provided you knew how to lie to them.

He found that the ends of the Z-trunks were connected together in a recklessly soft way. The designers of the system apparently had decided that it was sufficient to put the barrier codes on the outside of the trunks, and to employ a rather lax, easily manipulated system on the inside. A rowdy in such a system, Little Egypt observed, could really go berserk. In one brief experiment, he demonstrated that all the telephones of an entire city could be ganged together and caused to ring at once. It was possible to eavesdrop on any line, or on many lines simultaneously. All the powers of a senior supervisory operator were made available, and this required no more specialized equipment than the tongue in any mouth.

But now a dilemma began to frame itself in his mind, and it became clearer and more obvious the farther he went in his discoveries. The dilemma was this. The telephone company now lay at his feet, the secrets of its newest equipment entirely in his possession. These secrets were safe, of course, only as long as they stayed with him. The moment he put this information in the hands of Humberhill and the rest of them, he would lose the power to regulate it. His discoveries might be used to damage the networks, to cause havoc! This wasn't so farfetched! The power, the degree of control we are talking about here was substantial. The telephone systems of whole cities, of New York or Chicago, could be tied up and left to strangle by a single wrongheaded little fool! In fact, he told himself, this wouldn't even require wrongheadedness; carelessness would be enough. Someone with practically no knowledge could invade a Z-trunk, and once in there, could barge about, causing vast damage without even knowing what he was doing.

Thinking this, he felt pity for the telephone company. The rhythm-recognizing equipment was like a tender new plant, just pushing up from the soil, not yet protected against the danger of predators. He saw now that he must act as its defender as well as its investigator. It was no longer clear that Humberhill and the others should be told how to use his new discoveries.

He decided to bring Bell into his confidence and solicit his advice. Bell would have the judgment and experience to know what action the situation demanded. He would also have the contacts necessary to bring a suitable warning to the attention of the telephone company management. Some kind of warning would certainly be required to let them know that their new equipment was seriously flawed and vulnerable. After all, even if he were to keep secret every critical fact he had just learned, how long would it be until someone else came upon the same discoveries? The next person might not feel the same sense of responsibility.

He gave Bell an extensive demonstration of his knowledge and virtuosity. For the purpose, he rigged up an extra telephone receiver to his experimental instrument, so that Bell could hear everything he was doing.

The first thing he did was to grab a Z-trunk and tongue-click himself into a pay telephone in a bus station in Parkersburg, West Virginia.

"Dr. Fishman, please," he said to the man who answered.

"There's no Dr. Fishman here," said the voice on the other end. "This is the bus station."

"Oh, I'm sorry," Little Egypt said. "I thought this was Fishman's office, the dentist. I need him to pull my tooth."

He hung up, but he tongue-clicked back into the same number almost immediately. This time he put on a woman's voice. "Let me speak to Dr. Fishman," he said. "Tell him it's his wife."

"He ain't here," the same man said. "This is a bus station. I'm just standing here, waiting for my bus. I only picked up the phone because it was ringing. I don't know a thing about any Fishman."

The next time Little Egypt called, he used a deep voice. "This is Fishman," he said. "Have there been any calls for me?"

Apparently Bell had never heard that one before, because he laughed out loud. His laugh sounded like this: yaw-haw-haw.

They went together to visit the dying party-line number. It was busy with all kinds of traffic when they arrived. At least two Edison machines were playing in the background. Little Egypt commanded silence. When the line fell quiet, he said, "I brought someone with me. Let me introduce Professor Alexander Graham Bell."

"Oh, Jesus Q. Christ," the Walrus said. "That's the most banal name I ever heard. I don't think you should give him that name. Why don't you give him a name with a little imagination to it? Almost anything would be better than that. Why don't you call him Julius Caesar or something? I mean, your friend is welcome, but I really think you should get him a better name."

"Don't be such an old shrew," the Syracuse Stallion said. "If he wants to call himself Alexander Graham Bell, let him. I don't think we have any other Alexander Graham Bells yet, at least, none that I can remember." Then he said to Little Egypt, "Tell your friend to say hello."

Little Egypt passed Bell the instrument. "Hello," Bell said. Twenty or thirty other voices returned the greeting, including Bronx cheers and simulated belches.

"I wish you'd quit playing around and tell us what to do when this line goes dead," Humberhill said. "Every hour there's less of this circuit left, and you can't be bothered doing anything about it. You're not the one who's going to be cut off when this thing dies, I am. What I want to know is, when are you going to start getting us ready?"

"When I feel like it," Little Egypt said. With a chatter of teeth played out like a drum roll, he dropped out of the line.

Before long, Bell became something of a telephone enthusiast himself. Mourly Vold showed him the simple rudiments of hookswitch signaling, and Bell enjoyed pulsing his way into the lines of some of the shops he knew in Baddeck and Sydney.

"Is this Young's Mercantile and Smoke Shop?" he would ask. "Let me talk with old Mr. Young. If he isn't there, I'll talk with young Mr. Young."

When his party came to the phone, he would say, "Is your shop on the car tracks?"

"Yes, Dr. Bell," Mr. Young would say. "You know very well it is."

"Well, then, you'd better move," Bell would tell him, "because there's a streetcar coming."

In the beginning, Mourly Vold was pleased to see Bell enjoying himself this way, but before long he thought it was time that Bell began to appreciate the serious side of his work.

"This is something you might like to try," he said. "I call it 'Z-trunk shuttlecock,' because it's a way of batting the control of a Z-trunk back and forth from one end to the other."

When he demonstrated Z-trunk shuttlecock, Bell heard first one be-bip and then another, fainter one, coming from a great distance. Both sounds then repeated in an endless series.

"I can bring in another Z-trunk between switches of the first one, and then I get what I call the 'Z-trunk two-step.' "

Bell now heard an additional pair of be-bips added to the cycle of sounds. The net effect was a percussive beat like the famous sound of Binky Bishop sliding out to do a solo on the stage of the Sydney Palladium.

"Now, picture this," Mourly Vold told him. "You get one Z-trunk started, and it goes through its routine for a little while, and then it triggers off the Z-trunk next to it. They do the two-step for a bit, and then a third one joins them. So it goes, on and on, until all the trunks in an office are moving in step together."

This time, Bell heard the first Z-trunk begin its heel-toe rhythm. "Peep, be-bip; peep, be-bip," it went. Then the next Z-trunk came in, and the next, and the next, until the volume of the rattling, striding be-bips reached an almost uncomfortable level. The Z-trunks gyrated together in perfect synchrony, and every few seconds another one popped forward and took its place among the others.

"I don't even have to let it stop in this office," Mourly Vold said, shouting to be heard over the din. "If I set it up the right way, the last Z-trunk in this office kicks off one in the next office, and it can keep on going forever."

He demonstrated this. He set up a wave of Z-trunk shuttlecock which slowly began to roll out across the country, locking up the long-lines networks in a boisterous, clattering rhythm. The circuits heaved with the combined weight of so many Z-trunks doing the same thing; it was as if an army were marching in lockstep over a delicate bridge. Mourly Vold stopped it before the wave had gone very far. With a few accurately placed volleys of claps, he caused the lines to fall silent.

"Needless to say," he told Bell, "that sort of thing could annoy a lot of people if it happened regularly."

"My God," Bell said. "It was going out there and just taking them all over. All the telephones in the country!"

"Well, actually," Mourly Vold said, "it wouldn't stop at the borders of countries. It would keep on going. So you can see why this sort of knowledge could be dangerous. If it fell into the wrong hands, I mean. This is where I thought you could help me."

Now he explained what he had in mind. He took out a letter he had written to the telephone company management. The text of the letter was as follows:

To whom it may concern,

I am writing to bring to your attention a serious set of weaknesses in the new automatic equipment now being placed in service throughout the United States and Canada. I have discovered that Z-trunks routed by this equipment may be controlled by sounds introduced at the telephone microphone by several means, including snaps of the fingers, strikes with a wooden spoon, and clicks made using the tongue against the roof of the mouth. I have used all these methods successfully to take control of Z-trunks, employing both immediate and wink-start methods, without provoking glare.

I respectfully suggest that you delay plans to place any more of this equipment in service until methods can be found to protect it against intrusion.

I shall continue my investigations, and you may expect to hear from me again as I discover further faults. You may find that my investigations or the activities of my associates cause occasional minor disruptions. I apologize for these inconveniences in advance, and point out that if you had made the networks right in the first place, you wouldn't need us to help you fix them.

A friend

"What do you want me to do with this?" Bell asked.

"See that it gets to the right people," Mourly Vold told him.

"I don't even know who the right people are," Bell said. "I haven't had anything to do with telephones since long before you were born."

Even though he said this, he took the letter from Mourly Vold and mailed it, along with a covering note, to the executive offices of the Bell system at an address in New York he had never visited. Mabel found the address for him in the back pages of a telephone book.

CHAPTER 11

Not many days later, Bell received a telegram from the Department of the Navy in Washington, and by two o'clock the same afternoon he was on a train headed south.

The telegram had informed him that he was being granted an interview with the Matériel Procurement Board, Bureau of Ships. He was trying to interest the navy in placing an order for what he suspected might be his greatest invention, the hydrodrome.

It was already quite successful. Bell carried in his case photographs and notarized documents which proved not only the existence of the craft but also its speed. The photographs showed a tubular hull sixty feet in length, tapering to a point at either end. The secret of its speed lay in the lattice of hydrofoils underneath. These provided the force to lift it out of the water, so that the hull could fly along at a steady height of ten feet above the waves. Two enormous Liberty engines turning pusher airscrews had already driven this craft at more than seventy miles per hour, a new world's marine speed record.

Bell and his collaborators had made this machine to be not only the world's fastest boat but also the world's most deadly submarine chaser. Because it derived its power from aerial rather than marine propellers, it could not be heard by submarines. Tests made with sensitive hydrophones the previous year had shown that this craft could run directly over a submarine and never be detected.

And everyone said that the ride was so smooth and steady! Up on her foils, the hydrodrome was free of any influence of the waves, and so she bore along on a marvelously straight track, no matter what the sea conditions. This was exactly the opposite of what happens in a conventional speedboat, with its buffeting and hammering when as much as a ripple crosses the surface.

Bell himself had never been for a ride in the thing. He had watched it from the dock, and for him this had been entertainment enough. But Mabel had not been so cautious. Earlier in the summer, Bell and Mourly Vold stood together on the dock as Mabel climbed into the open cockpit. This was after one of the speed trials, and the crew was taking it out again for a victory ride. Bell all but forbade her to risk her life this way, but she had done it regardless. The engines were started and the hydrodrome slid away from the dock. A newspaper photographer recorded all this on film. Mabel was wearing a yellow bonnet tied to her head with a scarf. Only the top of the bonnet could be seen sticking out of the open cockpit. The engines came up to full power, and almost immediately the hydrodrome rose on her foils. A picture later published in the *Rochester Herald* shows that Mabel looked at the camera at this moment. A patch of that photograph, observed under a magnifying glass, reveals Mabel's face. The dots of the photograph become odd-shaped globs when magnified, but Mabel's features are still recognizable. She is wearing the expression of a woman about to lose her balance.

But when she had returned, she had been delighted with the ride, delighted with herself. "Casy let me steer it," she had said. "I drove it right around Bone Island. It isn't like driving a boat at all. I think it must be more like driving an airplane."

Sometime after that, as Bell, Mabel, and Mourly Vold walked along the shore, Bell happened to look at the narrow passage between Bone Island and the mainland. It seemed fantastic to him that anyone could get a rowboat through there, let alone a craft weighing five tons. Something was floating among the black, slippery rocks. It appeared at first to be a torn fragment of one of Mabel's dresses. How alarmed he had been then, over something that might have happened, but never did! He saw his wife's body floating. Her arms and legs were wide apart, and her hands, where they emerged from the sleeves, were blackened. Now he saw the moment it had happened: the hydrodrome at top speed striking the rocks, exploding into thousands of struts and splinters, the huge motors collapsing forward into the cockpit. This is how he might have lost his beloved wife, riding on the back of one of his own flimsy ideas.

But it hadn't happened, of course. There she was, standing on the path beside Mourly Vold. Their shadows fell beside them on the grass. Refracted light from Mourly Vold's spectacles made a star at eye level on his shadow.

Bell arrived in Washington shortly after dawn and immediately went to his town house on Connecticut Avenue. He lay down fully clothed on his bed, without even removing his shoes. Following his instructions, the staff awoke him at ten o'clock and summoned a taxi for him. He went to meet the admirals with a certain number of wrinkles in his clothes.

Nevertheless, he explained the hydrodrome project to them in bright and enthusiastic terms. There was a public magnetism about Bell that he never lost, not even in the last years of his life. When speaking, he first raised important and useful questions and then answered them. He introduced suspense whenever that could be effective. He spoke to his audience as individuals. He knew and used everyone's name.

His message for them, which he amplified using photographs and tables, was that the hydrodrome was a proven success. He explained to them what he called the "reefing action" of the foils, whereby, as the speed rises, the boat automatically lifts farther above the water, thus eliminating the drag of the upper foils and permitting a still-greater speed. The principles demonstrated here had a future far beyond their embodiment in the present boat, he said. In the future, there would be Zeppelins of the ocean which would steam across the Atlantic in a day. Passengers would ride inside the streamlined hulls and never feel the waves at all, no matter what the strength of the seas. The only way they would be able to detect the weather would be to look out a window. There would be an end to seasickness forever.

The admirals received all this information without comment. They did not have any questions for Bell. The chairman of the committee drew out his pocket watch and announced it was time for lunch. The group, including Bell, retired to a private dining room, where they were served bluefish and new potatoes. The topic of conversation around the table was a proposed change to the evening uniform. The admirals said that the new pants were so tight that they could only be worn by fairies.

After lunch, as Bell was leaving, he found himself standing next to his friend Admiral James E. Whitworth, and asked him what was going on.

"This was what we call a courtesy interview," Admiral Whitworth told him. "They've already made up their minds. They sent your proposal to Edison two weeks ago and he nixed it."

"He . . . nixed it?"

"That's right," Admiral Whitworth said. "He said it was useless. He called it an old man's toy."

"Who is he calling an old man?" Bell said. "We're the same age. Did you know that? Edison is exactly the same age as I am."

"I wasn't aware of that," Admiral Whitworth said.

"I think that's funny," Bell said. "Edison is going around calling me an old man now."

Bell left the Bureau of Ships offices in a daze. He found himself walking miles through the streets of Washington. It began to rain. The rain was falling out of a set of knotted clouds with black bottoms and white tops. Bell's thoughts were on Edison. His old, dear enemy! Nearly fifty years of sparring! Edison had tried to beat him to the invention of the telephone. He had built a device for analyzing the sounds of the voice electromagnetically. Only Edison's impaired hearing seems to have prevented him from winning the race. The sounds which came through the instrument were later shown to be intelligible as human speech, but Edison never heard these faint sounds and therefore never knew what he had. Too bad! He had beaten Edison fairly, playing by the rules of the game. Edison had so many other inventions to his credit, why wasn't he satisfied? Because he wanted to invent everything, that's why. He wanted to be the only inventor in the world. He saw it all as a contest—a battle, even. Bell had never understood Edison's ruthlessness. And yet he did see, when he forced himself to be perfectly objective, how Edison's ruthlessness was only another aspect of his determination, a quality that was popularly admired in inventors.

Bell recalled how he had offered the telephone to Western Union, and how they had rejected it disdainfully. And yet, only a few months later, when he made a great sensation as he demonstrated his instruments at the Centennial Exposition in Philadelphia, the Western Union men began to get frightened. They decided to call in Edison. The hired pirate! Edison set his huge staff to work in his typical way and tried to make a telephone transmitter by trial and error. He had his staff try every chemical in his laboratory one by one: calcium carbonate, copper sulphate, fiddlehead ferns, parakeet droppings. Does it really take genius to work this way, so desperately? It said in the newspapers that Edison worked fifty-hour shifts, and when he did sleep, it was under a bench in his laboratory. Under a bench! What kind of a man would do this to himself? He literally treated himself like an animal. The newspapers said he expected only slightly less than this from his assistants, but then he would hand out bonuses at the end, when he got what he wanted.

Bell walked the entire distance to DuPont Circle and then the few steps down Connecticut Avenue to his residence. Its three stories of brick and stone were disappearing under the long shadow of the house across the street when he passed through his garden gate. Although it was nearly dinnertime, he informed the staff that he was not hungry, and retired to his bedroom.

For the second time that day, he lay on his bed, alone except for the people who chanced to visit him in recollections. He could hear the evening birds through his open window. The colors of the elm branches were changing as the light left them. Something made him get up and open his closet. He removed several piles of books which were standing on the floor and withdrew a package wrapped in brown paper. He untied the cord and removed the wrappings. Inside was a portrait of a baby. He stood it against the wall and examined it in the diminishing light.

This was a likeness of the Bells' first son, Edward, painted from a photograph taken of the infant as he lay in his casket. Bell had commissioned a French artist to do this work. The portrait was now forty years old, but it had never been displayed in public view. The feelings it aroused in both parents even now, so long after the event, prevented them from treating it like an ordinary picture. It had the power to bring either one of them to tears at any hour of any day.

The baby had lived and died all in the span of a few hours on a day in mid-August in the same year that President Garfield had been shot. It had been born prematurely. It hadn't the strength to inflate its own lungs. It had appeared to be drowning, although the nearest body of water was more than a mile distant. The way it had clutched its mother's hand and gasped showed that it had badly wanted to live. Shortly before the baby's birth, Bell had been summoned to Washington for his ill-fated attempt to find the bullet in Garfield's body. In the years afterward, he wondered if this private tragedy might in some way have been a punishment for his failed role in the public tragedy.

In the months immediately after the baby's death, Bell had pursued a new invention which he called the "vacuum jacket." The patient would be placed inside an iron cylinder sealed around the waist and neck, and air would be moved in and out of this cylinder by a bellows. When the device was ready for a test, Bell's assistant John McKillop had permitted himself to be placed in the cylinder. When the bellows were operated, McKillop had found he could breathe with no effort. Bell had held a strip of paper in front of McKillop's mouth and manipulated the bellows. He had been fascinated to find that he could make McKillop breathe rapidly or slowly; he could make him sniff, or snort, or even sigh. The sensation of absolute control, of being the motive power giving breath to a man's body, had been so shocking that he had asked McKillop to answer a question at one point to prove that he was still alive.

Two years later, Mabel again gave birth to a premature infant son. Bell was at this time attending a scientific convention. No one in the house even looked for the vacuum jacket. It had been lost and forgotten. By the time Bell returned home, the baby had died. This time, the father wept openly. His tears expressed frustration and rage, as well as grief. He brought out the vacuum jacket and instructed everyone in its use—his wife, his daughters, the charwoman, the cook, his valet, the maids. He had wheels fitted to the bottom so that it could be rolled throughout the house. After that, the vacuum jacket had been kept in readiness in the north parlor for more than fifteen years, but Mabel never again became pregnant, and so it was never used.

CHAPTER 12

On the last day of the party line, Humberhill was very emotional. One by one, he discovered his oldest friends among the clutter of voices and said good-bye to them.

"Beetle," he said. "Listen, my boy. You're taking this thing too hard. We'll be together again in no time. I happen to know that for a fact. There's a whole new life for us just around the corner, when His Nibs decides that we're worthy of his secrets."

"I don't believe it," Beetlejuice said. "I don't believe he has any secrets. What kind of a person would just stand by and watch us get flushed down the toilet? Nobody would do that to his friends. It must be that he *can't* help us, not that he *won't*."

"I'm telling you, it isn't like that," Humberhill said. "I was there, don't you understand? I was there when he did all this new stuff. He *can* make a new party line anywhere."

"The son of a bitch," Beetlejuice said. "So you think he really is holding out on us, then."

"I swear it," Humberhill told him. "I don't know why he is, but he is."

"What's that?" Beetlejuice asked. "Did you hear that? It sounded like a crow."

The crow repeated again, followed by a diabolical laugh.

"It's him," Humberhill said. "He's just sitting out there somewhere, watching us sink."

"Is that you, you bastard?" Billy the Boozer chimed in. "Why don't you do something? Do you get a kick out of watching people suffer?"

"You won't get him to say anything," Humberhill told him. "He just waits out there. Waiting for the end. Now he never opens his mouth, except to make one of his fake little animal noises. I really don't know what's the matter with him."

"He's got a turd for a heart," Billy the Boozer said. "That's what's the matter with him."

There was the sound of a rifle shot. Then a terrible scream. Most of the commotion in the line fell quiet as everyone listened to hear what was happening. "Aaargh," a voice said. A body fell to the floor. Terrible moans and pants. "I never . . ." Billy the Boozer's voice said. "I never . . . should . . . have said that." Silence for a while, then more pants and gags. "I never should have said that my great leader . . . has a turd for a heart." Heavy wheezing. A horrible death cough. "Now I'm a goner."

"Very funny," the real Billy said.

Finally, the last hour came and went. People said afterward that it had been almost impossible to get into the circuit at the end. It was the biggest crowd the circuit had ever held. Old friends searched for each other to say one last good-bye.

"I baked some cookies," Bertha the operator said. "For all of you. If you'll give me your addresses, I'll send them to you."

"We don't live anywhere but here," the Syracuse Stallion said.

"Just a minute," said Beetlejuice. "You speak for yourself. I have an address she can send cookies to if she wants. Just wrap them up good and tie them with some kind of strong string so that my little brothers and sisters don't get them."

There was a hum in the background. The line went dead for a moment, then came back again.

"It isn't time yet, is it?" Humberhill asked. "It can't be."

"We have about one more minute," the Syracuse Stallion told him.

"Oh, God," Humberhill said. "I can feel the whole thing

shaking, getting ready to collapse. I had myself ready to take this like a man, but now it's here, I'm scared."

These were his last words. The end came suddenly, about thirty seconds ahead of schedule. There were a series of pops and clinks, and then the old party line went out of business forever.

Before Bell departed for Washington, Mourly Vold had borrowed from him James Clerk Maxwell's two-volume set *A Treatise on Electricity and Magnetism.* He now filled the silence left by the demise of the party line by giving himself over to the study of Maxwell's books.

This required a substantial physical effort as well as a mental one. He held the text within a few inches of his face. He used his left eye, the somewhat stronger of the two, exclusively for this work. The end of the double-lens system attached to his spectacles practically grazed the page. He needed to use a strong electric light to make out anything at all.

In spite of the eyestrain, he read on with an ever-growing pleasure. He noticed immediately Maxwell's perfect integrity. It was an integrity unlike any he had ever encountered. No human being he had known in his life had anything like it. Maxwell's arguments about the electrical nature of the physical world were absolutely trustworthy. The evidence he gave in support of these arguments was genuine and compelling. The farther he went, exploring Maxwell's competence and artistry, the more amazed he became.

He was aware that part of the sense of shock and pleasure he felt was due to timing. As he read the section of the first volume titled "The Electric Glow," he encountered plausible explanations of effects he had observed himself, only days or weeks earlier. Maxwell said that when a conductor having a sharp point is electrified, the superficial density of the electricity increases without limit as the point is approached. As a result, the electromotive intensity grows very large, large enough to overcome the insulating power of the air. The air close to the point breaks down and passes a portion of the electricity away. For these reasons, one can observe a steady glow close to the point, due to the continuous discharges between the point and the neighboring air. The charged particles of air, possessing electricity of the same sign as the conductor, are forced away from the point, giving rise to the electric wind.

As he read these words, Mourly Vold felt, for the first time in his life, that he had fallen into the presence of someone whose imagination flowed exactly parallel to his own. He discovered, from a dozen angles of view, the author's global purpose. Maxwell discussed electrification by induction, electrification by conduction, and the theory of two fluids. He discussed how vitreous and resinous electrical charges may be distinguished. He showed how Cavendish's experiments may be used to arrive at a proof of the law of the inverse square. With every separate illustration, the generality of his message grew greater. There is nothing that doesn't have electricity in it; nothing that isn't held together or forced apart by electricity. There is a natural order, not yet entirely revealed, and it depends upon electricity.

In the second of the two volumes, Maxwell took up magnetic phenomena, and the many interactions between electrical and magnetic behavior. He recommended that every student of electricity read Ampère's research, and take it as a model of a polished, finished piece, but one which does not permit the reader to know what paths of thought led to the final achievement. We can only think, he said, that Ampère discovered his law by some process he has not shown us, because he has taken down all traces of the supporting structure which he used to build his great construction. By contrast, Faraday lets us see both his unsuccessful as well as his successful experiments. The effect is that the student can learn from Faraday the cultivation of a scientific spirit, one which understands how to profit as well from the failure of an experiment as from its success.

Maxwell said that all of space is filled with fields of force, the lines of force being, in general, curved. Somewhere among these fields of force, bending among the curved lines, Mourly Vold recognized an idea of his own. In an instant, he gave pursuit, but this only startled it and caused it to run away. It moved like a swift snake, and wriggled out of one view and into another.

At last he cornered the idea, and saw it completely. It revealed itself as the solution to the problem of the bullwhip inductive coupler, the very question which had brought him to Baddeck in the first place.

This is what he saw. According to Maxwell, there is a magnetic field due to the current flowing in a long, straight wire, and the lines of flux are circles with the wire at their center. Mourly Vold now saw that if a second wire were coiled around the shaft of a flexible whip, and if the whip itself were wound around the long, straight wire, then the magnetic flux lines circling the straight wire would pass through the turns of the bullwhip wire like an arm passing through bracelets. The result would be an inductive coupling of very great strength.

In one of Bell's barns, among the stacks of old invention notebooks and disused furniture, Mourly Vold found a long buggy whip. He wound a thin copper wire around the whip and secured it in place with gum cement. With his homemade telephone secured to his belt, he set off to make a test. Outside, the sun was just falling below the horizon. A northeast wind bent the tops of the white pines and the spruces. They flapped their limbs up and down in slow, idiotic gestures. Mourly Vold walked along the road a half-mile toward Baddeck and followed the telephone poles where they entered the woods. The brown leaves were deep here. They made the ground invisible in the dwindling light. When he was certain that he was out of sight of the road, he opened his jacket and brought out the whip. Overhead, the telephone wire hung slack, unaware that it was about to take part in an experiment. It bisected the dark blue sky from east to west.

Mourly Vold now cracked the whip, sending the tip upward with the speed of a pointed spear. The whip caught the telephone wire and wrapped itself around it, exactly as he had intended it would. When this was done, he listened in his receiver and heard a telephone conversation as clearly as if he had cut the wires.

"Yesterday afternoon," he heard a woman's voice say, "I heard a knock at the door. And the knocks were coming from that world. I didn't go to the door, and I didn't let my grand-daughter go to the door either. Knock, knock. They came again. Just like that, knock, knock. Just like an ordinary person, coming to call. But I knew who it was, so I just sat there, very still. Went away. Then, later on, we saw lights going on in MacAskills'. Someone is going out of there tonight, I said. Wake up this morning, and they say that old Mrs. MacAskill is gone. They're making a box for her up there now."

Mourly Vold heard all this at a startling level of sound power. It was almost as if the voice were speaking from inside his own head. When this conversation was over, he took control of the line and pulsed into the central office in Englishtown. From there, he boarded a Z-trunk and rode it out to Hattiesburg, Mississippi, where he knew a waitress.

"Hold the phone out the window, Julie," he said. "I'm doing something differently up here, and I want to see if I can hear the chickens out in the yard."

"I'll do it," Julie said, "but you won't hear anything. They're all in their house, sleeping."

That night, Mourly Vold lay in his bed, but he found it impossible to sleep. In his imagination, the lines of flux orbited the telephone wire, and each one passed through the planes of twenty or more turns of his inductive coupler. He visualized his original design, the one which had failed completely when he had tried it back at the school. In that design, the wire had run down the center of the whip, and of course it hadn't worked! There, the antenna wire lay along the flux lines, where it would have no way of detecting their changing strength. It was all so obvious, once one understood what Maxwell was saying. He now had the ultimate tool for the clandestine investigation of the telephone networks, and it had come directly from the basic principles Maxwell described. In this way, Maxwell's treatise had become, in his hands, subversive literature.

This thought actually frightened Mourly Vold. He had made his invention almost instantly after reading the critical pages. Wasn't this proof that the concept was obvious, once one knew the facts? It was clear that only the greatest good luck had saved the telephone company up until now. Another large piece of good fortune for the telephone company had made him the first discoverer, rather than someone bent on harm. A misanthrope, armed with Maxwell, could become an invisible menace. He could connect himself to any circuit at any time, cause destruction without limit, and then disappear, leaving no physical evidence behind. A gang of people equipped with inductive bullwhips could take control of the telephone networks entirely, squeezing the life out of any wire careless enough to leave the main road and head off into the woods. They could make the relays in the register-senders jitter until their contacts fused together. They could short-circuit the battery banks, causing battery explosions that would send acid splattering everywhere. All of this danger was a consequence of the simplicity and generality of electromagnetic induction.

Whatever happened now, it was clear to Mourly Vold that no one else should be told of this new development. It was simply too powerful to be let out. He must put the whip away where it would not be found and mention it to no one until he had the confidence of high officials in the telephone company. When the time was right, he would disclose the whip, and with the collaboration of the telephone company scientific staff, he would search for a way to defend the networks against his own invention.

As he lay in his bed, Mourly Vold listened to the sound

of the arctic air rubbing past the needles of the pines standing all around Bell's house. This air flowed in an unbroken river from the northern edge of the world, a dry country where all the water is ice. He imagined that he was hearing the sound of the electric wind, which leaves everything it blows upon charged with its glow.

CHAPTER 13

The tyrosinase-negative albino is an individual with no melanin in his body. He has white hair, white skin, white eyebrows, and blue eyes so perfectly devoid of pigment that the harsh brilliance of the world beams through the irises without attenuation. Light is painful to him, and he may suffer gross nystagmus. His visual acuity is often very low. In Billy the Boozer's case, acuity tested less than 20/400, in both eyes, throughout his life.

Billy was born on a farm north of Orange, Massachusetts. While he was still in his crib, his mother painted him. She dyed his hair a light brown, the color she imagined Jeannie's to be in the song about Jeannie with the light brown hair. She painted his eyebrows with a number 6 sable artist's brush. As she did this, her baby's gaze jerked in silly directions. He seemed to be looking for something and never finding it. No one could watch him doing this for long without feeling seasick. As she applied his makeup every morning, his mother's eyes filled with tears. A recollection came to her of a time long ago when, as a child, she had painted the face on a little boy made of dough.

By painting her baby, she managed to fool the neighbors for a time. When the neighbor ladies came to visit, they saw only a sweet, if somewhat dizzy-looking, brown-haired child. Even the two grandmothers were taken in at the beginning. But, before the end of his first year, the neighbors and relatives who picked Billy up and held him began to ask why his colors were rubbing off. What was the deal here? Why would anyone want to paint up a little baby like a two-dollar whore?

At last, his mother stopped painting him, and all the color drained out of his face. The neighbors who saw this happen were astonished. Day by day, they watched an infant turn into a tiny white-haired old man. They knew, of course, that time is the thief of color in the body—it descends on this man or that woman with little warning and sucks away one's black hair and red lips faster than a spider can get the juice out of a fly. Even though they knew this, the sight of it disturbed everyone who watched it, because it was such a frightening speed-up of the transitions of age.

Throughout his son's painting and subsequent whitening, Billy's father stayed drunk every day. He had been an attractive young man in his school days, with many chums and many girls, and people said what a shame it was that he had been unable to amount to anything as an adult. He worked at a machine in the mill when he was dry, but most of the time he was wet and capable of no work at all. On an April day in the year Billy was two, Billy's father made the mistake of putting on his high-school letter sweater for the short walk to the local bar. As he was returning home, a group of young athletes from the same high school, all wearing the same letter sweater, spotted him weaving down the sidewalk. Unable to believe their eyes, they followed him. Who was this appalling creature—dressed exactly like themselves but twenty years older—reeling, stinking, and talking to himself? They ambushed him where his path led across a vacant lot and beat the shit out of him. Every blow was a blow of outrage and denial. They could not comprehend the horror of what they were looking at. It was the cruelest joke in the world, a humiliation upon them directly, that such a man could have once been one of them. They beat him almost to death, but with no effect, because even as he lay in a heap at their feet, his example continued to threaten their future lives.

The years passed and Billy grew larger. He spent his childhood alone. A quarter of a mile from Billy's house was an abandoned railroad bridge. It was one of the last covered bridges in the state, built entirely of wood, now badly rotten. Billy was forbidden to play here, because of the danger of its collapse, and because it was used as shelter by derelict men. Despite his mother's warnings, Billy formed the habit of walking to the bridge and sitting beside the river in its shadow. His vision was so bad that he saw the bridge only as a poorly formed mass. Its shadow moved on the riverbank. Billy learned to tell the time, more or less, from the place where the shadow fell on the rocks. He heard voices, often laughter, from inside. Once, when a man urinated through a crack, it splashed on a rock only a few feet from where he sat.

Billy's father often spoke in anger about the men who lived on the bridge. He accused them of stealing vegetables from the miserable garden he kept beside the house. He said they were no better than the river rats that lived in the watery basements of the mills and ate their own dead. He often spoke of burning the bridge to drive the men-rats away.

It is possible that Billy's father, acting alone or in league with others who also feared the homeless men, set the fire that destroyed the bridge. More likely, the fire escaped accidentally, since it was known that the men often made fires in there to keep themselves warm in the winter. However it started, a fire consumed the bridge on the night of a terrible blizzard in the year Billy was twelve. The glow and the flames could be seen from the mill buildings in the center of town, despite the heavy snow. In the morning, nothing was left; what remained of the bridge had fallen into the river and disappeared through the ice.

Two days later, under a gray sky, Billy returned to the rocks where he had sat so often before. The wind had blown the snow into curving, streamlined waves, so that the river ice was covered by many feet of snow in some places and left bare in others. Billy's eyes fluttered stupidly in all directions. The wind was beginning to rise again. He felt cold. He started toward home, walking on a narrow path of bare ice. A blackened shape appeared below him. There was something peculiar under the ice. He examined it on his hands and knees. A man's face looked up at him. His nose was flattened, as if he were pushing his face against a window. His hair and clothes were burned. As Billy watched, another man and another rose up and pressed against the ice. When Billy went home and told what he had seen, a party went out to get the bodies, but they never found a thing. The current had taken the bodies away.

In the spring of that year, Billy went off to live at Perkins. By this time, he had reached a rather marvelous height and weight, considering his age. He quickly found that his size and his residual sight, poor as it was, qualified him for a high place in the pecking order. The pecking order in schools for the blind is invariably based on handicap, with the totally blind and those with multiple handicaps at the bottom. Billy found that at Perkins he could be a king of sorts, but his pleasure was diminished by the knowledge that he was only a king of Bedlam. At night, the blind children who couldn't sleep stirred about, and some of them wept. He found the state of the toilets especially disagreeable. How can I live another day, he asked himself, in a place where everybody misses the pot?

In his third year at Perkins, he began the drinking that earned him the name Billy the Boozer to friend and foe alike. He kept beer, whiskey, schnapps, and several varieties of blackberry brandy in his room. He used the sweet drinks to introduce tender new souls to the joys of intoxication, a stage at a time. The strong waters he used on himself. Extraordinary stories, most of them lies, were circulated about Carol Jackson and Pamela Johnson and Alice Jefferson and how Billy plowed them one at a time in his room after getting them numb on Bronxes and highballs. He demanded absolute fealty from all the weak-sighted lackeys at his side. They kept their ears to the ground for news of food packages, and when one was received anywhere in the school, they exacted the customary 50 percent tax and delivered it to Billy's room. They extended invitations on Billy's behalf to women, and escorted them to his room for new experiences. Last but not least, they meted out punishments to blind children who fouled the conveniences.

"He's a little gangster," the teachers said among themselves. "But he makes them keep the toilets clean."

When the telephone experimenters first contacted the Perkins Institution, it was through a Braille letter received by one of the students who happened to have a Canadian relative. The letter was brought to Billy by Alfred Suet, also an albino, and Billy's second-in-command. It gave directions for reaching the party-line number and invited anyone interested in a little harmless fun to call in.

Getting the use of a telephone meant breaking into the director's office, which was kept closed up in the evenings. This was not difficult to do, but it did require pulling up to a high window in order to get in.

"This better be good," Billy said.

"You'll like it," his sidekicks told him. "It's really fun. It's like going into a different world where everybody is like us."

"Are you telling me you've already tried this?" Billy wanted to know.

"We had to, Billy," they said. "Otherwise, how would we know if it was really true?"

"I don't like that," Billy said. "You should have brought this directly to me. You guys took a chance on getting me salty. You know what happens when I get salty."

"You won't be salty when you try out the party line," they said. "You'll be happy there. Everyone is."

They were right, of course. Billy the Boozer became a famous hell-raiser in the telephone. Perhaps because he decreed it fashionable, many Perkins students joined him in this enthusiasm. Alfred Suet took the name Walrus and became a regular along with Billy—learning mischief, playing pranks, and dueling with wisecracks in the party line.

Sometimes, of course, they got down to serious business.

"There's something I want to know," Beetlejuice said one

evening in the party line. "It's about the Vaseline. Do you put it on yourself, or do you put it on her?"

"A question like that," Billy the Boozer replied, "shows exactly what you know. Nothing. You don't need Vaseline. Just get her good and hot first. Then it slides right in."

With the demise of that great old circuit, Billy and the Walrus, along with all the others, were cast adrift. For a week or so, it looked as if Billy might be satisfied to go back to the boozing and bullying that had been his style before he discovered intelligent life in the telephone. He made a halfhearted effort to enjoy being top dog at Perkins again, but it was no good. It was too easy to collect the desserts of the pathetic at mealtimes, to bloody their noses on the playground, to make them kiss his trouser legs. The truth was that most of them were so down-and-out that anyone could have made them cower. It occurred to him with a shock that they were like the men on the bridge, contemptible but helpless. He saw again the blackened faces looking through the ice. He wondered once more who had set the fire. A victory over such creatures is no victory at all.

But the telephone! This was something else! He had learned enough from the regulars—Humberhill, the Syracuse Stallion, and the others—to know what the power of a little knowledge could be. He had been with them once when they cracked open a central office step-by-step machine and caused it to grind its gears forward and backward until it went up in smoke. Little Egypt hadn't liked that. He had scolded them like a madman for that. As if he had a divine right over them! As if he were a little god! Just because he had been first on the scene, he thought he could tell everybody else what to do.

This business about letting the party line die was a perfect example of his arrogance. He had stood by and watched it collapse, although he could have done something to save it. Why? Why? Billy thought he knew the answer. To keep the troops in line. To make sure that no one else would ever rival his authority. Billy had used similar moves himself to take care of up-and-comers in the school. Sooner or later, Little Egypt would switch the party line back on, and when he did that, his control would be absolute once again.

Billy saw no reason to let himself be bested like that. With the Walrus to back him up, he went into the telephone on his own. He clicked away with the hookswitch as he had been taught, and gradually he made some progress. Yes, his telephone chicanery was by rote, and slow, and uninspired, but the methods all of them knew by then were effective enough. By pounding away at it for days, Billy and the Walrus managed to get into a central office and cause a short circuit in a linefinder. The result was a fire so small that the office electricians quickly extinguished it, but to hear Billy tell the story, you would think that they had destroyed an entire director system. Naturally, they called Humberhill to crow about it, fully aware that this news would get back to Little Egypt. It wasn't long before the boom fell.

"What's this I hear about you frying switches?" Little Egypt asked when he pulsed in.

"What do you want to know?" the Walrus said. "We did it. What's it to you?"

"I want to know how it happened," Little Egypt said. "Was it an accident, or what?"

"It wasn't an accident, was it, Billy?"

"It wasn't an accident at all," Billy the Boozer said. "It just happened. I don't see what it has to do with you."

A hostile silence.

"Well, let me see if I can explain it to you," Little Egypt began. "If you try anything like that again, I'm going to make you wish you were never born. I told you before that I don't permit destructiveness. Right now, I have the trust of a half-dozen or so of their people—linemen, engineers, and operators. They know what I'm doing. They know I'm working to find the flaws, to make the networks better. But all it's going to take is a couple of boneheaded moves like the one you just made to blow that trust away. You may think you're funny, but I can guarantee you that they don't."

"Oh, is that right?" Billy the Boozer said. "Well, you can mind your own business. We don't need you to tell us what to do. You can take your precious love for the telephone company and shove it where the crickets don't sing."

Upon hearing this, Little Egypt retaliated with a five-kilohertz whistle between his teeth that left his adversaries' ears ringing for days. Furthermore, he acted immediately through a Boston central office to disconnect all the telephones leading into the Perkins Institution. He regretted having to do this, but reasoned that whatever inconvenience it caused the school was more than justified by the need to contain the cancer he had discovered in his organization.

Later that week, Bell returned from his journey to Washington. He took to his bed, and two more days passed before he gave any attention to the pile of correspondence which had accumulated at his desk. One of the letters there was from a Mr. Adam Pfaltz, assistant to the president of the Bell Telephone Company.

Bell took the letter immediately to the carding room, where Mourly Vold was working.

"We have our answer," Bell told him. "They tell me I'm not to worry, because everything you said you could do is impossible."

Mourly Vold asked Bell to read him the letter all the way through. Bell sat on the edge of a table, took out his reading spectacles, and read the letter. His cheeks were flushed from having walked so fast from the house. With his white hair and white beard and red cheeks, he looked precisely like Santa Claus.

"They're very kind to me in this letter, wouldn't you say?" Bell asked when he was finished. "I was afraid they were going to talk down to me, but they really don't. They appear to remember who I am. I think that's nice. What do you think?"

"I think it's rubbish," Mourly Vold said.

Both were silent for a moment.

"The letter says it's impossible to control a Z-trunk using tongue clicks. That's a lie. I showed you how I can do it."

"Oh, yes," Bell said. "I see what you mean. Of course, *they* haven't seen you do it. Perhaps that's why they think it's impossible."

"It's time they had a demonstration," Mourly Vold said.

In contemplating his next moves, Mourly Vold felt a keen chill. The telephone company management had decided to stick its head in the sand. This was very bad news. Evidently, they were completely unaware of any of his own activities or those of the Perkins group. It was almost unbelievable that they had never yet detected his presence, but that was what they were saying.

Their attitude was also cause for concern. How could they think it was perfectly all right to assure Bell that everything was fine when things were in fact not fine? The tone of their letter was, "We don't know who this person is who has alarmed you, but you should just ignore him." Imagine that! How could they be so ignorant? The real truth, if they only knew it, was that not only were the weaknesses he told them of really there, but now there was a group of irresponsible bastards getting ready to draw blood the first chance they got. He had disconnected the Perkins phones for the moment, but that was only a finger in the dike. He knew the Perkins students now had rogue telephones. It wouldn't be long before someone complained and the school lines were turned back on again. It was true that Billy and the Walrus were a couple of ham-handed know-nothings, and probably would not be a threat to anything major even when they did their worst, but what confidence could he have that they wouldn't someday come upon one of the golden keys that the telephone company had left scattered around? What then? The prospect of such a day made him shiver. Those boys had no goodwill at all.

He telephoned the School for the Blind in North Sydney and asked to speak with Humberhill.

"I'm about to set off to do a little necessary mischief," he said. "Can I count on you when I need you?"

Humberhill was overjoyed. "Oh, do you mean it? Of course you can count on me! This is the happiest day of my life! Do you know what I've been *doing* since the party line collapsed? I've been listening to Froggy tell James P. Bishop what a great ass man he is. Does that sound like fun to you? They talk about dirty things all the time, even when they're playing checkers. Yap, yap, yap, all the time, and it's all so filthy and stupid. I just want them out of my goddamn *room*!"

With Humberhill's help, Little Egypt infiltrated the telephone company's main offices at 1016 Broadway in New York. Taking special care, he set up a temporary plane beneath the circuits leading to the telephones of each of the highest officers of the company. This temporary plane became a private electronic environment for Humberhill and himself to live in while they carried out their work.

After long consideration, Mourly Vold decided to build the electronic equivalent of a mantrap. His plan was to leave the circuits under any particular telephone balanced on a knife edge. This telephone would then be suitable for use without interference, provided that the speaker used an ordinary tone of voice. If, however, he should laugh, or make an exclamation, or raise his voice in anger, then this would cause all the telephones in the building to ring and be connected to the executive's telephone simultaneously. Anyone answering their phone would hear the rest of the conversation, but the executive would be unaware of any eavesdroppers.

All this required the most delicate manipulation of the automatic equipment in the building. Mourly Vold said it was like building a ship in a bottle. Every trivial piece of the construction had to be worked out, in a strict order, before he attempted it. Each new intervention had to be carefully considered to see whether it might knock down one of the others.

At last, he was ready for a final adjustment of the sensitivity of his trap. While Humberhill listened on a calling line, he experimented with his voice to see what was required to trip the eavesdropping circuit. When it was just the way he wanted, he armed the circuit and stood back to see what would happen.

The results were every bit as good as he had expected. At random times of day, telephones would ring throughout the office building, and the secretaries and mailroom staff would be treated to the latest episode in an executive's private life. They would hear Mr. Pfaltz shouting at his wife, or Mr. Blacker arguing with the police commissioner about a traffic ticket. After several days of this, Little Egypt changed the sensitivity of the hair trigger so that only a soft, intimate voice would ring the phones and bring in the eavesdroppers. This setting proved much more popular, and brought to light certain scandalous behavior within the company which need not be discussed here.

Of course, none of this chicanery was worth anything unless Mourly Vold owned up to it, and this he did in an extraordinary way. One morning, the operators in the message register room said that the paper tape machine had filled up their entire room with paper tape the night before. On the tape, printed endlessly, were these words, "I told you so . . . I told you so . . . I told you so . . ."

After a week of this, someone in the company leaked the story to the newspapers. The Hearst papers picked it up, and for some reason made a big thing out of it. Joseph Malachy's *Journal* and Edward Blum's *American* called the perpetrators of these strange happenings "vandals." The stories said the police were investigating.

Bell read the *Journal* story aloud to Mourly Vold and Mabel at the breakfast table. Before them stretched the empty dishes which had recently contained Bell's customary breakfast: salmon in wine sauce, wheat toast browned in a pattern of longitudinal bars, fresh butter, rose-hips preserves, a dark fall-flower honey, segments of apple with cinnamon, a poached egg, and tea.

"The investigation to date has not revealed how the vandals gained access to the building," Bell read.

He paused here and said, "That means they think it was someone who works for them."

"I can't imagine why they think that," Mourly Vold said. "I practically told them it was me."

Several more days went by and it appeared the matter was forgotten. Nothing more could be found in the papers. No letters or telegrams came from them. Mourly Vold grew impatient. It was clear that they had thick skins. What would he have to do to get their attention?

At last, when he could wait no longer, he pulsed into Adam Pfaltz's phone directly.

"Listen," he said. "Suppose I was a foreign power. Suppose I wanted to take out all the phones on this continent. I could just do a little number like *this,* and that would take care of it."

He clicked up a tame Z-trunk and let it loose. It thrashed through the networks, spinning the strowager switches like eggbeaters, starting and stopping the message registers, hopping from New York to Trenton to Baltimore, flipping whole panels into the make-busy condition as it passed. After letting it run wild for a minute or so, he halted it and pushed it back into its normal state.

A short time later, he called Mr. Pfaltz back. "Well, what do you think of that?" he asked. "Do you still say your system doesn't have any weaknesses?"

"Who are you?" Mr. Pfaltz said. "How did you do that? Do you realize what kind of trouble you've just caused? I've been getting reports of malfunctions all up and down the East Coast."

"It's all back to normal," Little Egypt told him. "I was careful not to cause any permanent problems. But I could have. Do you believe that now?"

"Tell me what you want," Pfaltz said.

"I want you to listen to me," Little Egypt said, "and I want you to fix the networks. They are full of funny little problems at the moment; I think you should admit that. I don't know how you could go on doubting any longer that I'm your friend and you need me. You know where to find me when you want me."

With that, he broke the connection and left Mr. Pfaltz to think about it.

Several days later, Mabel was working in the flower garden in front of the house when two men drove up in a new Pierce Arrow sedan. They asked to see Dr. Bell, and spoke with him for over an hour. At the conclusion of this interview, Bell left his guests and went to find Mourly Vold. He finally tracked him down in one of the upper pastures, where he was helping Donald G. Morrison to repair a fence.

Bell was quite tired from having climbed the hill. He sat down on the green grass and puffed for a few minutes. Finally he told Mourly Vold why he had come.

"I have been meaning to talk with you for days on this subject," he began, "but I've always put it off. Now it's practically too late."

"What do you mean?" Mourly Vold asked him.

"There are two detectives here," he said, "from the company. They want you to go with them to New York."

"Excellent," Mourly Vold replied. "I'll go with them today."

"Just a moment," Bell said. "You're under no obligation to do any such thing. We can send them away if you want. I haven't told them anything about you, not even your name."

"I *want* to go with them," Mourly Vold said. "It's clear that they're ready to cooperate."

"Nothing is clear," Bell said. "Not to me, at any rate. One of the things I wanted to say to you was that I don't think you're negotiating with the company very effectively. You're putting them on the defensive."

"They *should* be on the defensive," Mourly Vold said. "They're vulnerable. They could be attacked. I want them to know that."

"They do know that, now," Bell said. "But you won't help your cause by putting them in a panic. If you really want them to cooperate with you, I'd advise you to be more diplomatic. Try to see matters from their point of view. They're not grateful now; they're frightened of you."

"Why should they be frightened of me? I'm only one little person and they're a great big company."

"That's true," Bell said. "But it doesn't change anything. They have feelings the way you and I do, and right now they're frightened of what you can do to them."

Mourly Vold was quiet for a moment. He was clearly taking satisfaction in hearing this. "Maybe that will make them want to listen to me," he said.

"It's possible," Bell said. "They're reasonable men, as far as I know. I've met one or two of them. But it's *human,* don't you see, to be offended when someone calls attention to your shortcomings in a mocking way."

"Is that what you think I've done?"

"Yes," Bell said. "That's what you've done."

Mourly Vold picked up his tools and took them to Donald G. Morrison. He shook hands with his old friend and said good-bye to him. Then he joined Bell, who was already walking down the path toward the house.

"I appreciate your advice," he said. "I just don't know how to make use of it. I'm afraid I'll have to get their attention in my own way."

CHAPTER 14

When Mabel was told that Mourly Vold was planning to go to New York, she raised an enormous fuss. She said that there was no need for him to go; that his health would be placed in jeopardy by the pockets of influenza that still lingered in the cities; that the newspapers were full of stories of gangsters shooting each other in crowded restaurants. At the end of her tirade, she said that he was simply not to go.

Ordinarily, a pronouncement like this from Mabel would have closed the matter. She did not put her foot down often, but when she did, there was no precedent for any other outcome than the one she wanted.

The following morning, Mourly Vold walked with her through the garden. He took her arm as they climbed together toward the field where, in times gone by, Bell had flown his enormous tetrahedral kites. A piece of the red silk, faded now after so many summers and winters, remained stuck in the thorns, a reminder of those years.

"I must go," he told her. "It's time for me to do my real work."

"That's a peculiar way to put it," she said. "Your real work."

"What other way is there to say it?" he asked her. "I have this chance to do a big and important thing."

"You're important to us here."

"I know," he said. "I know."

Mabel's eyes filled with tears. It was not clear that she had understood everything. Sometimes her lipreading failed to give her every word. At these times, she made out the most she could and pretended to understand the rest.

Bell met them as they came down through the gate. For a moment, the three stood looking at each other. Finally, Mourly Vold passed one arm around Mabel's waist and the other around Bell's, and they walked with their arms around one another toward the sheep pens. They stopped when they passed a particularly large raspberry bush, loaded with fresh fruit.

"Hoy, hoy," Bell said. "What do you think of these raspberries? Aren't they the kitty's whiskers? Let's pick a quart for you to take with you in the car."

Each of them worked for ten minutes or so in silence, and when they were finished, they had nearly filled Bell's cap. Bareheaded, Bell worked in the brilliant sunshine, and his white hair stood out from his head like the fur of an Angora rabbit.

"I'll tell you what makes that bush grow so nicely," he said, stepping out of the berry patch. "I've been watering it myself this summer, using nature's watering can."

In the morning, Mourly Vold put his few articles of clothing into his old carpet bag. He embraced both of the Bells. Mabel held him for a long time.

"Who will go with me now to find the lambs?" she asked.

Mourly Vold kissed her forehead. At last, he climbed into the Pierce Arrow with the two men from New York and drove away.

The sky was clear and a wind was blowing. The wind slid over the long fetch of inlet between the mainland and Boularderie Island. The water there was as blue and rough as the open sea. When the wind reached the land, it combed the tough grass so flat that the sheep had to pick it up with their tongues.

The detectives said very little to Mourly Vold. They smoked their cigarettes and talked between themselves. As this familiar and beautiful landscape passed by the windows of the car and out of his life, Mourly Vold felt a moment of panic and regret. He had been happier here than anywhere else. It suddenly seemed crazy to be leaving this place where love and understanding were taken as the most ordinary things in the world.

And yet, he must go! The opportunity for a vast new life, full of terrors and grand achievements, had arrived for him, and he felt as much obligation to take this opportunity as to take his next breath. Even so, as Baddeck fell behind, he resolved to return as soon as his improvements in the telephone networks should be completed.

They drove to Sydney and boarded a train for New York. At Port Hawkesbury, the train was put on a ferry, to cross the Strait of Canso to Port Hastings. From there, the train rattled on through the pine forests to Moncton, to Saint John's, and then over the border into the United States. In Bangor, they boarded the Boston and Maine's *Northeaster* to Augusta, Portland, and Boston. From Boston's South Station, they took an express operated by the New York, New Haven, and Hartford to Grand Central Station in New York.

The journey required three days. They arrived in New York late in the evening on a day in the third week of September. The detectives took Mourly Vold to the old Eagle, a midtown hotel on the West Side. In the morning, the lace curtains at the windows were pushed aside by a dirty, hot breeze. The noise of the traffic came up from the street. The detectives stood at the sink in their underwear while they shaved. They were obviously pleased to be back in the city. There were millions of people out there, and the detectives loved one or two of them. They whistled as they put on their clothes. They wore their hats at all times when they were not actually sleeping.

The detectives took Mourly Vold to the main offices of the Bell system on lower Broadway. Mourly Vold was very pleased and excited. All around him, behind this door or that one, were the people of the telephone company. Here were the route engineers, the traffic supervisory engineers, the switchbar service technicians. Mere mortals! And yet, they were part of something magnificent! Right here, in this very building, was the center of a world he had seen before only in his imagination. Testboards, toll switchboards, step-by-step selectors! All here! Voice path cuts, E- and F-type signaling modules, all here!

The detectives took him up in the elevator to the tenth-floor executive offices. After a wait, he was taken into the office of Mr. Adam Pfaltz.

Mourly Vold had declined to give his name to the detectives, and now he declined to give it to Mr. Pfaltz. He said he wished to be known only by the name he had been called in the newspapers, "the telephone vandal." Mr. Pfaltz said it would be necessary for him to prove who he was.

"Fine," Mourly Vold said. "Let me show you."

In the company of Mr. Pfaltz, he visited the engineering laboratories. The technical staff there was very friendly. They showed him into a large room filled with step-by-step signaling equipment. He was given a telephone at a desk.

"The first thing you have to do is pulse into a local office and look for a Z-trunk that isn't doing anything," Mourly Vold said. He showed them. "I give that trunk a cadence interrupt, and I'm on my way." He fluttered his tongue against his palate, and the sound was like a flock of woodpeckers digging a meal out of a hardwood forest.

By this time, a crowd had assembled around the desk where he was working. After a little experimentation, he found the Z-trunks controlled by the switching equipment in this very room. One by one, he took control of them all, and made them play Z-trunk shuttlecock with each other. The strowager switches danced back and forth in unison. On an impulse, he made them play a bit of rhythm from an Irving Berlin song. The switches belted out the drum rolls from the title song of *Yip, Yip Yaphank*. A cheer went up from the laboratory personnel in the room, followed by applause.

His virtuoso performance continued. He demonstrated off-and-cold wink starts, using knuckle cracks and tongue clicks. He showed them high-low signaling done entirely by rapping the receiver on the desk top. For a finale, he pulsed into the central office in Flats, Nebraska, and made all the telephones in the town ring at once.

"Hello?" everyone in Flats, Nebraska, said to everyone else. "Hello? Hello?"

"All right," Mr. Pfaltz said, "I'm convinced you're the guy. That's enough."

But he was wrong, that wasn't enough! The switchmen, the traffic service engineers, the home office operators roared their approval. They lifted Mourly Vold on their shoulders and carried him throughout the building. Everyone wanted to talk to him, to show him where they worked and what they did. He was treated like a liberator. These were the personnel Mr. Pfaltz and the others referred to as the "little people" of the company, the workers who made it all go, but it was clear that they didn't think of themselves as little people—they thought of themselves as citizens of their own state. Here they were, handing Mourly Vold the keys to their capital city.

And so it happened that he was occupied the rest of the day giving demonstrations for technical people and trading shop talk with them. The experience, for Mourly Vold, was like dying and going to heaven. Everyone marveled at how deep and complete his knowledge of the networks was. Even the top electrical engineers wondered how he could know so much without any formal training. Many of them said afterward that he knew enough to do their jobs right now, with no further instruction.

At the end of the day, the technical people brought him back to Mr. Pfaltz and said good-bye to him, with much handshaking all around. They even gave him gifts. An attractive young operator named Suzanne gave him her headset, with ribbons tied on top and earrings dangling from the earphones, and a lineman gave him his favorite tool belt.

A senior supervisor of linemen called Red summed up the feelings of many when he said, "You can come back and see us anytime. This is the best thing that's happened around here in a long while, finding out that there's a bright young person such as yourself coming along. Today I don't feel as sorry for the future as I usually do."

CHAPTER 15

Mourly Vold spent another night at the Eagle with the detectives. In the evening, he went with them to a jazz room where a young woman did a shimmy dance with a yo-yo. The yo-yo was covered with rhinestones to catch the light. She made the yo-yo climb her leg like a snake gliding up a tree. At the top of the yo-yo's flight, as it paused before the next dip, the green glass eye at its center paused and surveyed the room.

Everyone was drinking gin out of jelly jars. One of the detectives disappeared under the table during the yo-yo dance. His partner had to carry him back to the hotel. The one who did the carrying was indignant and muttered complaints under his breath. "There's always a drunk to spoil the party," he said. "There's always one. I've never seen it fail yet."

Both of the detectives were miserable the next morning, but they managed to get Mourly Vold to the telephone company offices in time for his eleven o'clock appointment with Bertram Fairchild, president of the company. Mr. Fairchild was to take Mourly Vold to lunch.

"I'm glad you're here," Fairchild said, when Mourly Vold arrived. He was a tall, athletic-looking man with white hair. He stood up and shook Mourly Vold's hand. "We can go right away. If you'll wait a moment, I'll get some coats. Here, sit in Elsie's chair while you're waiting. Elsie cleans up at night, and she always sits in that chair while she's eating her supper. She tells me it's the best seat in the establishment."

When Fairchild returned, he was carrying two woolen navy jackets. "I thought you might like to have lunch on my boat," he said. "I brought a jacket for each of us in case there's a wind."

Going down in the elevator, he remarked, "You made quite an impression here yesterday. Everyone I've spoken to this morning wants to talk about you."

As they walked through the lobby, a cheer greeted them from the employees who happened to be present.

"See what I mean?" Fairchild said. "I'm sure that wasn't for me. The one time I got a cheer like that was the day I told them they could chew gum at work."

Out on the sidewalk, the crowds of New York pressed in on them. For a moment, Mourly Vold lost track of his host. Fairchild was with him one moment and gone the next. Hats passed in a blur at high speed. The noise of the traffic bounced back from the polished stone fronts of buildings on both sides of the street. Mourly Vold's handicap was such that he could see well enough to make his way without assistance in sunlight, but he was as good as blind here in the shade. When Fairchild reappeared, he offered his arm. Mourly Vold took it, and walked with him north on Broadway toward Greeley Square.

Fairchild's courtesy in offering his arm came as a surprise, since most sighted people don't know what to do in such a situation. They will grab at a blind person and pull or push him where they want him to go, rather than extending an elbow for a lead. Had someone taught this to Fairchild? Did he have a weak-eyed friend or relative? Or did he have enough common sense to know the right way to behave without being told?

"I can't walk through this part of town without remembering the old days," Fairchild said. "I suppose that time must be forty years ago now, although it doesn't seem as long as that. We had no money then. Western Union was destroying us with

Edison's transmitter. Business was miserable. Still, we weren't unhappy. Some afternoons we'd close the office and walk up the street, and we'd stop at the various hotels and have a drink. The Metropolitan, the Bakersfield, the Broadway Central. Those were beautiful old buildings, every one of them. Inside, they had marble on the floor and red silk on the walls. Some of the hotels even hired women to sit there in the bar, just to talk with you. Nothing else, only talk. These ladies didn't serve drinks, or bus the glasses, or anything. They were just there for conversation. Some of them were very beautiful.

"We knew the telephone was good, but we didn't know *how* good. There was no way to know who was going to be left in the business in five years. Bell's patents were standing up, but Western Union was going after them with their big guns. They had Edison filing for a new patent every week. We never knew when Edison was going to grind us under his heel. I don't know what made us think we should stay with it. We were young, I suppose, and we had the heart for it. This is where we get the bus."

They boarded a crosstown bus and climbed the curving stairs to the top deck. Sitting here under the open sky, Mourly Vold felt the sun on his head and shoulders as the bus crossed the avenues. Flocks of pigeons flew above, in the narrow air corridors between the buildings, and cursed each other in the foulest language. At Twelfth Avenue, the bus turned north, and Fairchild indicated that they were to get off.

He led Mourly Vold across the avenue, past a collection of trucks parked at warehouse loading docks, and out along a narrow pier. They descended a ramp to a float, and here Fairchild untied a dinghy. He held the boat steady while Mourly Vold climbed in.

As they rowed out on the Hudson, the traffic noise gradually receded. A pile driver was working somewhere to the south. The sound of the steam exhaust gave a warning before each blow. Fairchild's strokes with the oars were not quite synchronized with the strikes of the pile driver: sometimes the crash came when his oars were in the water, and other times when they were in the air. Fairchild had removed his coat for the exercise. It lay folded on the seat beside him. His arms reached out and pulled back, reached out and pulled back. It was obvious he was enjoying the rowing. A tugboat passed, pushing a scow loaded with garbage and sea gulls. Mourly Vold felt happy for no reason he could put his finger on.

Before long, they reached a large white steam yacht moored in the river. This was the *Nancy,* a vessel one hundred and seventy feet long, built originally for a wealthy tire magnate. Until Fairchild brought the little boat under the shadow of the yacht, Mourly Vold had been under the impression that the dinghy was the boat they would be taking their lunch in. They stepped onto a wooden platform at the side of the yacht and ascended a stairway to the deck. Fairchild spoke to one of his staff and ordered a light luncheon to be served on the Captain Drake Deck.

He gave Mourly Vold a tour. He showed him the bridge, and introduced him to the captain, whose responsibility was to keep the *Nancy* always ready for sea. He showed him the radio room, the billiards room, and the salon. The floor of the salon could be drawn back by electric motors to reveal a glass bottom; Fairchild said that this was a pleasant accessory to use in Florida, but that the view beneath the surface of the Hudson was disgusting.

Lunch was served on a high deck toward the stern. An umbrella shaded the table. Three waiters hovered and swooped; before it was over, they had swooped in with terrapin bisque, followed by médaillons of veal in a lemon-and-onion sauce, asparagus tips with almonds, and a fresh sourdough bread.

"As I mentioned earlier," Fairchild said over coffee, "you caused quite a stir yesterday. This morning, all my technical people kept telling me I ought to hire you, and my legal people were saying I ought to prosecute you."

Mourly Vold felt a sharp jab in his stomach. What? Prosecute? This word certainly hadn't come up before. He waited to see what Fairchild would say next.

"I have decided to do neither," Fairchild continued. "Neither seems like the best plan at the moment. Now, given that those two alternatives are put aside, what do *you* think I should do?"

"About what?"

"About you," Fairchild said.

"I don't get it," Mourly Vold said.

"Why have you been trying so hard to get our attention? What's your message?"

"I came here to show you that your new in-band signaling equipment can be manipulated by anybody who can click his tongue," Mourly Vold told him. "As I told everybody yesterday, I'm willing to help you fix it, but it will be a big job. Until I can figure out how to safeguard your equipment, the only thing you can do is to take it out of service."

Fairchild looked straight ahead and said nothing. He folded his hands in his lap and then unfolded them again.

"We can't do that," he said. "We're committed to signaling in the voice band not only now, but for the foreseeable future. By the end of next year, that equipment will be in every central office in this country. It's going to make telephone service faster and cheaper every year of your lifetime."

"Not if I can help it," Mourly Vold said. "Not while it's as badly built as it is."

"I don't agree it's badly built," Fairchild said.

"It's vulnerable."

"Only to you," Fairchild said. "If you really feel as protective toward us as you say you do, you could agree to be discreet with that information."

"I could," Mourly Vold said, "but that would do no good at all. The cat is out of the bag. What I found, another person could. You don't need to fix *me*. You need to fix the networks. I don't know what could be plainer than that."

Fairchild brushed some bread crumbs to the edge of the table and into his hand. He deposited these neatly on the saucer of his coffee cup.

"I don't think you have any idea of the magnitude of what you're suggesting," he said. "You're talking about shutting down more than half of our operating plant. You want me to do that, and put up with all the service loss that entails, and then wait while you make up your mind what I should do next?"

"That's about it," Mourly Vold said.

"I can't," Fairchild said. "There's no way in hell I can do what you're asking. I can't afford it. The company would never recover from the revenue losses. I've worked all my life to make this organization go. We've beaten Edison's microphone and Dolbear's patent suits. We've been in debt up to our eyebrows and we've fended off raids from Western Union more times than I can remember. Now, just because you say there's a nuance you want to change in our equipment, which happens to be the most powerful innovation any communications company has ever put into service, I'm supposed to roll over and play dead, and let the company go bankrupt. Well, I can tell you I'm not going to do it. Not after all I've been through."

"It isn't a nuance."

"What?"

"The thing that's wrong with your stuff. It isn't a nuance," Mourly Vold said.

"I don't care *what* it is," Fairchild replied, raising his voice.

"I'm simply telling you that you're asking for the impossible. I'm also telling you this. From now on, I expect you to exercise better judgment."

There was a short silence.

"Are you telling me to leave you alone?"

"Yes," Fairchild said. "I'm telling you to leave us alone, and leave telephones alone."

"I could leave them alone or not leave them alone," Mourly Vold said, also growing angry. "But if you don't fix them, then they won't get fixed! Is that so hard to understand? All I did was discover what's wrong with them. I didn't make them that way! Don't you realize that? Once a discovery is made, it's made! You can't put it back where you found it!"

Fairchild stood up. "It's time we went back," he said.

They rowed across to the pier in silence.

As Fairchild tied up the boat, he spoke again.

"How shall we leave matters, then?"

"That's up to you," Mourly Vold told him.

"Look," Fairchild said. "I've told you the facts. I simply can't afford to scrap our percussive signaling system. I'm willing to put that before you and depend on your sense of fair play to tell you how to behave."

"How do you know I have a sense of fair play?"

"You do," Fairchild said. "My technical people tell me you do. And I believe them. Otherwise, you wouldn't be so concerned about us."

"Listen," Mourly Vold told him. "It wouldn't be fair play for me to drop my work now. It would be desertion. You're in deep trouble, whether you know it or not. You're lucky that I was the one to find the way into your system, and not some other people I could name. For the moment, I have it all under control, but how long can that last? The ways of getting in are so obvious that sooner or later someone will discover them again. I can't quit on you now. I have to finish my investigations.

Furthermore, I'll need your cooperation when I know what needs to be done."

"Young man," Fairchild said. "If you do anything more, it will be at your own peril. You have your freedom. Use it wisely. Don't let something ugly get started that neither of us expects or wants."

CHAPTER 16

The Hearst newspapers in New York, the *American* and the *Journal,* jumped on the story right away. Sources inside the telephone company reported what they had seen and heard on the day of the telephone vandal's triumphal demonstrations. At first, the stories emphasized the freakish aspects of the matter—the fact that the perpetrator of such outrages had been a nearly blind boy. When it was discovered that he had been living with Alexander Graham Bell in Nova Scotia, the mystery deepened. What, exactly, was his connection with the inventor of the telephone?

In these days, the Hearst press was forever telling the people that the revolution in Mexico had created conditions that were an outrage to Americans. The rebels had taken over property belonging to Americans and would certainly try to get more unless the U.S. government had the guts to stop them. Hearst himself owned extensive estates in Chihuahua and Campeche, but this was not mentioned in the editorials and the news stories. Instead, it was emphasized that the lives and homesteads of American citizens were being threatened by little brown people with guns.

A link was suggested between the telephone vandal and the Mexicans. It was entirely possible that he was a Mexican agent. The nonsense with the phones could be a Mexican plot. This suggestion appeared so frequently that it was obviously straight from the imagination of W. R. Hearst himself.

After leaving the company of Bertram Fairchild, Mourly Vold sat on a bench in Central Park and read the newspapers.

The weather had turned cold. A severe wind was carrying heavy clouds across the sky.

In his pocket was a railroad ticket which would take him back to Nova Scotia, a gift of the telephone company. He read about himself with a growing sense of wonder. The news stories and editorials somehow were talking about a Mexican spy. The inversions of truth were so blatant that they were laughable, but he was not even slightly tempted to laugh. The thing which disturbed him most was the fact that Bell's name was often dragged in. It was implied that Alexander Graham Bell had sold out to the Mexican revolutionaries.

Mourly Vold saw now that he could not return to Baddeck. He must do nothing more to compromise the Bells and their good name. If he returned to their house, it would not be long before the newspapers sent reporters and possibly more detectives. This would be an unhappy way to live for the Bells as well as for himself.

He cashed in his rail ticket and bought a bus ticket south. From the bus terminal, he wrote Mabel Bell a long letter. I must get myself out of the way for a little while, he said. I haven't finished the work I came here to do, but I can't do it in New York. I will write again when I know where I'll be. I love you and Dr. Bell very much.

The destination he had in mind was Hattiesburg, Mississippi, where his friend Julie served hashbrowns to motorists in the Pig's Poke Inn. He had a dozen other friends scattered around the country, people he had met by accident as he jumped out of a Z-trunk during some random wandering. There was Peter, who worked in a live-bait store in Empire, Louisiana, and of course Bertha, the long-lines operator based in Toledo. There were very few parts of the country where he did not know someone. He picked Julie to aim for without any particular reason, but once he had done so, he was satisfied with his choice. She would be the least surprised of all of them when he popped up in person. Nothing surprised her. Furthermore, she might have some work he could do in exchange for his keep.

He boarded the bus, feeling pleased with the prospects of new adventures. In his imagination, he saw the South stretching before him. The roads that would take him there were like footpaths leading into a warm garden. Beside these paths grew every fruiting and flowering plant in the world, their roots parting the hot soil like slow-moving worms. He tried to imagine what cotton plants might possibly look like, and decided that they would have the appearance of miniature sheep supported on green stalks.

On the trip from New York to Washington, the bus was filled with cigarette smoke. Not only men, but women were smoking. Newspaper editorials were saying these days that women were intent on taking over all of men's liberties. Frail young girls in slippery skirts were driving automobiles; they were smoking cigarettes; they were expressing themselves using words that could make a Greek sailor lose his lunch. The next thing they might try would be urinating from a standing position.

Curiously, there was only one man in America who raised his voice against cigarette smoking. This man was Henry Ford, who had published, at his own expense, a pamphlet against cigarettes titled *The Little White Slaver.* He believed the source of the harm was in the paper, and advocated the substitution of corn husks for those who rolled their own. He said he got this information from his friend, Thomas A. Edison.

In Washington, where the bus stopped for two hours, Alan and Francine got on. They took the two seats just ahead of Mourly Vold. They had with them two suitcases and a motorcycle engine.

"Say, do you mind if I put this on the floor beside you?" Alan asked. "There doesn't seem to be any other place for it."

"Please do," Mourly Vold said. "I don't mind at all."

"I told you there wouldn't be any room for it," Francine said.

"Now, darling, this just isn't any of your business," Alan told her. "There's a good little old place for it right beside this gentleman, and he says I can leave it there."

Francine looked around. She was sitting in the aisle seat directly in front of Mourly Vold. Her face was close enough to allow him to see that she was very beautiful. Her hair was blonde, full of light, and very long. It came down past her shoulders. She was wearing a black Martindale cap trimmed with daisies. "Thank you," she said to him.

"It's no trouble," Mourly Vold answered.

Before long, the three became friends. Francine shared their lunch with Mourly Vold. She gave him a chicken wing, a hard-boiled egg, and an apple cut in pieces. Alan told him about the motorcycle engine.

"It's for an old Indian my brother gave me," he said. "Mine threw a rod. I picked this one up at the army junkyard outside of McLean. We have a field across the street from us. Nothing there. No people or anything. That's where I learned to ride. I went out there with a chum and we dug holes and everything. Jumped up out of the holes, va-voom! There was a tree there, right in the middle of the track. We tied a mattress around it. And we had our own rules of the road. There was really only one. You ever hear of the front-wheel rule? The fellow who gets his front wheel out there has the right-of-way.

"This was when I was still in high school, before I ever met her. I got to be a pretty good rider then, but I'm better now. She didn't want me to race at first, but now she's used to it. She's seen me race. She knows I can take care of myself. It used to bother her, but now it doesn't."

"Ha!" Francine said. "Listen to him!"

"You said it doesn't bother you."

"I never said any such thing!" Francine told him. "I let

you do it because you act like such a miserable child if I say you can't. But what happens if you break your leg, like your awkward brother? Then who would do your work? I can't teach school and do all the farm work, too."

"She's a teacher," Alan explained.

"Very nice," Mourly Vold said.

"I have half a mind to get rid of you and your motorcycles both," Francine said. "Then I could get a man who's serious about farming."

"She never could do that, though," Alan said. "She's too attached to my cooking. Especially my pies. She can't leave my pies alone."

Throughout the afternoon, the bus traveled across northern Virginia. It crossed the Shenandoah at Riverton over a wooden bridge and continued west. By evening, it was starting to climb into the mountains. The driver used low gear on the steepest grades, and the bus slowed to a walking speed. The straight-cut gears in the transmission whined loudly. On the downhill segments of the road, backfires from the exhaust returned as echoes from the mountain walls all around. The windows in the bus had sashes made of wood. Every one of them was open to admit the cool air draining down from the high ridges.

At sundown, the driver stopped at a mountain store to let the engine cool. Here some of the passengers left the bus to stretch their legs. Alan and Francine did not get up; they were asleep. Francine's head rested on Alan's shoulder. Mourly Vold settled in his seat and listened to the evening birds. In the silences between their songs, he could hear the slow, steady sleep-breathing of his friends. A bird landed on top of the bus. Its toenails made a scratching noise as it hopped about before it flew away.

Days later, as the police tried to reconstruct what had happened, someone suggested that the driver had been drunk. He would have had an opportunity to buy excellent homemade corn whiskey under the counter at that mountain store or any other in West Virginia. There was also the possibility that the driver was fine but the brakes had failed. Whether either of these conjectures was true or not, there need be no speculation about the other details of the accident. Only twenty miles farther down the road, just outside the village of Talcott, the bus failed to negotiate a turn and left the road. The police reports say that it turned over twice as it slid down the bank. It finally stopped when it struck a large red oak. It did not burn.

The investigators said it was red oak, and we can be confident they were correct. There can be little opportunity to mistake the identity of a red oak—it is made conspicuous in summer by its dark gray, ridged bark and its bright green crop of leaves. The leaves are an alarming, almost luminous green above, but paler beneath, with an oval outline and deep lobes. In autumn, at the end of their lives, these leaves turn a bloody color between blue and red.

CHAPTER 17

The survivors were taken to the Summers County Hospital in Beckton. This structure, built ten years earlier of white granite blocks, stood by itself on a grassy knoll. Sheep grazed in a pasture which began just behind the hospital and climbed slowly upward toward the ridges.

Mourly Vold's injuries were not severe. He had sustained cuts to his face and hands, and bruises on his arms and legs. Francine had also been cut by flying glass, and she had suffered a mild concussion as her head struck the ceiling of the bus. Both were treated and released the day following the accident.

Alan's condition was much more serious. A tree branch had gutted the side of the bus where he had been sitting. He had spilled out through the open hole and fallen more than eighty feet down the ravine. His neck had been broken in the long fall.

Francine stayed by her husband's bedside day and night for the first five days. Mourly Vold sat with her through periods of each day. The room Alan occupied faced south, toward sheep pastures and mountains. Flies from the sheep pastures bumped against the window screens from the outside. Alan remained unconscious for the first thirty hours. When he awoke, he was in great pain and he could not make his arms and legs work. He wept and screamed. The doctors gave him morphine to send him back to sleep.

Francine took lodgings in a nearby guest house called the Summersville. Mourly Vold took a room there also. The accident had shattered his plans the way it had broken Alan's neck. There seemed no point in continuing on his journey, even though his injuries would not have prevented that. When he was not in the hospital sitting beside Alan's bed, he wandered through the sheep meadows, following the gravel roads by their white glare, crossing and recrossing Meadow Brook until the road started down again, just under the summit of Briery Knob.

After a week had passed, the doctors said that Alan was not going to get better. They kept him awake each day only long enough to feed him. They told Francine that he would never move his arms or legs again. They said that inevitably in such cases, a respiratory infection would come along and turn into a fatal pneumonia.

The afternoon she received this news, Francine walked into the town in search of a job. The money she and Alan had been traveling on had nearly run out. Mourly Vold accompanied her. The only jobs available in the town were with the county high-way department, painting railings. They were told to report for work at seven o'clock the next morning. Between them they had a dollar and fifteen cents. They ordered a supper of beans and fried hash at the Lookout House, a restaurant not far from the hospital.

When the waitress brought their meals, Francine picked up her plate and threw it across the room. It hit the wall just above the head of the Reverend Horst Winkel of the Little Birch Lutheran Church, who had just begun to eat his fried cabbage. She took the dollar and fifteen cents from Mourly Vold's hand, smacked it on the table, and walked out.

He followed her out the door. Once he was standing on the porch, his poor vision would not allow him to find her in the gathering darkness. He groped ahead, and nearly fell down the front steps.

"I'm over here, you poor fool!" Francine said. She was sitting on the steps, weeping. "Just tell me where the sense is in that! He rides his goddamned motorcycle around and around, missing trees and rocks by that much, and nothing ever happens to him. Farm work, too. He works up on ladders, and down in wells. Nothing ever happens to him! What do you think of that? Nothing ever happens to him! And then, he takes a ride with me on a bus, and a tree opens up the side of the bus and scoops him out. Pretty funny, wouldn't you say? Don't you think that's funny?"

Mourly Vold gave no answer.

"He's such a bastard for letting this happen. When we got on, I said I would sit by the window. But no, he had to sit by the window, so he could look down under the seat and check on his motorcycle engine. If it hadn't been for that, we would have changed places, and he'd be perfectly fine today. We'd both be fine, in fact. If I had been sitting there, I never would have let myself fall out of a bus, even if there *was* a hole in it."

In the morning, they left the rooming house before the light touched its roof. Fog persisted in the hollows. It would last in the deepest places until midmorning. The fog produced strange effects. Tiny droplets of water grew spontaneously on the hairs of Mourly Vold's arms. When the sunlight coming over the ridge reached the top of the fog, the light scattered dimly in all directions, so that Mourly Vold had the illusion of walking in a glowing cloud.

They were transported by truck, along with several other members of the painting crew, ten miles out along the Charleston highway to where the work was under way. There the supervisor handed each of them a bucket of white paint and a brush.

Mourly Vold's first hour of gainful employment went badly. He had to position his good eye within a few inches of the guardrail to see any of its details. This made it a big problem deciding where to put the paintbrush. He finally worked out a procedure involving several steps. First, he would inspect the place where the paint was to be applied, touching it as well as looking at it. Then, with the image of the area fresh in his mind, he would apply the paint. Finally, he would inspect the area again, by touch and by sight, to be sure that he hadn't missed any spots.

Even this painstaking technique produced something less than a perfect job.

"Look at this," Francine said. "You can't leave big holiday areas like this. You'll get yourself canned."

After that, she came by every half-hour or so and touched up his work.

At noon, they took the ham sandwiches they had brought with them to a field full of long grass and blue flowers. They sat under an oak and listened to the sound of a waterfall somewhere down below.

"I want to thank you for taking care of my mistakes," Mourly Vold said.

"Don't mention it," Francine replied. "I suppose you're doing as well as you can. I'm getting a better idea, now, of what you can see and what you can't."

Something about this remark, he didn't even know what it was, hurt his feelings. Neither one of them said anything further until they had finished eating.

"Over that way," Francine said, "that's Kentucky. That's where our farm is. The nearest town is Beauty. I was born there, in the town. But then we moved to the farm when I was five years old. My mother wanted the farm. She was the one behind it. My pa was as bad a farmer as Alan is."

So they continued, for the next two days, painting railings along the Charleston highway. Each day, the sun moved slowly overhead, and the shadows under the railings moved in the opposite direction. Motor traffic on the highway blew dirt and pine needles into the paint. Flies stuck themselves randomly to the painted railings. Mourly Vold's accuracy improved, but Francine continued to inspect his work for mistakes. He grew accustomed to her presence. When she was working nearby, he could tell where she was by her sounds and by the blurred

THOMAS McMAHON

colors of her clothes. She wore her hair braided and gathered
on top of her head to keep it out of the paint.

In the evenings, they ate at the Lookout House. The management had accepted Francine's apology for the dish-throwing
incident. Their new wages allowed them to eat what they wanted.
The trout and the fruit pie were fresh; the hamburger wasn't.
They ate their meals under the curious stares of the local people.

"I wonder what makes them think they can stare at us
like that?" Francine said. "In Kentucky, we'd call that impolite."

"They're looking at me," Mourly Vold said. "Don't let it
bother you. It happens all the time. I'm funny-looking."

"What makes you so sure they're looking at you?" Francine
asked. "They might be looking at me. Don't tell me you're stuck
up. I don't want to find out you're stuck up, just when I'm
getting used to you."

After supper, they would spend the rest of the evening
with Alan in the hospital. Most of the time they were with him,
he was sleeping. When visiting hours were over, Francine would
kiss him without waking him. Then they would walk back to
the rooming house.

"Can you see the fireflies?" Francine asked one evening.

"No," Mourly Vold answered.

"I'll tell you about them, then," she said. "They're all
around us, little bugs flying so quietly you can't even hear them.
Each one seems to be turning its light on every minute or so.
They're very pretty."

She touched his arm.

"Stop a minute," she said. "I want to look."

Mourly Vold waited for her. Several minutes went by. He
heard her begin to sob, and then stop.

"It's very hard for me," she said. "I wouldn't want to be
alone with all of this. I don't know why you're staying in this
town with us. I don't even really know you, I suppose. I just
want to say that I'm glad you *are* staying, that's all. It's helping."

• •

Toward the middle of the next afternoon, the railing they were working on descended a long grade, turned a corner, and came to a bridge. Another painting crew was already at work on the bridge, painting the high steel trusses. Francine spoke to one of the men doing this work and discovered that they were being paid much more money.

"I'm going to ask for a job up there," she said. "Alan and I are going to need the cash."

"I think I'll do the same," Mourly Vold said.

"What? You can't do that. It's *high*!"

"Of course it's high," Mourly Vold said. "Why wouldn't it be high? It's a bridge."

With this, he put down his paint can and climbed up into the trusswork, reaching out above his head to feel the branch points of the columns and beams, touching the cables and their turnbuckles and using them for footholds as he passed, until he reached the top. Here, eighty feet above the roadway, there was only the moaning sound of the air flowing past the girders. The hiss of the water far below in the creekbed had almost disappeared.

When he came down, Francine said, "Well, I'm impressed. Where did you learn to do that?"

"I used to climb a lot of telephone poles," Mourly Vold told her.

And so the aerial phase of their lives as painters began. The sky cleared and for many days the weather was perfect. It was a time that Mourly Vold remembered afterward as one of great happiness. High up in the steel, he felt a sense of calm and isolation. He spanned the cables and beams like a spider clinging to the network of its own web. The logical organization of the trusswork pleased him deeply. If there was a certain angle between two girders at one corner of the bridge, then that same angle would be mirrored at the other three corners. A technique he worked out here could be duplicated exactly there—the same sequence of brushstrokes, the same resting place for the paint can, the same handholds. In many ways, the symmetries of the bridge were the steel equivalents of symmetries he had discovered in the telephone networks. Formerly he had lived in latticeworks of links and nodes that were only as real as he could make them in his imagination; now he lived in a symmetrical web that was actually in his hands and under his feet.

"If you could see where you were, you'd be scared," Francine told him. They were working together on a scaffold near the top of the main arch.

"You don't want to see where you are?" Mourly Vold said. "Then close your eyes."

"That doesn't do any good," she said.

Of course, part of Mourly Vold's sense of exhilaration derived from his feelings toward Francine, which seemed to grow stronger with the altitude. He could hear the fright in her voice. Everything seemed to be heightened in her when she was on the scaffold. Her breathing and pulse were fast. Several times a day, she grabbed him when she thought one of them might be falling. Her arms and her body were taut when she held him. She was thin and yet strong, like the steel cables that held the bridge together.

He wondered what her feelings toward him might be. There were many signs that she had begun to regard him differently. Up here, their earlier roles were reversed. She now depended on him, rather than the other way around. He could scamper over the ironwork, rerigging the scaffold, reaching inaccessible places, and he did this all without giving any regard to the height. It was apparent that she attributed this to courage on his part. The courage in her admired the courage in him. Mourly Vold took great satisfaction from this, but the more tenderly he began to regard her, the more he wanted her to know who he really was.

Who he really was! His other life. His real life! He longed to tell her about the other world he had first discovered and then mastered. The opportunity refused to present itself.

One morning, Francine failed to appear for breakfast. Neither did she show up at the highway department garage a half-hour later when the trucks departed for the work sites. All day, Mourly Vold worked alone. It was a strange and uncomfortable feeling to be without her. He had grown accustomed to the touch of her hand on his back as she passed on the narrow scaffold. He recalled the smell of her hair. He invented a hundred reasons why she might not be there. The work suddenly seemed pointless.

When he returned to the rooming house that evening, Francine had already packed her bag and was preparing to leave. She said that Alan had died. She would take him home to be buried.

They sat together on the glider on the front porch. "It was very bad," Francine said. "Several times when Alan was awake, he asked me to help him die. I could have just put a pillow over his face. He was always a big, strong man, but that's all he would have needed to go."

She wept for several minutes.

"I couldn't do it," she said. "And so he suffered needlessly, all those hours. He died by himself. I could have helped him, but I refused."

CHAPTER 18

In April 1921, Albert Einstein arrived in New York on the *Rotterdam* in the company of Chaim Weizmann. They had come to enlist American support for a lunatic idea in Weizmann's mind, a Jewish State of Israel. Einstein was at this time already a public figure. A crowd of several thousand people came down to the pier to see him get off the boat. Einstein's English was dreadful. A dozen reporters from the various Hearst papers wanted to talk to him. He shook their hands instead. He shook hands with the purser, the first mate, and the young man in charge of the ship's kennels. John F. Hylan, the mayor of New York, was holding a large reception for him at city hall. A limousine took him into the city. Einstein shook hands with the limousine driver. Arriving at the reception, he shook hands with the doorman.

Finally he encountered someone who spoke German, a reporter for the *New York Times*. He seemed relieved to be able to talk at last. He said he didn't understand why the Americans were so interested in him. The reporter tried to explain that, in America, when a child showed any kind of mathematical talent in school, he was called a "little Einstein." Americans regarded the potential for achievement, particularly when it appeared in their own children, as the most valuable thing in the world. Americans, he said, were enthusiastic about science because the scientist thinks like an immigrant. The scientist cares only for the future, and how he can live in it and change it with his own hands. Thus Einstein's person was more important to Americans than his discoveries, great as those certainly were, because in his person was the potential for untold new developments, new ways of going about life.

The reporter then asked Einstein for an explanation of relativity, suitable for the practical man.

"The practical man does not need to worry about it," Einstein told him.

On the day Einstein first set foot on American soil, he had been famous for approximately a year and a half. He had not courted this notoriety. It had come to him as a consequence of Arthur Eddington's observations of a total eclipse of the sun on the island of Principe off the west coast of Africa. The photographs Eddington and his assistant took then were besmirched by clouds, but there were enough stars visible to determine once and for all whether it was Newton or Einstein who now smelled like a goat. The measurements Eddington made showed the bending of starlight as it grazed the sun, and confirmed Einstein's theory of general relativity. When H. A. Lorentz wired this news to him, Einstein sent a postcard to his mother in Switzerland telling her about it. His mother propped the postcard up on her night table. The picture on the front of the postcard showed a kitten playing with a ball of yarn. At a joint meeting of the Royal Society and the Royal Astronomical Society, J. J. Thomson introduced the results, saying that Einstein's work was perhaps the greatest achievement in the history of human thought. The newspapers of England and the rest of the world took this up and tried to explain what Einstein's theory was. It soon became clear that no one without extensive mathematical training could understand beans about it. The newspapers hired mathematical consultants to put the theory in simple language, but this proved to be no good. Nothing they said was compatible with common sense. The difficulty was put to Einstein on this same trip to America as he visited Princeton University and received an honorary degree. Einstein said that the problem was not with his theory but with common sense. He implied that common sense was no longer valuable. An editorial in a New York paper expressed outrage at the assertion that there was anything worthwhile knowing which could only be understood by the chosen few. It said that such an assertion was an insult to the Declaration of Independence.

In Germany, the hostility toward relativity was much more venomous. In August 1920, there had been a mass meeting in the Berlin Philharmonic Hall to protest against relativity, pacifists, and Jews. Speakers at this meeting gave reasons why pacifists and Jews had contributed to Germany's defeat in the recent war. Relativity was only another fraud in the long line of dangerous horseshit offered up by the pacifists. Einstein had attended this meeting as a spectator, unnoticed.

Again in the same year, Einstein had been vilified at the annual Congress of German Scientists and Physicians. In still another meeting, the nationalist leader Rudolph Leibus had urged Einstein's murder. The German State of the time decided that this was going too far and required Leibus to pay a small fine.

So much controversy over matters which had no practical consequence! Einstein was surprised that everyone cared so much about ultimate philosophy. He had been under the impression that people cared most for their families and loved ones. His own family circumstances were in a sad way. His first marriage had ended, and his children were in Switzerland with his ex-wife. His father's ashes were buried in Milan. His mother had recently died in Berlin as she visited him for the last time.

Now he was in America, and he wished to put aside all blue feelings, at least for the brief period of his stay. He told the *Times* reporter, "In Europe, you would not see so many signs with Edison bulbs. You give the light away as if it cost nothing. I like that." The press was astonished by his sincere and informal manner. They had expected that a famous European scientist would be a stuffed shirt.

Then, as now, physicists were fond of baseball, and one of Einstein's physicist friends took him to see Babe Ruth play.

During the game, a man died of excitement as Ruth hit a home run. Afterward, Einstein was taken to meet the great Babe, who apparently confused Einstein's identity with someone else's. There was in those years a brand of frankfurt made and sold locally in New York by a pair of brothers named Einstein. Ruth may have thought the man he was meeting was one of these brothers. When Einstein was gone, a reporter tried to explain who he was. He was the inventor of the theory of relativity, the most difficult idea that had ever been discussed in the newspapers. "I don't care what you say about him," Ruth replied. "He still makes a great hot dog."

When Einstein returned to Europe, he stopped in France and spoke to reporters. His statement to them was a message of thanks to the Jewish doctors of America. On reaching Germany, he found that the mood had grown uglier during the weeks he had been away. Internationalism was practically dead. Some of Einstein's scientific colleagues no longer wished to sit with him at meetings. His friends told him that by openly espousing Zionism, he had shot himself in the foot.

Even the weather was bad. There came two weeks of solid rain. Most of this time, he stayed in his Berlin apartment. His cat developed a cranky mood.

"Poor darling," he said to the cat, stroking her chin. "I know what's troubling you, but I really don't know how to turn it off."

Meanwhile, in America, most people seemed willing to forget their loathing of pacifism. The soldiers had come home, and even though they had won the war, their dissipated behavior made many of their parents ashamed of them. They had returned from France with lice, venereal diseases, and dirty photographs. Instead of putting the war aside and getting back to business, they seemed to want to live in an imaginary world. Nothing was too strange for them. This mood infected people who had not even been at the front. When the famous dancer Irene

Castle accidentally singed her hair, she regarded herself in the mirror and knew what to do immediately. She cut off practically all the rest, the undamaged part as well as the damaged, leaving only a fringe which ended high above her shoulders. Immediately, every other young woman in the country rushed to do the same. The style became an emblem of sexual freedom.

The most anyone could recall of pacifism was that William Randolph Hearst had been in favor of it before the war. Hearst had been forced to become a pacifist by his hatred of the English. He regarded the English as a bunch of stuck-up sissies. Even after the war started, his papers had urged Americans to keep our boys home. We should arm to the teeth and let them come to us, he had said. Some of this was popular, particularly among German-Americans. In order to prove that this point of view was patriotic, Hearst had ordered his papers to carry little American flags at the tops and bottoms of their front pages.

It was during the war, when he was in his fifties, that Hearst took a new woman into his life. He was a big man—robust, still handsome. He did not admit that any part of life's adventures were over for him yet. The woman was known as Marion Davies, but she had been born Marion Cecilia Douras in Brooklyn. He picked her out of the crowd in Florenz Ziegfeld's *Follies of 1917*. Somewhere in there among all the other arms and legs he noticed a particular set which fascinated him. He fell in love not with Billie Dove, Carol Crystal, Dotty Dugs, Beverly Bush, Maude Lushleben, Cissy Sweet, or the beautiful Justine Johnstone, but with Marion Davies, a seventeen-year-old girl who could barely say her few lines without stuttering or breaking into laughter. Every evening for seven weeks, he bought two tickets to the performance. He sat in one seat and placed his hat on the seat beside him. He watched Marion Davies prance and giggle with her companions, regarding carefully each one of her dips and glides, so that the hair at the back of his head slid over his coat collar the way the feathers slide on a hawk's neck when it turns its gaze.

Before long, he was escorting her about town. He took a lavish apartment for her at the Beaux Arts Building on Sixth Avenue. A special telephone girl was hired to sit at the switchboard of the Hearst offices. This girl's duty was to know where Miss Davies was at any hour of the day or night. He neglected his wife's feelings entirely. He ground the usually accepted standards of discretion under his heel. He went about New York in the open company of Miss Davies and John Hylan, the heavy, redheaded hayseed he had installed in the mayor's office. Hearst delighted in Miss Davies's humor as well as her appearance. Once, as they visited the mayor in his apartments, she had waited until the mayor was indisposed in the bathroom and then had short-sheeted his bed.

Hearst conceived the ambition to make Marion Davies into the most famous film actress in the world. He wished to push her higher even than Mary Pickford in the public's esteem. He bought Sulzer's Harlem River Park Casino at Second Avenue and 127th Street and made it over into a well-equipped film studio. An academy of tutors was hired to fill in the many gaps in Miss Davies's education. There was a speculation that Hearst was doing all this on a bet. It was said that he had wagered with Orrin Peck that he could pick any one of Ziegfeld's dunghill flowers and make her into a star. The point was that the public would go for anything his newspapers told them to go for. It is important to state that there is not a shred of evidence that Hearst ever had such a wager with Peck or anyone else, even though the circumstances support the speculation.

Marion Davies's first starring role was in *Cecilia of the Pink Roses*. Hearst redecorated the Rivoli Theater for the premiere. Hundreds of thousands of real pink roses were arranged about the interior. The Hearst *American* gave the event and the picture a three-column headline. It called Miss Davies's performance an unqualified triumph. There was a quote from the mayor of New York, who said that he had seen the picture and recommended it to every citizen of the city. Hearst's *New York Journal* was even more effusive, mentioning Miss Davies and the picture in four separate news stories, the theater reviews, and the "notable people" page. The independent papers were less enthusiastic. The *Times* and the *Daily News* ignored the film entirely, and the *Telegraph* said it was meant to be a sob flicker but was worth no more than a snuffle.

In the winter of 1920–21, Hearst and Miss Davies were working on *The Young Diana* in Lake Placid. The scene of the story was supposed to be St.-Moritz. Hearst had a clear vision in his mind of how Miss Davies should look as she stood on the ice in her brief skating costume. As she could not stand up on her skates, two assistants had to lie prone on the ice and hold her ankles. The scene required snow, but the weather refused to cooperate. Two army JN-4 aircraft were flown from New York and landed on the ice. The airplane propellers blew three thousand bags of goose feathers past Miss Davies as she contemplated the horizon.

Even as Hearst managed all this, he continued to supervise his newspapers closely. At the Oberlander Lodge in the evenings, he spread out the day's copies of his newspapers on the floor. The *New York American*, the *Journal*, the *San Francisco Call*, the *Syracuse Evening Telegram*, the *Rochester Evening Journal*, all these and more were dropped by air every day and inspected by Hearst each night. He would mark the papers with red and blue crayons and send them to their editors to show what he wanted. Everywhere in the country, Hearst reporters were expected to climb trees or fire escapes, to go down in sewers and mines, to disguise themselves as rescue workers or nurses, to risk their lives, pay bribes, or even to invent stories as the occasion demanded. Hearst required absolute loyalty and devotion, and would pay cash for these things when they were delivered in a timely fashion. He often gave two executives the same job and let them fight it out to see who could cut the mustard. His executives, Brisbane, Goddard, Kobler, Carvalho, Merrill, and all the rest were paid fantastic salaries for behaving like brutes when the occasion demanded. And the public loved it! Hearst was certain that it was not only the common man who was buying his newspapers. He was confident that the snobs in Boston were sticking a copy of his *Boston Record* between the pages of the *Christian Science Monitor* in order to read the story under the headline MUM TOOK SIS'S LIFE WITH PINKING SHEARS.

That spring, when Hearst returned to New York, he resumed his daily working schedule at home at the Claremont, arising just before noon and retiring at three the next morning.

It was 11:26 P.M. on April 2 when he first picked up the story of the telephone vandal. It was in a short piece toward the back of the *New York American,* just one column, twenty lines or so, saying that the telephone company had discovered acts of vandalism that had been accomplished from within.

Hearst circled the story with a blue crayon and sent it to the editor. "Get going on this," he wrote in a large scrawl. "See if you can get two or three weeks out of it. Work the sabotage angle."

Thereafter, he paid close attention to the story and supervised its development day by day. "What do you think of that?" he asked Marion Davies. "The little fellow does it all by clucking his tongue."

"I wonder if he works parties?" Marion Davies said. "I'd love to see what it's all about. Do you suppose we could get him for our Fourth of July party at Mother's?"

When Einstein arrived in New York, Hearst was too upset to meet him. Instead, he got Hylan to give Einstein a reception at city hall. There was a serenade by the Sanitation Workers' Band. At the reception, Hylan told Einstein his life's story. "I used to be a judge," Hylan said. "That was terrible. I never knew whether they did it or not. I used to look at their eyes. They say that when a man sees his own crime, it makes one eye bigger than the other. I could never tell. It's much easier being a mayor."

Not until October did Hearst make the connection in his

mind between the telephone vandal and Mexico, and by then it was too late. The weak-sister management of the telephone company had had him, but they let him go. As he contemplated the dangerousness of the telephone vandal, Hearst's angry feelings freshened into a rage. He called the editor of the *Journal* and said, "I want you to polish Fairchild's nuts in pepper sauce for this. It will be on his head if his little friend breaks his telephone company in half."

One evening soon afterward, Hearst took Marion Davies, her mother, her sister, and a group of film people on board his steam yacht, the *Oneida,* for a cruise. When Hearst was in New York, the *Oneida* was kept staffed and fired for his immediate use at all times. It was over two hundred feet long, weighed seventy-five tons, and was fully equipped with a set of staterooms and common rooms that would accommodate a large party.

As the *Oneida* steamed south past the Battery, past the Statue of Liberty, toward Staten Island and finally out into Lower New York Bay, Hearst felt his mood lifting. This was a man who spent more than fifteen million dollars annually on his own private expenses. He regarded the operating revenues of his papers as available money and frequently raided the till of any Hearst newspaper he happened to be near. In addition to newspapers, he owned magazines, mines, and land. In his youth, he had manufactured a war with Spain. All his life, he had badly wanted to be president, and in his middle years he had spent a lot of money trying to accomplish this. His ambition to be president had been a joke to everyone but Hearst. To him it had been no joke at all; it had seemed, for a while, like a sure thing. Standing at the rail on the aft deck, Hearst turned and looked at the lights of New York receding in the distance. The *Oneida*'s wake stretched back to the city like a curving arrow on a newspaper map. This was the city that had caused him so much frustration and pain! It had many times tried to ruin his life. It had never accepted him, possibly because he was a westerner. It had no real place for a man with a heart as large and enthusiastic as his. New York, from this view, looked like a satanic city. The smokestacks of northern New Jersey pumped hot filth into the night air. The tops of the tall buildings disappeared behind the white gases trapped in the temperature inversion higher up.

The trip had been planned as a three-hour excursion to escape the noise of the city, but now Hearst suggested that they continue on to Mexico. He made the plans sound like wonderful fun. The guests all agreed. The following morning, the *Oneida* stopped at Baltimore, where Hearst handed out large sums of cash to each guest to buy clothes and other equipment needed for the journey. When they reached Mexico, Hearst hired a private train to take them into the interior. Hearst's spirits were as high as at any time in his life. He wrote a hoss opera in which everyone on the train took part. He gave Marion's mother and sister roles as townspeople. William LeBaron, the film director, was cast as a bad guy. Marion Davies was, as usual, the heroine. Just this once, he gave himself a speaking role, that of the avenging angel, the unknown stranger who rides out of the desert and changes a small world through swift justice.

Hearst put them through various versions of the performance more than twenty times as the train rattled across the dry plains of northern Mexico. He had the men run through the coaches and climb over the roofs. In each succeeding version, he made the miracles of the play more fantastic. After days of this, Hearst's guests gave up trying to hold on to their own personalities and let him manipulate them exactly as he wished. He would not let them slip out of the character he had assigned them, not even at mealtimes. In the mornings, as his guests were asleep, Hearst would stop the train in tiny towns in Coahuila and Chihuahua to buy fresh fruit and vegetables for their breakfasts. As he walked through these towns looking for the produce market, he wore a beautiful white ten-gallon hat.

After visiting his vast properties in Chihuahua, Hearst turned the train south toward Mexico City. Here he took Marion Davies to meet the new Mexican president, Álvaro Obregón. Obregón's hospitality was generous and compelling. After a long visit, Hearst convinced himself that Obregón was not the bomb-throwing lunatic he had imagined. He left Mexico feeling reassured that his properties were in no immediate danger.

CHAPTER 19

Winter had arrived by the time Hearst and his party returned to New York. As soon as the *Oneida* anchored, Hearst learned from his editors that the police in Syracuse had apprehended a blind youngster monkeying with his home telephone. A neighbor on the same line had heard and seen strange things. Acting on the neighbor's tip, the police had watched through a frosty window and seen a young man hammering on his telephone with chestnut shells and wooden spoons. Satisfied that they had cornered the famous telephone vandal, they burst in and put the cuffs on him. Over his mother's passionate objections, they took him to jail.

"Tell the chief I said to throw the book at him," Hearst told his editor at the *Syracuse Evening Telegram*.

"They say he's just a cute little kid," the editor in Syracuse said. "He looks as harmless as they come."

"So does a baby rattlesnake," Hearst said. "If he gets away again, I'll take it out of your hide."

Hearst worried considerably over this development. He had President Obregón's promise for the safety of his Mexican properties. If the telephone vandal wasn't working for the Mexicans, who was he working for? It now appeared likely that the young man was a Bolshevist.

In those days, millions of people believed that a Red revolution was about to begin in the United States. The infection was spreading from Russia across Europe and already its angry boils were rising here. The Hearst papers devoted considerable space to stories of Bolshevist atrocities. Radicals had fired guns at members of the United States armed forces in an Armistice Day parade in Centralia, Washington. To teach the Bolshies a lesson they would never forget, a group of American patriots took a self-confessed Wobbly out of the local jail and pushed him off a bridge with a rope around his neck. A clerk in the New York post office put aside sixteen identical packages wrapped in brown paper. The Bolshies had neglected to put enough postage on them. The packages were addressed to J. P. Morgan, John D. Rockefeller, Justice Holmes of the Supreme Court, Commissioner of Immigration Caminetti, and other important men. Each one contained an identical bomb.

This was just too much for the returned soldiers and sailors. Every town in the country had given them a victory parade, but no one would give them jobs. The war industries had all closed down. There was no work and nowhere to live. In New York City, men slept eight or ten to a room. Their lives were ruined by vice. In spite of this, they loved their country. When the Hearst papers carried the news of the Red bombs, the soldiers and sailors naturally ran out into the street, looking for the enemy. In the Palm Garden, uptown, the Women's International League was holding a meeting in support of Revolutionary Russia. The soldiers and sailors ran there and surrounded the building. They tried to smash their way in. The women inside feared for their virtue. None of them wanted to be raped. These were the same soldiers and sailors who had looked so fine in their uniforms before they went away to the front, but now they resembled nothing more than a pack of crazy hyenas. The soldiers and sailors knew that the Reds inside were young women and this knowledge made their dicks swollen. Fortunately, the doors held and the women were saved. Hours later, they were taken away by Mayor Hylan's police, some in a highly excited condition.

Hearst's papers ran scare headlines identifying the telephone vandal as an agent for Red Russia. The people were told that, as with the mail bombs, they had narrowly missed disaster.

A political cartoon ran in the Hearst papers showing the telephone vandal as a blind mole under the ground, eating at the roots of the American Freedom Tree.

Meanwhile, in Syracuse, the telephone vandal the police had in their custody was not Mourly Vold at all, but the Syracuse Stallion. Here was a totally blind boy of very modest physical size. His skin and hair were very fair, and his chest was built along the lines of a chicken's. A reporter noticed that his face looked something like that of Barney Google, the Hearst cartoon character. When the police questioned him, he told them all he knew, which was not much. Telephone company engineers and officials present at the questioning said that this certainly was not the young man who had dazzled them with his power some months ago. This boy knew only a few simple procedures for making free telephone calls. He had no knowledge of the theory behind the percussive signals he used. The engineers advised the police that they were holding the wrong person.

When Hearst heard this, he concluded that he was up against a whole network of conspirators. There was no doubt that the telephone vandal was actually more than one person. His papers screamed this fact everywhere in the country. SPY NEST ACROSS U.S., said a headline in the *Philadelphia Mail*. RED PLOT DEEPENS; "BARNEY GOOGLE" ONLY ONE OF MANY.

The Syracuse Stallion's mother visited him in his jail cell every day. She was a handsome woman with big breasts, an immigrant from Latvia. In spite of her strong physical appearance, she was obviously a tender character. She wept all the time, both inside the jail and at home. Her neighbors, her friends, and the members of her church had all withdrawn from her. The newspapers were saying that her son was a Red agent, and the terrible thing was not to know whether this was true. She knew he liked to play with the telephone, but can such a simple thing as that threaten a whole country?

The Syracuse Stallion had been a student at the Sister Mary McWilliams School for the Blind since he was seven years old.

He had been the smallest child in his class in every grade. The bullies with partial sight had stolen his food and pushed him down. They had depantsed him and left him to find his way back from the horse barn behind the school. None of this had diminished his curiosity and his enthusiasm for life. He discovered interesting ways of navigating about the school grounds, based on the slant of the land under his feet. In winter, he opened his window and listened to the snow fall.

There had always been something naïve and fragile about his perceptions of the workings of the world. Take banisters, for example. The Syracuse Stallion presumed, from a young age, that the banisters which follow staircases were put there for the use of blind people. When, one holiday season, his mother took him to a department store, he was surprised and even irritated to find that people with normal sight used them also. He collided with several persons of apparently normal vision who were creeping up the stairs with one hand on the banister. What good can vision be if you still have to cling to a rail?

After he had been in jail for a week, he asked his mother to bring him his Braille stencil and stylus. He used this to write a letter to Humberhill. The letter began cheerfully, but anyone reading it could feel the fear growing in the Syracuse Stallion's heart. It was all about Little Egypt, how he admired him and had faith in him. He believed that somehow Little Egypt would find a way to get him out.

Humberhill wrote back to him. Don't worry about a thing. Just hold on. Sooner or later, they'll get tired of looking at you and send you home. Try sticking out your tongue at them whenever you think of it; that should help wear them down. But he said nothing about Little Egypt, since no one knew where Little Egypt was at this terrible moment.

Granting her son's request, the Syracuse Stallion's mother brought him his Boy Scout sleeping bag. He promptly crawled inside and refused to come out. The police put his food on his Boy Scout plate and his water in his Boy Scout canteen. They passed these into the opening of the sleeping bag. Days went by. When they wanted to question him, they had to speak to him through the mouth of the sleeping bag.

Meanwhile, Humberhill and the others were stunned by the arrest. Blind telephone experimenters throughout the country had their family members buy the Hearst papers and read the stories to them. A typical story of this time, one which appeared in the *Cleveland Banner-Chronicle,* began with the headline WHO'S TROTSKY? SAYS "BARNEY." It reported on an interview with the Syracuse Stallion in which he disclaimed any knowledge of the famous Russian revolutionary.

Humberhill went on the rampage, contacting every member of his cadre individually. "It could have been me," he said. "It could have been you. It could have been any one of us. I'd really rather that it *had* been someone else. The Syracuse Stallion is not the boy I'd have picked to take our knocks, if you know what I mean."

"He's not that tough," Beetlejuice said.

"He's not tough at all."

"Do you think they'll let him go?"

"I suppose they'll let him go eventually, but I don't know when," Humberhill said. "Until then, he's one miserable boy."

"I wish we could do something," Beetlejuice said. "Have you got any ideas?"

"No," Humberhill said. "For ideas, we need Little Egypt, and there's no telling where he is. I wish to God he'd show his face. Sometimes I imagine that he's here right beside me, but I know it's only an illusion. For all I know, he could have gone to another planet."

Another week passed, and still the Syracuse Stallion refused to come out of his sleeping bag. He would not talk to anybody, not even his mother. He seemed to be very sad and confused.

The jailors who watched him saw only a quiet little lump in the sleeping bag. His dreams of this period were the dreams of a very depressed person. He dreamed he was actually in the telephone, and there he met Little Egypt face-to-face. Little Egypt was a great bird with glowing silver wings. His face was the face of a very old man. He spoke in riddles. Without once smiling, Little Egypt turned away and disappeared.

The Boy Scout sleeping bag had been designed well. On the inside was a soft cotton blanket. Next came a layer of cotton batting. Then came another layer of cloth, and finally an exterior sheath of a waterproof material known as NoDamp. The NoDamp was almost perfectly airtight.

At a few minutes past three in the morning of his last day, the Syracuse Stallion came out of his sleeping bag to use the chamber pot. When he was finished, he sat on the edge of his bunk. He slid his hand over the blankets until he found his musical mouse. This rag-toy mouse had a simple music box in it which played a fragment of a Chopin waltz. The name of his mouse was Disgusting. He had loved this musical mouse since his mother had made it for him when he was very young. Now he wound it and listened to the melody play over and over until it stopped.

Taking Disgusting with him, he crawled into the sleeping bag headfirst and pulled the drawstring tightly closed. In this way, he accidentally escaped from jail, using a route no one thought he was likely to try.

CHAPTER 20

After the Syracuse Stallion suffocated in his sleeping bag, the Hearst papers finally quit calling him Barney Google. Although nothing of the sort had happened, the news stories asked if maybe the Bolshies hadn't sent someone in to take care of him before he exposed the whole ring. Or, it could have been, as the police maintained, that he had taken care of himself.

The Bolshies were known for their suicide missions. Still fresh in the public's memory was the pathetic incident a year earlier when a Red had rushed into the house of the Postmaster General in Washington. He had clasped his arms around a plumber who had come to repair a pipe. The plumber had heaved the man out a window and left him there, stuck in a rosebush, furiously trying to defuse himself before the bomb went off. The Postmaster General had not even been at home. The astounding thing was not so much the Bolshie's audacity as his mistake, since there had been only the most superficial resemblance between the plumber and the man's target, the Postmaster General.

As sloppy and foolish as the Bolshies were, Hearst was willing to give them credit for finally having come up with something in this telephone vandalism. At last they seemed to pose a genuine threat. They seemed to know things about the telephone networks that even the Bell company didn't know. Worst of all, the telephone company seemed to have fallen under an evil charm. It showed no interest in defending itself.

As the winter eroded into spring, it crossed Hearst's mind that he might hire Thomas Edison to find out how the Reds were getting into the telephones. Of course! That was it! Edison and his men would discover their methods and trap them. Then Mayor Hylan's police would fix their wagons. Hearst also reasoned that adding Edison to the story wouldn't hurt the circulation of his papers, since Edison was currently the world's most famous American. His papers could make Edison into news anytime, after all. He dispatched a special representative to put the proposal to Edison at West Orange.

If this had happened a few years earlier, it is unlikely that Edison would have found the time to cooperate. During the war, Secretary of the Navy Josephus Daniels had made Edison chairman of the Naval Consulting Board. Edison announced that he would turn his entire laboratory over to war research. A great number of important ideas came to him. He worked on a shell which would release oleum in a cloud to ruin the enemy's eyes and lungs. He conceived of a super-powerful underwater searchlight for melting holes in submarines. He tested a directional sea anchor which was supposed to allow ships to turn quickly to avoid torpedoes. In the course of his war service to the navy, he submitted over forty new developments for the use of the fleet, and not a one was accepted. His disappointment was enormous. He wrote to Secretary Daniels saying that, as far as he was concerned, the entire naval staff had shit for brains.

After the war, Edison's competitors in the phonograph business prospered. The public liked the fact that Victor, Columbia, and Brunswick records could be used interchangeably, since they all used a lateral cut. Edison's records used a hill-and-dale cut, and were not compatible. Edison's disks piled up in his warehouses. His cylinders, although still for sale, were now bought only by hayseeds.

An even greater threat to Edison's fortunes came from radio. In the month Einstein visited America, there were over two hundred thousand radio sets in the hands of the public, and all it wanted was more. Edison's staff advised him to get into radio manufacturing, but he said nix. "The Radio Craze will blow itself out," he said. "The Crooks in Radio are mean Pups & will lose their shirts as the Public becomes bored."

Edison was soon obliged to borrow heavily to meet his payrolls. He had bitter arguments with his son Charles, who was supposed to be managing things at the phonograph factory. He tried to understand what people liked about the radio. He put a pair of earphones on, but heard nothing. Charles showed him where the volume control knob was, and he turned it up so loud that the sound was horribly distorted. People standing ten feet away could hear screeches and clicks coming from Edison's ears. The static sounded like automatic weapons firing. Edison put the earphones down, bewildered.

Hearst had offered him a lot of money to go after the telephone vandals. This was certainly a consideration in his decision to accept, since the phonograph business was failing. Another factor must have been the adventure involved. Edison enjoyed a good fight. In the early days of electric power, he had gone head-to-head with George Westinghouse over AC versus DC. Westinghouse had been offering for sale a competing electric power system based on Nikola Tesla's scheme of alternating current. Edison's district managers were saying that they would all be busted by Westinghouse unless Edison introduced an alternating-current system of his own.

Edison had called in the newspaper reporters. With his assistant, "Professor" Harold P. Brown, he had demonstrated the dangers of Westinghouse's system. Dogs and cats were coaxed onto grids and electrocuted by alternating current in full view of the reporters. The dogs and cats had been purchased from schoolboys at twenty-five cents each. Responding to a request from the New York State legislature, Edison and Brown put together an electrical cap and shoes and sold them to the state for the purpose of executing criminals by alternating current. Edison's idea, and a clever one it was, was to associate execution and alternating current in the mind of the public. As it happened, the operators of the equipment were inexperienced and did a poor job with the first criminal. He came back to life several times and had to be recooked, making everyone who saw the execution lose his breakfast. Nevertheless, a new way of dying had been invented, and the newspapers needed a name for it. Edison proposed that a new verb be added to the English language—"to Westinghouse." He predicted that Westinghouse would kill a customer within six months of putting alternating current in residential houses.

The Hearst agent told Edison that the telephone vandals sometimes connected their own instruments to telephone wires. This fact suggested to Edison a simple way of stopping them. He would merely add a Westinghouse voltage to the telephone lines. An ordinary citizen could continue to use his telephone safely, since he would never touch any bare wires in the course of his lawful use of the service. Anyone attempting an unlawful use could touch the wires at his own peril.

Edison put an assistant in charge of working out the details for electrifying the telephone wires, then returned to the private experiments he had been working on before the Hearst man arrived. His experiments were aimed at a theory of memory. In a special room of his West Orange laboratory, he had built a smaller room supported on rubber legs. Pressed against the walls, ceiling, and floor of this room was a skin of glass photographic plates.

Edison's idea was to record the passage of tiny elements of memory as they flowed through space. He entered the room and closed the door. He sat in a chair and wrote down all his thoughts, exactly as they occurred to him, in a notebook. His plan was to develop the photographic plates later and look for traces of the memory particles which had penetrated them.

Edison presumed, from his own experiences, that the particles of memory moved in swarms. Arcing through the air, they would find a brain to alight upon and live there for as long as harmony remained in that brain. They would join the swarms of memory particles already present, some of which might be very old, having been transmitted to the brain before birth by the parents. The man capable of great inventions owed his ideas to memory swarms of the highest quality and greatest vigor. But sometimes, the various swarms fell into disagreement with one another. Rival queens could appear within the colony, with the result that struggles for power would erupt. Unless the minority factions were willing to let themselves be ruled by the majority, the discord created could threaten a man's sanity. Occasionally, a group of minority particles would gather about the eyes, which Edison took to be the entrance to the brain, and then fly off in their thousands, following their queen to a new nest. By this process, the brain of some fortunate young man became enriched, and the brain of an older man became weaker.

Edison himself had a truly fine memory, but recently swarms had been escaping from it at an alarming rate, leaving behind holes he feared were big enough to poke your thumb through. In the old days, he could remember price lists, catalog numbers, railroad timetables, the mass densities of all the elements, and the names of the presidents, vice-presidents, and secretaries of State since the founding of the republic. Much of this information was no longer at his command, and, paradoxically, it was useless things he could recall without effort. As he sat on the chair in the memory-swarm room, he suddenly shouted out loud, "Holy Moses!" as he remembered the name, Michael Oates, of the childhood playmate he had once given a great quantity of Seidlitz powders to swallow. He had expected that the gas developed in this way would cause Oates to rise up into the air. Instead, Oates had merely become ill and complained to his mother, leading to Edison's receiving a thrashing.

Edison wrote in his memory-swarm notebook, "Mike Oates. Seidlitz powder = farts. Are farts hydrigin? More like water-gass. Could be usefull to propell bicycle."

But now another memory returned to him, and this one made him shiver. He was back in Ohio, in the small town where he had grown up. Below his father's house was the canal basin, and here he had gone swimming with a boy whose name he could no longer recall.

Toward evening, he had returned home and gone to bed. By lifting himself on one elbow, he could see out the window. In the darkness, adults were walking around, carrying lamps and calling. Very late at night, the searchers had questioned someone who remembered seeing the missing child with Edison. The search party had come to Edison's bedroom. They had brought their lamps in with them, filling the room with a harsh light. At first, he told them nothing. Then, under their pressure, he admitted that the missing boy had been swimming with him in the canal. He had seen the boy's head go down. Then he had waited a long time, not knowing what to do. Finally, he said, he had returned home.

The following morning, Edison had again leaned on one elbow to look out the window. The boy's body lay floating in the canal. Edison sank back into his bed and closed his eyes. It was late in the morning when he looked once more, and by this time, someone had taken the body away.

The Hearst man had arrived at West Orange a month before Edison's departure on his annual camping trip with Henry Ford and Harvey Firestone. Each spring, they met in Pittsburgh and drove south through the mountains. This year, the party, including the staff, numbered twenty-six people. There were cooks, valets, drivers, guides, mechanics, and riggers. They traveled in three large touring cars, followed by six trucks. One of the trucks held a generator to power the electric lights for the tents. The guides shot small game for the table, and the chefs served it up in elaborate style. As Edison was fond of pie, there were rabbit pies, blackbird pies, pheasant pies, and pies made with apples, blueberries, strawberries, and rhubarb.

Carloads of newspaper reporters followed them as they drove out of the valley of the Monongahela into the high country of West Virginia. Harvey Firestone had plastered the trucks with signs saying BUY FIRESTONE TIRES. Some of these signs can be seen in the photographs that appeared in the Hearst papers.

In one of these photographs, Ford and Edison are standing together, Ford the thin one and Edison the heavy one. Both are looking down into a brook. Wherever they went, Ford estimated the industrial potential of each river, stream, and brook. With jerky motions of his hand, he showed where the dam would go, where the iron smelter would be built, where the body plant, the foundry, the steel mill, and the machine shops would be placed. His imagination constantly bulldozed the landscape in front of his eyes.

Other Hearst newspaper photographs show Edison asleep under a tree, asleep in a hammock, asleep under a pile of greasy rags in the back of one of the trucks. The story that everyone in the country had been brought up to believe, that Edison went without sleep, seemed to be exposed as bunk by these photographs. There is a particularly famous picture of Edison asleep on his stomach in a grassy field. For this photograph, Ford had carefully pushed the stem of a large mountain daisy between Edison's legs, so that the stalk, capped by its flower, appears to be escaping from Edison's rear end. Above Edison's outline, curving to imitate the general shape of his enormous hams, is the famous vista of Brewster's Knob.

CHAPTER 21

Edison's camping party came through Beauty, Kentucky, midway through the second week of their trip. Mourly Vold was now living here with Francine on her farm. When Edison's touring cars and trucks went by, they raised a cloud of dust high enough to reach the topmost leaves of the oak trees standing beside the road.

Edison rode in the front seat of the lead car. He had appointed himself the navigator and selector of campsites. The cars and trucks bumped over the unpaved roads at a good clip. "Keep this bucket of tin moving," he said to the driver. "I want to give Ford's bony bum a few sore spots." At the end of each day, he told the newspaper reporters that he enjoyed a good shaking-up.

It is important to remember that, at this moment in U.S. history, no other American enjoyed as much popular recognition as Edison. Mothers who had learned about Edison in their school texts were now watching their children learn about him from the same texts. Mr. Phonograph! Mr. Electric Light! Edison the little train boy, with his baggage-car chemical laboratory and printing press! A letter was once delivered to Edison bearing no name or address, only his picture. His heavy, unsmiling face and his white hair were known to millions. Even Francine recognized him immediately as his caravan passed her house on its way to the town square.

It was now seven months since Alan's death. For the most part, the normal operation of the farm had resumed, and this was largely due to Mourly Vold's help. He milked and fed the cows. He looked after the sheep. He cleaned barns and mended fences. He climbed in the apple trees and pruned dead branches. Francine was surprised that he could do all this in spite of his thin frame and his weak sight.

She insisted upon paying him wages. Otherwise, she said, she could not permit him to stay and work. He ate all his meals with her in the house, but slept in the barn. In spite of this perfectly proper arrangement, eyebrows were raised among the neighbors. One of them even spoke to Francine on the matter. "I need the work," Francine told her. "If you don't like what I'm doing, maybe you'd rather send your husband over."

They often worked together in the fields. One day, not long before Edison came through, they were putting in a fence around the pond to keep the goats from wandering away. Mourly Vold dug the holes for the posts. He labored with his shirt off under the hot light. Francine noticed how his face and arms had darkened, and how the movements of his body were strong and manly. She watched him swing the shovel, and with each stroke, it flashed. These flashes looked like strikes of lightning, but they were only reflections from the bright surfaces of the shovel. For the first time, she wondered what Mourly Vold's age was, and tried to estimate it. She guessed that he was eighteen or nineteen, which would make him either three or four years younger than herself.

Immediately after making this calculation, she reproached herself for it. So what? she asked herself. So what?

When he had dug each hole deep enough, he placed a post in it, and held it while she struck the post with the maul. Steady, she said to herself each time she lifted the maul. If I let this thing slip, I'll brain him. He knelt and held the post with both hands, his head bent down. He's thin, she thought, but his back and arms are powerful. He doesn't look like much with his shirt on, but with it off, he's not bad.

Francine knew that men are aroused through the eyes. Her life with her husband had taught her this. In changing her clothes, she had always to remember to keep her breasts covered to avoid giving him an erection. Once he had one, he would want to put it to work, no matter what time of day it was. What a powerful reflex! And so dependent on sight! She wondered if Mourly Vold's weak eyes meant he could not be excited in this way.

As he dug the next hole, she wandered away to the edge of the pond. There were lilies growing just beyond the edge of the water, about ten feet out. The blossoms floated on a compact raft of their own green leaves. They turned slowly in the breeze. She picked up a stick and reached out to them. For a time, she played at trying to pick the lilies by winding them around her stick, but they were too slippery; they slithered away.

She looked around and saw that Mourly Vold was standing beside her.

"Can you help?" she said. "I'm trying to get some of those lilies. I want them for the house."

He listened to her splashing with her stick for a moment. "You're not doing very well."

"I know," she said, squinting into the bouncing glare and the ripples.

"Take off your boots and go after them."

"I don't want to," she said. "I don't like the mud."

Mourly Vold climbed the far bank of the pond and sat down. He filled his pipe and had a smoke.

"How come you aren't doing anything?" Francine called to him.

"It's noon," he said. "Time for lunch."

Francine put down her stick and brought the lunch pail up the bank to where he was sitting. She brought out a table-cloth, spread it on the grass, and unpacked the lunch.

"Isn't it nice here?" she said. "The forest smells so pleasant."

She put fried chicken, sliced country sausages, and raw carrots on a plate and passed it to him.

"Right out in front of us," she said, "there's a little valley, and the schoolhouse is down there. I used to walk home along a path that goes over the ridge, and when I'd get to the top, I'd just stand there for a while. I would pretend I was a lookout, looking for trouble. I'd look all around, and see if there were any burning houses or drowning children. I wanted to be a heroine, you see. I'd read about them in books. In books, heroines had nice lives. From here, on a perfect day, you can see five miles."

"Nobody can see five miles."

"Oh, yes," Francine said. "Yes." But it was obvious to her that she should not follow this line of conversation any farther, since it had come to rest on what one could do with normal sight.

"There are just two things I've always dreamed about," Francine said, "and one of them is saving somebody's life. I think the opportunity is always lurking there, like money hidden in the grass. You just have to be alert. It would be such a marvelous thing to save somebody. I really want to do that someday."

"What's the other?"

"What?"

"What's the other thing you want?" Mourly Vold asked her.

Francine turned her head away. For a long moment, it appeared she might not answer this at all.

At last, she spoke again. "The other is to have everything I want sexually."

Mourly Vold said nothing. He finished eating his lunch, then walked down to the pond to rinse his plate.

Francine instantly regretted what she had said. She had embarrassed him; perhaps she had even frightened him. She had broken a taboo, but which one? She had taken unfair advantage of the years between them. It was entirely possible, she thought for the first time, that he had no experience at all.

She followed him to the water and rinsed her plate. Bending

close to the surface, she saw her own image—her face surrounded by a curtain of wheat-colored hair, and all this planted
in the center of a white fair-weather cloud. Mistake! Mistake!
Why had she said such a thing to him? It would have been so
much better to have kept her mouth shut. There had been no
reason to tell him such a personal thing. She had not meant it
as a come-on, but only as a confidence to a friend. It had been
an unwelcome confidence. And it could be taken in such a
terribly wrong way! She wondered if she were about to apologize.

The moment she straightened up, a ball of soft mud struck
her left ear. She whirled in his direction, just in time to catch
another glob of wet muck on the front of her shirt.

"You little . . ." she screamed, and shoved him into the
pond. He sat down heavily in six inches of water, then stood
again, immediately. He was laughing. She realized she had not
seen him laugh before. "You little . . ." she said, and pushed
him again, but this time he held her wrist, and pulled her down
in the water beside him. She squirmed and thrashed in the mud.
He held her fast. The black water filled her boots and ran down
her shirt. It soaked her coveralls and wet her hair.

"You'd better let go of me," she said.

"What if I don't?" he asked her. "Are you going to tell
me another secret?"

"I think you're horrible," she said, and wrestled away from
him. She waded out of the pond. "I don't think that kind of
behavior is funny at all. If you try anything like that again, you're
out, Buster. I mean it." With that, she walked to the house,
went in, and locked the door.

He didn't see her again for the rest of the afternoon.

After she was gone, Mourly Vold stripped off his clothes
and went for a swim in the pond. The water felt wonderful
after his morning's work. He swam to the middle of the pond,
where it was deep, and lay on his back. The water at the surface
was as warm as a bath, but it was cold only a foot or so down,
where his heels stroked through the deeper layers. The pond was

full of aquatic plants with brown-and-green leaves climbing up toward the sunlight. In the canyons between these plants, families of bass went about their business.

Toward the middle of the afternoon, Mourly Vold rinsed the mud out of his clothes and hung them to dry on a sumac bush. He returned to the pond, and paddled among the lilies for another hour. After four o'clock, he came out and dug six more postholes, working in the nude except for his boots and his spectacles. When his clothes were dry, he put them on and returned to the barn for a short rest before dinner.

That evening, he found his meal set out for him on the screen porch. Francine was nowhere in evidence. He sat down at the rough table and removed the white linen napkin that covered the plate. She had prepared ham with raisin sauce, asparagus spears with butter, and a magnificent baked potato. By the side of the plate was a stein of cold beer. He had not been eating long before Francine came silently through the door and stood by his side. She was wearing a thin cotton dress printed with yellow flowers. He looked at her for a moment and then went on eating.

"I didn't know you could be such an animal," she said.

"I didn't know *you* could."

"Oh," Francine said. "I thought so. I offended you. I can see I'm going to have to be more careful. That was it, wasn't it? What I said?"

Mourly Vold didn't answer.

"Don't take it so seriously," she told him. "Everyone does that now. They say the first thing that comes into their heads, without thinking what it will mean to anyone else. It's just the style. Say, what's that?"

Francine looked out on the lawn. When she recognized what it was, she stood up and held out her hand. "Come," she said.

"I'm not finished eating."

"Then I'll wait one minute. Exactly."

Mourly Vold finished his beer and blotted his lips. Then Francine took his hand and they went out on the lawn.

"You really are an old-fashioned boy, aren't you?" she said, as she stooped to pick up the lily. "It's beautiful. And it smells so nice, too. Oh, look! There's another one. Did you put that there, too?"

"I don't know what you're talking about," he said.

He followed her as she moved across the lawn, picking up the water lilies he had placed there, until she reached the barn where Mourly Vold made his bed. The moon was just rising above the boughs of the old oak standing beside the house. She slipped her fingers between his.

"What now?" she asked.

"Now," he said, "you have to decide if you're going to leave the lights on in the house all night."

On the day Edison's party drove by the house, Mourly Vold was shingling the roof of the barn. Francine walked to town to buy a loaf of bread. When she returned, he was still working on the roof.

"I just saw Mr. Thomas Edison on the town square," she said.

Mourly Vold stopped hammering and looked down in her direction. He could not see her, of course—she was well out of his range. "Oh?" he said.

"He was kicking his leg up in the air. Mr. Henry Ford was right beside him, doing the same thing. They were having a contest to see who could kick the highest. There were newspaper reporters and photographers all over. Mr. Edison won."

"Are they still there?"

"As far as I know," Francine said. "Come down."

They walked together to the town of Beauty, where, just as Francine had said, a large collection of cars, trucks, and pedestrians had taken over the two acres of green space that people called the town square. Here, at the edge of the baseball diamond, a dozen large tents had been erected. A crew of men were stringing wires to the various tents from the generator truck. One of the tents was open at the front. Inside, Francine could see a long table spread with a white tablecloth. On top of this table were a vase of flowers and several settings of china and heavy table silver.

"Where's Mr. Edison?" Francine asked a reporter.

"Sleeping in his tent," the reporter said.

"Is he coming out again?"

"You can count on it," the reporter told her. "In about an hour, I would say. I've been watching him for two weeks now, and I haven't seen him skip a meal yet."

They waited for Edison in McCracken's pharmacy. Each of them drank a phosphate. Mr. McCracken's stone countertop felt cool under their hands. Through McCracken's window, Francine saw Henry Ford emerge from his tent, carrying an ax. He disappeared into the woods, then returned later, pulling a small tree. It was a red oak, the same species that had killed her husband. Several people walking past stared at Ford, but no one stopped. They did not recognize him. Ford knocked the branches off the tree and cut it into firewood. In the course of an hour, he did the same thing twice more.

When Ford had accumulated a pile of wood, he made a campfire and heated a pan of milk. While the milk was warming, he opened a box of dried figs. He spread a tablecloth on a folding camp table and opened a folding chair. Then he set out his evening meal, which consisted of a warm glass of milk and three figs.

Ford had discovered that all the diseases of mankind were due to wrong mixtures of food in the stomach. Through careful experimentation, he had arrived at a method for eating his figs and milk which kept them in the correct proportions. He would first eat a fig, and then take a swallow of warm milk, and then wait exactly one minute by his watch before doing the same thing again until the meal was finished. The important thing was to eat no sugar except the sugars of fruit. He believed that granulated sugar scratched the walls of the blood vessels.

At last, Edison emerged from his tent. Francine and Mourly Vold joined the crowd of reporters and townspeople who surrounded Edison to hear what he might say. Several pies were now cooling on a table outside the cooking tent.

The reporters really wanted to know only one thing: what was Edison going to do to stop the telephone vandal and his gang?

Edison stood before them with his clothes wrinkled and his trousers sagging. "That's an easy question," he said. "You fellows ought to ask me something hard."

"Why don't you answer the easy question first?" said the *Times* man.

"The machine that will stop them is already being built," Edison said. "I can tell you it's a honey. When it is placed into service, no one will monkey with the telephones and live to tell about it. The problem will be ended."

The interview over, the newspaper reporters dispersed. Mourly Vold said he wanted to buy a paper, so they returned to McCracken's drugstore and bought the *Knoxville Banner* and the *Washington Democrat*. As they walked home, Francine read the papers to him. This is how Mourly Vold learned about the death of the Syracuse Stallion. The papers were full of the story in all its various aspects. They gave great attention to the fact that Edison was now a part of the hunt for the telephone vandals. One of the most recent developments was that a Hearst reporter had discovered the name of the mastermind; he was said to call himself "Little Egypt."

When they reached Francine's house, Mourly Vold sat down in a chair at the kitchen table. He acted quite subdued. Francine began to prepare their supper.

"A moment ago," she said, as she washed potatoes, "I was wondering why you were so interested in those stories about the boys who play with the telephones."

There was a silence.

"Now I'm not wondering anymore. I figured it out."

"Is that so? What did you figure out?"

Francine put down her work and walked to his chair. She put her hand on his head, then pulled him tightly against her. His spectacles pressed against her magnificent lollies. The buttons of her dress flattened his ear. She held him this way for several minutes. "You're him," she said. "You're Little Egypt."

"Good guess," Mourly Vold said.

"Am I right?"

"Of course," Mourly Vold told her. "Who else would I be?"

He was delighted and relieved that Francine had at last seen through his disguise. On her own, she had peered through the thin and weak-sighted Mourly Vold and had seen the powerful Little Egypt shining beneath the surface. Without anyone telling her the secret, she had discovered it herself, the truth about him.

In celebration, they went for a wild ride together through the networks. He walked with her to a maple grove he had found earlier, where a telephone wire left the road and crossed into the woods. With a ruthless crack, he wound the tip of the bullwhip coupler around this wire, and within minutes he had taken control of a Z-trunk. Now he took her up into the circuits, revealing himself splendid in his own country. In Hattiesburg, he found Julie feeding the truckers their dinners.

"Hey, what are you doing here?" Julie said. "I haven't heard a peep out of you in months. I thought you might be dead, or in jail. Maybe both, from what the papers say."

"I brought somebody to meet you," Little Egypt said.

"Hello," Francine said.

"Pleased to meet you," Julie said.

"Now look," Julie said, returning to Little Egypt. "Are you really a Red? Because if you are, I've got a job for you. The man that owns this place is getting to be a pain in the ass, and if you're really a Red, I want you to send one of your boys down here with a bomb or something to teach him to mind his manners."

After leaving Julie, he went to Columbus, where he knew the owner of a tobacco store.

"Your friends have been calling for you," the tobacco-store owner said. "They must have called twenty times, over the past few months. I told them I hadn't heard from you. They want you to get in touch with them."

"I'll do that soon," Little Egypt said. "Meanwhile, I want you to meet Francine."

"Hello, there, Francine," the tobacco-store owner said. "Glad to know you. Any friend of Little Egypt's is a friend of mine. He's been quite a pal to me this last year."

"He's been a pal to me, too," Francine said.

At last, Little Egypt went looking for Humberhill and the others. He poked around in some of the utility trunks they had once used for party lines, but no one was there.

Giving up on Humberhill for the moment, he pulsed into a long-distance cord-board office in Chicago, so that Francine could listen to the operators at their work. He explained to her in great detail what they were doing. He wanted her to have a perfect mental image of the board in front of them and all its controls. She listened as the operators patched calls through and made signaling-integrity checks. The operators worked their voices in buzzing monotones, endless speech which was part jargon and part gossip, getting their jobs done and at the same time being women.

Meanwhile, in Baddeck, Alexander Graham Bell fell ill. A chill lodged in his lungs and would not come out. His heart beat faintly. The doctors said he was slipping into idiopathic anemia. At his request, Mabel made a bed for him on the couch in the living room.

She sat with him most of each afternoon. He seemed to want to review his life. Each day, when his strength permitted it, he spoke with his wife for hours.

He said much about his long and close friendship with Helen Keller. Her beauty and innocence were still perfectly intact in his memory. Helen had once traveled with the Bells to Niagara Falls. To let her feel the power of the water he had taken her to the porch of a hotel near the falls and placed her fingers on a windowpane. He recalled the puzzled expression on her face as she struggled to understand what was causing the window to shake. She had imagined, before this time, that sound traveled on a beam of human intelligence. She saw it passing between people without disturbing anything in its path. The fact that it had a physical power, a strength to move objects on its own, was something she had not found reasonable.

As Bell grew more feeble, he stopped talking. He took Mabel's hand and spelled into it, using the manual alphabet. This is the way he had communicated with Helen Keller half a lifetime ago. He revealed to Mabel what he had never told her before, that he had once inadvertently observed Helen and Anne bathing nude. He asked her what she thought of him for that. Mabel replied that she didn't think that was terrible at all, and recalled that they had both been very beautiful when young.

Drifting in and out of sleep, Bell watched his wife, now fully in his gaze, now in the corner of his eye, as she went about her household chores. His head was full of spaces, gaps, and disconnected memories. A question occurred to him: how common is the love of a good woman? The question seemed to have no answer—at least, none that he would ever know. He put the question another way, in language he had used in speaking with himself a thousand times before. Suppose he had never met Mabel. Whom would he have married then, and would she have been anything like as fine? There was still no answer. I have had a good bargain in this life, he said to himself, but I don't know whether the bargain is in my own dear wife or in marriage itself. It could be that marriage is always a good bargain for the man.

On two different days, near the end, he signed, "Where is our boy?"

To this, Mabel replied, "He is free and happy."

CHAPTER 22

The newspapers Francine brought home reported Bell's death, but treated the news as unimportant. It was taken for granted that more people would be surprised to hear that Bell was still alive than to hear that he was dead, since he had been obscure in the public's mind for more than a quarter of a century. The stories about him recounted his life as a teacher of the deaf, as the inventor of the telephone, and then they seemed not to know how to go on. There was the implication that the news-worthy part of Bell had died long ago.

In the Hearst papers, the news of Bell's death was all but eclipsed by lurid headlines exposing new details of the menace of the telephone vandals. A long account was given of the life and death of the party line. The stories said that the conspirators had met together in a special telephone connection for the purpose of planning their takeover of the country. Here they passed around information about how to do dirty tricks in the service of Red Russia.

Of course, these stories were ridiculous; they were larded with details concocted out of the imaginations of their writers, but what disturbed Mourly Vold was not their lies but their truths. A very substantial fraction of what the public was being told had actually happened. The papers now knew where Little Egypt had been born and where he had gone to school. It was plain that someone he had trusted had been giving information to the press.

He suspected it was Humberhill. The details that were showing up in the Hearst news stories and editorials included things that could only be known by the old-timers among the telephone experimenters. These included himself, Humberhill, Beetlejuice, Billy the Boozer, and the Syracuse Stallion. Of these, the Syracuse Stallion was dead, and Beetlejuice and Billy would be too frightened of him to cross him this way.

He fell into a blue mood, deeper and stranger than any he had ever experienced. Day after day, he rose early and began his chores around the farm. He avoided contact with anyone. In the evenings, he climbed alone to the top of the ridge and smoked his pipe.

On one such evening, Francine followed him. She pushed her way through the pitch pine and large-toothed aspen to the gravelly trail and saw him climbing ahead of her. The dust rising in miniature clouds from each of his footsteps glowed in the red evening light. The sky was darkening, and already there was starlight. She saw him leave the trail several times and stop just before colliding with a tree. In the gathering darkness, particularly in the shadows beneath the pitch pines, he was as good as blind. Even so, each time he walked off the trail, he found his way back to it. Because of these forays off the track, Francine had no trouble keeping up with him. Finally he reached the top of the ridge and sat down to light his pipe. A bright field of stars surrounded his head. From where Francine was standing, the coal in the pipe's bowl made a light as bright as the planet Mercury.

He looked up as she approached. She sat down beside him and put her arm around him.

"I came to see what you were doing up here," she said. "I thought you might be meeting another girl."

"Nope," he said.

"Come on," she said. "Don't give me one-word answers."

A breeze washed up to them, bringing the pleasant stink of the pines.

"Talk to me," she said. "Don't keep me out. I didn't keep

you out when I was sad and in trouble. You feel betrayed, don't you?"

"That's it."

"Who do you think betrayed you?"

"I don't know," Mourly Vold said. "But I have my ideas."

"Who?"

"I think it was Humberhill. He had more information than anyone else. The thing is, I can't figure why he did it."

"I don't think it was him," Francine said.

"Why do you say that?"

"Because, from what you've told me about him, I don't think he would do anything to harm you. Furthermore, also from what you've told me, I think he could tell the difference between something that could harm you and something that couldn't."

"If you know all that, then maybe you can tell me who did betray me," Mourly Vold said.

"Yes, I can," Francine answered. "But you may not want me to."

"Try me," Mourly Vold said.

"It was Dr. Bell."

As soon as she said this, Mourly Vold sat upright and looked at her.

"You think he let you down," she said. "Not by telling your secrets to the newspapers, because he didn't do that. You think he let you down by dying."

"I don't even believe that he *has* died," Mourly Vold said. "The newspapers make things up to suit themselves. He was perfectly healthy the last time I saw him."

"He was old, though. Sometimes illnesses take old people quickly."

"But there was nothing wrong with him!" Mourly Vold's voice was full of rage. "I wasn't finished with him! I'm not ready to do without him!"

Francine took her arm away from his shoulders and lay back on the grass. "I said the same things," she said, "when Alan died. I had the feeling he was running away from me. That was the biggest, worst feeling, that he had gotten rid of me. But finally, only just a few weeks ago, I realized it wasn't his fault. He didn't do it deliberately. Thinking about it that way, I finally stopped being angry at him."

They sat together without talking for over twenty minutes. A dog on a distant farm barked for a long while. It sounded like a monster with saucer eyes and terrible teeth.

Mourly Vold finally spoke. "For the first time in my life," he said, "I don't know what to do."

"Then don't do anything," Francine said. "Just let things rest, and see what happens."

The following day, as Mourly Vold worked in the vegetable garden, Francine used her telephone to place a long-distance call to Humberhill in Nova Scotia. She had previously made his acquaintance in Little Egypt's company; now she called him on her own. She invited him to come and spend a few weeks with them in Kentucky, saying only that his friend was very low and needed him.

"It sounds good to me," Humberhill said. "I don't know if I could do it, though. The only way I know how to get places is with a telephone."

"You'll have to get to us on a bus," Francine said. "Maybe a train first, then a bus."

"I can hardly hear you," Humberhill said. "This is a terrible connection. Are you paying for this call?"

Francine told him she was.

"That's the problem," Humberhill said. "The phone company does a miserable job with these long-lines connections. Little Egypt knows how to get here using a snazzy route that cuts out all the hum and fuzz. The next time you call, get him to show it to you."

"Just a minute," Francine said. "Don't go yet. There's something I should tell you. He thinks you might have talked about him to the newspapers."

"He thinks that? It isn't true."

"I'm glad," Francine said.

"Of course I wouldn't blab to the papers," Humberhill said. "But I happen to know who did. I'll bring the evidence when I come."

Humberhill showed up in person a week later. He arrived by taxi from the bus station, accompanied by a worn leather suitcase. Nothing Francine had been told about him had prepared her for his size. He was quite enormous. His height was about average, but his breadth was very great indeed. His trousers had a shiny spot on the seat as large as a roasting pan.

Humberhill emerged from the taxi with his white cane in one hand and a funny-looking cigar in the other.

"Look at this," he said to Francine. "Do you believe this? It's fantastic. I've got to show it to him. Where is he?"

"He's working in the orchard," Francine said.

"Do you know what this is?" Humberhill asked. "It's Edison's Perpetual Cigar, invented by our good pal, Thomas A. Edison. It's refillable. Isn't that amazing? You put the tobacco in this little hole, here."

Francine took Humberhill on her arm and walked with him to the orchard where Mourly Vold was working. They walked slowly, as the weather was very warm. Humberhill chattered on without stopping.

"God," he said. "You have no idea how great it is to be with someone who isn't talking about Mah-Jongg."

They found Mourly Vold planting young apple trees in a new orchard. When Humberhill's shadow fell over him, he stood up.

For a moment, he looked Humberhill square in the face without speaking. Finally, he said, "Well, I don't believe it. It's a walking left-handed horse turd."

Humberhill threw his arms around his friend and squeezed hard.

"Easy, easy," Mourly Vold said.

"Don't break him, please," Francine said.

Humberhill released his grip. "I wouldn't think of breaking him," he said. "I have big plans for this boy."

Humberhill reached into his shirt pocket and took out a letter written in Braille. "I hear you think I've been doing you dirt," he said. "Here, read this." He passed the letter to Mourly Vold.

Francine grew impatient. "What does it say?"

"It's not a pretty story," Humberhill said. "It's a letter the Syracuse Stallion wrote to me before he died. Most of it is about Little Egypt, and how he expects Little Egypt to show up at the jail and get him out. The little kid was really in mental agony, sad to say. He was afraid we were throwing him to the wolves. There's a bit in there at the end where he says that he's answering every question the cops ask him and they still won't leave him alone."

"So, you think he was the one who gave the information away," Francine said.

"I'm sure of it," Humberhill replied. "There's the proof."

Over the next few days, dozens of telephone calls arrived in Francine's house. Every one of them was from one of Little Egypt's friends, with a message of encouragement.

"You don't know how much I've cried over this," Beetlejuice said. "I guess it doesn't mean as much to you as it does to me. Let me tell you what I've never told anybody. I'm twenty-one years old and I live with my mother in a walk-up in Queens. My hands shake, my eyes don't see and my legs don't work. From the time my mother goes out in the morning until she comes back in the evening, I sit by the window and listen to the traffic. Before I found you people, I never had a friend who didn't pity me.

"When I'm in the telephone, all that goes away. I can be

as clever and happy as my cousin Sandy. For a whole year, I lived like an ordinary person. Now they say you want to give it all up and let Hearst and his bunch make us go back to the way we were. I say that's the bunk. I say we give them a fight."

Calls came in from the old gang everywhere, including Bertha from Toledo. "I feel awful sorry about that little fellow, the one that died," Bertha said. "He was such a sweetie. He looked up to you, oh so very much. Yes, he did. He always told me how you could do this and you could do that. I remember how he said we'd all be happy again when Little Egypt comes back to life."

"This is breaking my heart," Mourly Vold said to Humberhill. "Did you put them up to this?"

"They put themselves up to it," Humberhill said. "I just told them where you were."

It worked, of course. Hour by hour, Mourly Vold's mood changed. The Little Egypt inside of him emerged, glowing. A fierce heartbeat pumped in his chest.

Taking the bullwhip coupler in one hand and Humberhill's arm in the other, he led his friend to the remote clearing where the telephone line passed overhead. With a mighty crack, he wrapped it solidly around the wire, and, within seconds, he was up in the networks. With several half-wild Z-trunks coiling and gyrating about him, he descended upon Beetlejuice, the Walrus, and some others he found hiding in a disused verification trunk he had discovered for them in the old days. He carried Humberhill in with him, and together they blew military fanfares on kazoos and whoopee cushions. Most of what any of them knew about military life they had learned from the pages of *Captain Billy's Whiz Bang*. Little Egypt used an echo in a wink-start network to make an effect that sounded like a salute from a ten-inch naval gun.

"You're in the army now," he said in a voice modeled on that of a three-hundred-pound drill instructor. "I own your fat white butts! And so help me God, I'm going to make men out of you. Go home and settle your affairs, and report back here at seventeen hundred hours. You're all going to be killers!"

The cheer that came back rattled the networks from Akron to Birmingham.

Later that evening, as they lay together in Francine's big maple bed, Mourly Vold said, "Do you want to hear something amusing?"

She curled closer to him and spoke into his ear. "Yes," she said.

"Humberhill has let me know that he feels sorry for me."

"Why does he feel sorry for you?"

"He thinks blind girls are more passionate than girls with sight," Mourly Vold said. He turned to Francine and grinned.

"Oh?" she replied. "What did you say to that?"

"I told him that this time, he was so *very* wrong."

Francine put her head on Mourly Vold's chest. One of her breasts cradled his chest from below, the other from above. He closed his eyes and the next moment he was back at the house in Baddeck, standing among its beautiful gardens. In his reverie, he could walk all the way around the house, looking at it from the water side and the land side, standing now in its shadow and again later on its southern aspect, where it reflected light back powerfully from the sun. He continued walking, and passed under the boughs of the black spruce, until he came to the porch. He climbed the porch stairs and sat in a wicker chair. There was a glass of lemonade there Mabel had made for him. Bell was nearby, asleep on the glider, covered with his old tartan rug. His white hair moved in the sea breeze. A goat's bell hanging from the porch railing stirred in the wind, and made faint sounds. But Bell was only asleep, you see, not—

"Tomorrow I'll write to Mrs. Bell and ask her if he really did die," Mourly Vold said. "I'd rather speak with her, but there's no way to do that. The telephone is no good to her at all."

. .

Mabel answered Mourly Vold's letter immediately. Her reply was five pages long, written in a large, open hand that was beautiful to read. She gave few details of Bell's illness and death, but said more about his simple memorial. Donald G. Morrison had made a box for him using the wood from a strong white oak that had grown by the water. The box was lined with the red silk he had used for his kite experiments. Bell's friends from the town had come to supper. As the sun went down, they had put the coffin in the rocky ground. A piper played some of Bell's favorite Scottish highland songs, and it was over.

At the close of her letter, Mabel said that she understood Mourly Vold's grief, but told him that he must now accept the fact that Dr. Bell was gone. To imagine or hope otherwise was to live outside of reality. She enclosed a separate envelope containing a letter of introduction addressed to the electrical scientist Nikola Tesla. She instructed Mourly Vold to present this to Tesla in New York.

"I send you to Tesla," she wrote, "confident that this is the one thing my husband would have wanted to do for you himself if he were still alive. You know that I love you more than my own life, and that the only thing I wish for, now that he is gone, is that you should use your gifts to be as great a man as he was."

CHAPTER 23

Nikola Tesla awoke after noon in his room at the St. Regis, and the first thing he did was to check the pigeon nests. Under ordinary circumstances, a bird will build its own nest, but these had been made for the birds by Tesla from wooden packing crates he had purchased particularly for the purpose. They were hospital nests, ones occupied by sick birds he had found around the city and brought back to his room. The windows of his room were left permanently open; sometimes hundreds of pigeons were here at one time, feeding on the seed he sprinkled about on the floor.

Tesla still wore his silk pajamas as he made his rounds. His initials were monogrammed above his left breast. He was a tall man, above six feet, and yet he weighed less than a hundred and forty pounds. The sleeves and pantlegs of his pajamas were several diameters larger than they had to be to contain his skinny limbs. We see him here sixty-five years old, but his head is still covered with hair, and not all of that is gray. His face is thin, but it is not gaunt. It is still possible to picture him as the attractive bachelor he was thirty-five years ago, when his inventions had made him rich and every young woman in the city of New York desired his company.

In fact, Tesla had once been the object of special attentions from Sarah Bernhardt, who apparently picked him out for some quality of his face. This had happened in Paris, in Tesla's youth. Tesla was then employed as an engineer at the Edison Company of France. Each morning, before dawn, he would swim in the

Seine, and then walk five miles to work. In the evening, he would always eat in the same restaurant near Notre Dame. One night, the Divine One passed by his restaurant in a large carriage. Suddenly she gave orders to stop. She got out, surrounded by all her entourage. Tesla sat by himself at a table near a window. Sarah Bernhardt stared at him. "What a beautiful man," she said. Tesla did not notice them, or at least gave no indication. Sarah watched him eating his asparagus. He lifted a spear to his mouth and bit off its head. Bernhardt jumped. There was something about the sight of his teeth at that instant that both frightened and moved her. One of her retinue asked her if she would like to have this man approached. "No," she said. "I don't want him disturbed. We must leave him just as he is." With that, Bernhardt led her troupe back into the carriage, and they continued on to the Porte-Saint-Martin Theater, where she was starring in *Froufrou*.

Of the six nest boxes Tesla had set up on dressing tables and bookshelves about the room, only three were occupied. Two of these contained birds that had been victims of human attacks. One bird had suffered a broken wing, the other a gash on its head when human beings had thrown bricks or rocks at them. From previous experiences, Tesla knew that the prognosis in such cases could be decided within hours; if a bird lived through the critical early period, it would almost certainly recover. Both of these birds were nearly mended, and would shortly be joining their associates in the city flocks. He fed these first, and then gave his attention to the last bird, a little female with white wings.

Her case was different from the others, and the differences worried him considerably. She had been born in his hotel room, in the very nest box where she now lay. Her mother had been an injury patient who had stayed long enough to raise a family before finally flying away. This little female had been Tesla's darling since she had been a chick. She had been his constant companion for over a year. He had confided to her things he told no one else, ideas for inventions that were too important to write down.

Now she lay ill in her box, and the illness was one he could not recognize. She had been in this fragile condition for over a week. He put his ear close to her head and listened to her breathing. He feared to hear her cough, because he knew that a pigeon that coughed would almost certainly die. As far as he could tell, her breathing was quiet.

He gave her the last of the birdseed. No, that couldn't be true! He looked in the large sack; he looked through all the drawers of his dressing cabinet; he looked in his several closets, and nowhere could he find any more. It seemed impossible, but there was no more food for the birds. He had never before allowed the cupboard to go completely bare like this.

He telephoned Western Union and asked that a messenger be sent to a feedstore where he had an account. The messenger should bring twenty pounds of seed immediately.

"We're not going to do it, Mr. Tesla," the dispatcher said. "There are a number of bills you can pay us before we do anything further for you."

"There's no need to take that tone of voice," Tesla said. "You'll be paid when I find it convenient."

He telephoned the feedstore directly, but they were even ruder and said they were not prepared to let him have anything more until he paid his entire account in cash.

Tesla had known this day was certain to arrive, but it seemed unfair that it had come now, with the little female so weak. He had ignored the inevitable connection between his needs and his income all his life and had gotten away with it. Until today, he had found it possible to leave separate the questions of what was to be done and how it was to be paid for, but now a life he treasured trembled under the double threats of death by disease and death by starvation.

He looked again at the little female with white wings. Here

was his dearest friend, the happiest heart in the world in other times, his devoted partner! Now she lay so still that she might not be breathing at all. He had lined her nest box with velvet cloth. Beautiful quilted comforters intended for the newborn infants of the wealthy supported her little body. He bent close to speak to her.

"I'll go out," he said, "and I'll find my friend, Mr. George Westinghouse. Do you remember, I told you that I once gave him something worth many millions of dollars? He's a good man. When he hears that the birdseed is gone, I'm certain he'll help us."

Tesla removed his pajamas and put on silk undershorts, black hose, and a white silk shirt. He selected a suit with a waisted coat and a red-and-black silk tie done in a stylish pattern of thin stripes. He took a silver-plated brush in each hand and pushed back his hair, parting it carefully in the middle. The man in the mirror caught his eye.

"Who is that old guy?" he heard himself say.

The man in the mirror stared at him.

Tesla was aware that Helmholtz had shown that the fundi of the eyes are luminous. According to Helmholtz, a man may see the movements of his own arm in complete darkness, depending only on the light of the eyes for illumination. The brain provides the power for this light, using the energy of the thoughts.

Tesla wondered now what he had wondered before, whether or not the images of a man's thoughts appear on his retinas as the thoughts escape. He looked closely at his own pupils, but saw only blackness there. It would be necessary to take a photograph and blow the image up many times, so that patterns in the faintly luminous portions of the retina might be discerned. Unknown to Tesla, this same idea was beginning, coincidentally, to have some currency in forensic science—the district attorney of Davenport, Iowa, would in this same week request that photographs be taken of a young rape-murder victim's dead eyes to see if the image of her attacker remained there.

Tesla took the elevator to the lobby and walked out the front door of the St. Regis. He was on his way to the New York offices of the Westinghouse Electric and Manufacturing Company. It would be pleasant to see old George Westinghouse again after such a long time. He tried to recall when they had last met, and decided that it must have been more than thirty years ago. He remembered clearly the day that Westinghouse had come to his laboratory at South Fifth Avenue and purchased his entire set of alternating-current patents, covering every aspect of modern power generation and distribution, for one million dollars plus royalties. Within a few years, Westinghouse had used these patents to build a series of far-reaching power grids. These made Edison's direct-current systems look like the second-rate trash that they were. All this success, in spite of Edison's depravities, his public executions of cats and dogs! It was clear, also, that Edison had used his influence to persuade the New York State Prison Authority to give alternating current a bad name by using it to kill murderers. The word was that Edison himself had made the electric cap and boots which had been connected to an alternating-current dynamo. George Westinghouse had witnessed how miserably they had used it—he said the job could have been done better with an ax.

Despite Edison's chicanery, Westinghouse had expanded his operations, but by too much—the bankers had obtained a large interest in his business. Tesla recalled the day Westinghouse came to visit him four years later. He said that the bankers had him by the short hair and would dissolve his company unless he were able to make Tesla give up all royalties in his inventions. That day, Tesla had put his arm around his friend and torn up his contract. No one, he said, had wanted the idea before Westinghouse had expressed interest in it. Edison had laughed at it and sent him away in scorn. The only important thing now was that Westinghouse, his friend who had believed in him and fought for him, should keep his company. If this meant an end to the royalties, then so be it. Westinghouse had been over-whelmed by this generosity. The royalties due at that moment were counted in the millions; it is impossible to calculate how many hundreds of millions would have become due eventually.

Now, as Tesla walked through New York, he felt better. When he began his mission, he had thought of asking Westinghouse for ten dollars for birdseed. Now it seemed to him that this would be altogether too little; the smallest disbursement a man like Westinghouse would be accustomed to making would be much more; a thousand, perhaps, or ten thousand. He looked at his watch and saw that if he hurried, he might catch Westinghouse before he left his office for lunch. As he passed Delmonico's, the doorman recognized him and bowed.

"Charles," Tesla said to him, "I don't have time to stop. Would you please tell Maurice that I will have my usual table at lunch, and that I will return with a gentleman in one hour?"

"What usual table is that?" Charles asked.

"It hasn't changed," Tesla told him. "The one by the mirror on the west wall. Now, I must go along. Please accept this for your tip. I haven't any money in my pocket at the moment."

He scratched something quickly on a piece of paper. When he was gone, the doorman saw that it was Tesla's IOU for five dollars.

Tesla reached the offices of the Westinghouse Company shortly after one o'clock. He was kept waiting by a young receptionist, who was obviously confused by his request to see Mr. Westinghouse. At one forty-five, a man who identified himself as a member of the executive staff came out to speak with him.

"Whom did you wish to see?" asked the man.

"George Westinghouse," Tesla said. "Just tell him Dr. Tesla is here. Tell him I came to take him to lunch."

"You can't take him to lunch," the man said. "He's been dead for eight years."

■ \ ■

Tesla left the Westinghouse offices and walked to the corner of Fifth Avenue and Fortieth Street. He climbed the steps of the New York Public Library and whistled once. Immediately the air was full of wings, and great flocks of pigeons landed all about him, their drafts sending feathers and street dirt in curling vortices down the steps. Some of them landed on his head, others on his shoulders.

"I have nothing for you, my friends," he said. "Nothing but the sad news that the little one is weaker."

He stood for many minutes, looking at the traffic on Fifth Avenue. Some of the birds despaired of being fed and flew away. Others remained faithfully.

Throughout his life, Tesla had an uncanny ability to see imagined objects in front of his eyes as vividly as if they were actually there. He could see a blackboard full of mathematics, and read answers from it as easily as if he had just written them there himself. He could design complicated machine parts by visualizing them in space, even to the point of fitting them together and watching them perform their intended operations. At this moment he saw, looming over Fifth Avenue, casting a shadow as real as the shadow of a low-flying airship, a paper bag of birdseed a hundred meters high. He saw the bulge of the bag near the bottom where the kernels pressed it out and the wrinkles in the brown paper near the top where a giant hand had squeezed it closed. The top of the bag had a serrated edge. The serrations were a series of notches more than a meter on each edge, and above their severe peaks the clouds and the sky and the sunlight resumed.

He recognized this bag of birdseed as the one he had pressed into the hand of his secretary, Mrs. Geraldine Sitz, the day he had closed his offices years earlier. On that terrible day, the sheriff and his men had arrived, ready to take everything away. The sheriff had confiscated the laboratory equipment and the typewriters, but in private Tesla had handed each of his employees a full bag of birdseed with instructions that they were to hide it somewhere on their persons in order to sneak it past the lawmen, and after that they were to distribute it to the pigeons of New York.

Tesla walked to the West Side apartment house where Mrs. Sitz lived with her family. In this neighborhood were many Poles and Lithuanians. It was after five o'clock, and the smell of boiled cabbage came from the open windows. Tesla found the building and rang Mrs. Sitz's bell. It turned out that he had come exactly at their dinnertime, but Mrs. Sitz was so delighted to see him that she didn't mind at all. When she heard what he wanted, she disappeared for a few minutes and then came back to the door, carrying the brown paper sack.

"I was keeping it as a souvenir of you," she said.

"You don't mind letting me have it?" Tesla asked. "Some-day I will bring a much larger bag back to you, filled with every kind of seed there is."

"That will be wonderful," Mrs. Sitz said.

"Now you must go back to your dinner, to your family."

"You won't join us?"

"I must not," Tesla said. "There is someone waiting for me."

"Then take care of yourself," Mrs. Sitz said. She took Tesla's arm and pulled him down until his face was at a suitable height and kissed him on the cheek. "You're so thin," she said. "I worry about you."

As Tesla was walking back to the St. Regis, he opened the bag and found that Mrs. Sitz had enclosed, along with the birdseed, a ten-dollar bill. Clipped to the bill was a note: "For feeding Dr. Tesla."

Two days later, when Mourly Vold and Humberhill arrived, the little female with white wings had died. Tesla sadly opened his door to receive them. He invited them into his room. It now resembled the parlor of a funeral home. Most of the ten-dollar bill from Mrs. Sitz had been spent on inexpensive flowers, which filled vases in every corner. The shades had been pulled down to give the room a subdued light. In the center of the carpet lay the nest box containing the little female with the white wings. This unusual wake was attracting pigeons from all over New York, who arrived at the windowsill, hopped into the room, and availed themselves of the birdseed spread on the floor.

Tesla read the letter of introduction from Mabel Bell. When he had finished, he said, "You're welcome to stay with me as long as you like, and learn whatever I can teach you. I should tell you at the beginning, however, that there isn't any money in being an inventor. The boys at the bank get it all in the end."

With great solemnity, Tesla closed the cover of the nest box and tied it with a piece of insulated wire. He put on a black topcoat and a bowler. "Come, now," he said. "We go."

They accompanied Tesla as he carried the nest box through the streets of New York to Pennsylvania Station. After purchasing three tickets on the Long Island Rail Road to Wardencliff, Tesla took his young friends into the Streamliner, the most expensive restaurant in the station. With the last of Mrs. Sitz's money, he bought three small bowls of leek soup.

"Hey, this stuff isn't bad," Humberhill said.

During the journey, Tesla was quiet. His thoughts seemed to be somewhere else. He held the nest box on his lap, and looked down at it often.

When they reached the Wardencliff station, they left the train and walked for several miles along roads lined with goldenrod and daisies. Finally, Tesla led them down a long gravel drive sprouted out in many places with milkweed stalks. At the end of the drive lay the ruins of a large, flat building, and beyond that, the broken remains of an enormous tower.

Tesla fitted a key into a padlock securing the door of an outbuilding and emerged carrying a shovel. He led the way to the hill behind the ruined laboratory building. At a point just below the crest of the hill, among a stand of white pines, he began to dig, and he didn't stop until he made a hole more than six feet deep. When this was finished, he asked Mourly Vold to pass the nest box down to him. He placed the nest box on the floor of the hole, then dropped to his knees and curled his long body around it. He remained that way, lying on the cold floor of the pit, sobbing, for many minutes. Finally, he climbed out of the hole and filled it in. His expensive clothes were now covered with clay.

Tesla searched among the rubble of the tower at the top of the hill until he found timbers to make a suitable cross. He lashed the cross together with scraps of wire and planted it at the head of the grave.

When he was finished, he said, "She was a wonderful friend. No one ever had a little friend so cheerful. How she loved life! It was a privilege to see her every day, and to hear her voice at the window. That privilege has now been taken away forever."

He wept again, then dried his eyes with his handkerchief. "That's all," he said. "Now I'll tell you what this is, this mess around us, if you want to know."

"We do, indeed," Mourly Vold said.

"This is all that's left of Tesla's World System," he began. "I abandoned it here more than twenty years ago. The bankers strangled me before I could finish it. It was to make possible transmissions of voices and other intelligence to all parts of the world. In that respect, it was similar to what radio has become today.

"But there was more to it, much more. This pile of timbers was once a tower more than a hundred and fifty feet tall. It was designed by Stanford White, the famous architect. At the top was a dome a hundred feet in diameter, covered in copper. In that building over there were dynamos capable of many hundreds of horsepower. This is all very big stuff, yes? But it was nothing compared to what I was doing at Niagara. There, everything would have been ten times, a hundred times bigger than this. There, we would have put out ten million horsepower, enough to make the whole world ring with high-frequency electricity.

"Picture this. You're in a house in the country. There are no wires anywhere for miles. But you have electric lights in your house, and a telephone! A metal ball attached to your chimney brings the power down, out of the air. High-frequency currents light the lamps in your house, which are actually vacuum tubes. The currents also operate your electric clocks, in perfect synchrony with a central clock at the falls.

"In addition to electric power, the high-frequency currents do many more things for you. With the cooperation of the newspapers, they send you news. They connect telegraph and telephone offices all over the world. They coordinate the action of stock tickers everywhere. And, if you're on a ship, they allow you to know your position exactly and to steer without a compass. All this is possible because the Niagara station has set the whole earth into resonant vibration. I know this can be done, because I have shown it happens each time lightning strikes the earth."

"Wait a minute," Humberhill said. "Go back. What did you say about telephones?"

"Telephones are only a part of it," Tesla told him. "The World System would have made it possible to have telephones without wires. Everything that depends on wires now could be run more efficiently without wires, using high-frequency currents propagating through the air."

"So why didn't it catch on?" asked Humberhill.

"The bankers got nervous," Tesla said. "They pulled their money out only a few months before I could have had this all working. I never knew why they did that, but somebody once told me that Edison had a hand in it."

"Edison?" Humberhill said. "What does Edison have against you?"

Tesla sat on the ground. "I've wondered that myself," he said. "I used to work for him, you know. First I worked for his company in Paris, and then I worked for him here. He promised me a substantial sum of money for a set of improvements I made for him in his dynamos, but he never paid me. When I asked him for the money, he said, 'You don't understand our American humor.' He said the promise had been nothing but a joke. I quit, then, and went into business for myself.

"Years later, after Westinghouse made a fortune with my alternating-current patents, they wanted to give me the Nobel Prize in physics jointly with Edison. I told them I would not take it. I'll take nothing jointly with Edison, especially not the Nobel Prize. That would be a very bad joke. Edison is not a scientist. He has no understanding of electricity. He is a bad-tempered businessman. He should get the Nobel Prize for Bad-tempered Business."

"Funny you should mention Edison," Humberhill said. "Because, at the moment, he's after *us*. He's been hired to get us because we know how to do things with telephones."

It was obvious that Tesla was not in the habit of reading the newspapers, because he had no idea of what telephone vandalism was. Once Mourly Vold showed him, he was very interested.

Mourly Vold opened his battered carpetbag and took out his bullwhip induction coupler and his rogue telephone. When Tesla asked about the coupler, Mourly Vold explained how it worked, and even showed him the spiral windings which made the inductive coupling so successful. Tesla understood it right away. "By God," he said. "That's beautiful. It is a piece of genius. I like it very much."

They walked to the road, where a telephone wire made its way languidly along the coast of Long Island. With a flick of his wrist, Mourly Vold sent the tip of the bullwhip upward to do its wickedness. He performed a set of complex manipulations using tongue clicks, cracks of his knuckles, and percussive sounds created by striking rocks together. When he had established the condition he wanted, he passed the receiver to Tesla.

The sound Tesla heard in the earphone was a musical note with the tone of a flute, a note which wavered up and down ever so slightly, the way the light of a candle flickers to illustrate its own tiny turbulences. "What's this?" he asked.

"It's the vital sign," Mourly Vold told him. "That's what the traffic service managers call it, the vital sign. It's an acoustic signal they have on their board to tell them the state of health of an entire operating region. It has in it information about the number of calls, the number of available lines, the rate at which calls are left incomplete, and other things that indicate the stress on the networks and how well they're doing. When the vital sign is quiet and smooth, it means they're doing well. When it's loud and uneven, it means things are going badly for them.

"Now, watch this," he said, and started a game of Z-trunk shuttlecock in the northwest corner of the Bronx. As it marched toward Manhattan, tying up all lines in its path and throwing local offices into convulsions, the vital sign for New York developed first a background hiss and then a roar, while its musical note grew louder and more shrill until it sounded like an undulating fire siren.

"The equipment is worried about itself," Mourly Vold said. "Now, let's give it a little problem in Queens." He connected several Z-trunks in a loop, so that the tail of one was in the mouth of the other. On his cue, one of them bit down hard, and started a wave of anguish rocketing around the circle. As soon as he did this, the vital sign for New York became a desperate howl.

"You can bet there are a lot of people trying to find out what's happening now," Mourly Vold said. "Needless to say, I could make their lives really miserable if I went on with this, but that's not my purpose." With a few well-placed tongue clicks, he restored everything to normal, and the vital sign became quiet and mellow again.

"That's truly amazing," Tesla said. "I didn't know it was possible to take over like that."

"But it *is* possible, as you can see," Humberhill said. "The system is loaded with weaknesses. He hasn't even begun to find them all. We're trying to get the big boys to fix the networks, to make them tamper-proof, but instead Hearst has hired your friend Edison to put us out of business. It's a sorry state of affairs."

"I should say so," Tesla said.

"You could help us," Humberhill said. "If you wanted to."

That same afternoon, at the Perkins Institution, Billy the Boozer and the Walrus had finally pieced together enough information to become dangerous again. It had been months since Little Egypt had cut them off from the flow of information. In that time, they had tried several times to establish themselves as a separate and rival group. They now called themselves the Venetian Blind, and claimed a large membership, although, in fact, the Venetian Blind was a conspiracy of two.

Billy the Boozer had been experimenting with tongue-clicking into the telephone, but so far he had been unable to figure out how Little Egypt did his dirty tricks this way. He clicked, then listened, then clicked again, but the Z-trunks refused to obey him. None of the regulars would help him, or even so much as talk with him. Whenever he tried to reach Beetlejuice or any of the others, they would break the connection. Little Egypt had made it a federal offense among his people to say a single word to Billy. In this way, he had attempted to keep the Venetian Blind furled in a void of silence.

But now Billy had an idea. He and the Walrus would physically walk into a telephone company central office and steal a cadence generator. They would give up trying to acquire know-how and get themselves a machine that had the know-how built into it. With a cadence generator in his possession, Billy planned to become great and powerful, more powerful even than Little

Egypt. And when he ruled the world, he intended to settle a few scores.

"Wait a minute," the Walrus said. "How big is this thing we're supposed to steal?"

"It's about the size of a box of doughnuts," Billy the Boozer told him. "I heard him say so one time. In fact, that gives me an idea for how we can get it. We'll say we're delivery boys from a bakery. We'll take a dozen doughnuts in and come out with the gadget in the box. There'll be nothing to it. When we get through with them, every last one of them will wish they had never heard of the Venetian Blind."

When Mourly Vold, Tesla, and Humberhill reached the railroad station at Wardencliff that evening, Tesla at last had to face the fact that all his money was gone. He tried to write a check for three fares to the city, but the ticket agent found his name on a list and refused to take his check.

Mourly Vold discovered that there were several pay telephones against an outside wall of the waiting room. As the light was poor, he asked Tesla to read the numbers on each of these telephones so that he could memorize them.

"I want you to stand by the coin box of the first phone in the line and be ready," he said to Tesla.

Tesla had no idea what was about to happen. "Be ready for what?"

"A generous loan of money."

Mourly Vold went to the telephone on the far end and made a call to Information. Before the connection could be completed, he used raps and tongue clicks to perform a fancy maneuver roughly equivalent to jumping from a speeding train into a tub of water. He fell deep into a pool of step-by-step relays and coin-sound recognition equipment. Before long, he surfaced in the place he wished to be, the remote coin-management center. Here he did a little discreet tickling. In perfect unison, the four telephones in the station regurgitated all the coins in their coin boxes.

Humberhill and Tesla went from one telephone to the next, scooping up the take.

"Is there anyone watching us?" Humberhill asked.

"No one at all," Tesla said.

But before they did anything else, Mourly Vold had Tesla count all the money and tell him how much was there. He then telephoned Francine at home in Beauty and asked her to get out the wages he had put aside from his bridge painting and deposit an amount equal to what they had just collected into the first pay telephone she could find. It is important to remember that in all the time Little Egypt was a famous outlaw, he was never once a crook.

CHAPTER 24

Francine arrived in New York at ten o'clock one morning, and by two that afternoon she had rented a furnished two-room flat on 109th Street, in the block between Broadway and Amsterdam on the Upper West Side. The first thing she did, following Mourly Vold's instructions, was to note the location of the telephone service coming in from the street. Then she went to a department store and bought a frying pan, several place settings of cheap dishes and flatware, and a plumber's plunger. The plunger was necessary to deal with a stopped-up sink. On impulse, she also bought a set of white cotton curtains.

Walking through New York, she felt the thrill of a new beginning. Here was a landscape and a population entirely unlike any she had ever lived among before. Here was a freedom so complete that no one she met on this street, or the next, or the one beyond that need ever know a thing about her, if she chose to keep herself a secret. So much anonymity, the very thing that was unobtainable at any price at home, and here it was all free!

Francine was wearing the clothes that made her a sensation in her own town, but here they were nothing extraordinary. She had on her knee-length white silk skirt, her black silk blouse, her Marlene Appleton jacket with the thin stripes, and a new black cloche hat. At home, the entire female population of the county looked up to her for her daring dress, but here in New York she had already seen four or five women on the street dressed in material so diaphanous that in certain lights it appeared transparent. What a place this must be! The people here were entirely unshockable! No experiment in appearance, no matter how outrageous, had the power to lift an eyebrow! Francine decided that at last she had arrived at the one place that suited her. She should have found a reason to come to New York long ago.

People were walking around an obstacle on the sidewalk some distance ahead. As she drew closer, she saw that the obstacle was a man. He was in a posture that she recognized as the glide of some swimming stroke. After she thought about it for a moment, she realized it was the Australian crawl. His body was prone, and his left arm was extended over his head, while his right arm was pressed against his side. His face was turned toward the right and his mouth was open. She peered at him over the top of her new frying pan. As she watched, a young woman and her male companion approached from the west, stepped over the man on the sidewalk, and continued on.

They continued on! They didn't investigate him or interfere with him in any way! And, to prove that this was the accepted protocol in the city, the thing to do, several other people stepped over the motionless body as she watched.

She could see that the man was inebriated. In the hand that had just finished the propulsive stroke, he clutched a bottle of blackberry wine. Yes, Francine said to herself, yes. They're respecting his privacy. I was thinking a moment ago that this is all I would want if it were me. But something kept her from walking on. The man's face was dirty and unshaven, but it was fairly young. She estimated his age at not more than thirty years. His clothes were torn and foully soiled, but they had been of good quality once. The more she looked at him, the more puzzled, the more interested she became.

"Listen to this," she said to Mourly Vold when she reached him at Tesla's hotel room later in the day. She was speaking from a coin telephone at the corner drugstore. "You'll never believe it. I found a place that should be perfect for us. There should be room enough for everybody. And who do you think I've got up there right this minute? None other than Sparky Edison, the great man's son. He knows about us, and he could be willing to help."

Twenty minutes later, Mourly Vold arrived by cab, accompanied by Humberhill and Tesla. As Francine prepared chili for their supper in her new frying pan, she told them what Sparky Edison had said about himself during the afternoon. Sparky was now asleep on the bed in the other room, and the first thing they did was to go in and look at him.

"The resemblance to his father at the same age is extraordinary," Tesla said, whispering. "I wish I had a nickel for every time I've seen Edison looking just like that, sleeping on a pile of newspapers in a closet or on the floor somewhere, and snoring like a bull seal."

Sylvester Edison, the youngest of Edison's children, had been given the nickname Sparky by his father. If the name implied that Edison hoped his son would follow him to glory in the electrical arts, then something must have caused Edison to forget these hopes, because he ignored the boy almost completely throughout his growing years. The adult Sparky told anyone who would listen about his memories of his father from childhood—the sarcasm and practical jokes which his father offered as humor, and the black rages which he put forward as discipline. For Sparky's fifth birthday, Edison made a trick glass which would spill its contents down the front of anyone who attempted to drink from it. Sparky said he used the glass dozens of times, and was laughed at by his father each time for spilling his milk, until his mother discovered the trick and explained it to him. On the Fourth of July, the famous Edison would send the sissies running by setting off enormous firecrackers of his own design on the lawn. When a particularly potent one of these caused Sparky to dampen his trousers, Edison proposed afterward to call his biggest firecrackers "Sparky wetters."

At the age of ten, Sparky developed an interest in matchbox

puppets. He made these from matchboxes and pipe cleaners, and dressed them in clothes that he cut from pieces of silk, cotton, and velvet salvaged from his mother's old dresses. He created an elaborate puppet stage in his room, using boards from packing crates he found discarded behind his father's laboratory.

Over the course of a week, he wrote out the script for a grand puppet show by which he intended to win his father's love. The story was the story of his father's wonderful life. Here was the Reverend Engle's schoolhouse in Port Huron, where his father and a girl of his acquaintance had let down a baited hook from a window and caught a chicken which happened to be loose in the schoolyard. Here was the tray of candies and fruit his father wore around his neck when he was a train boy, and there was a tiny pile of paper squares representing his father's newspapers. In a corner was the railroad desk his father worked at as a plug telegraph operator. At this point, Sparky's information gave out. How his father actually became an inventor was hazy in his mind. So he jumped the narrative all the way forward to the present, and showed their house as it looked at the time, with the long, two-story laboratory next to it, including its dozens of windows and their hundreds of panes of glass. On the path between the house and the laboratory he showed, using dots of brown crayon, the places where his father had spit tobacco juice in the snow.

Sparky remembered that he had made a playbill advertising the event, lettered in red, black, and gold. He had mailed this to his father, along with an invitation giving the time and place of the performance. The name of the puppeteer was also mentioned. The letter had been collected by the postman and brought back by him one day later, the stamp canceled, in a mailbag containing more than a hundred angry demands for payment by creditors. Edison had returned home at dinnertime, in a hurry and seething as usual. He was, in those years, always in the midst of a battle with everyone about money. His wife sent money to her relatives and left the household bills unpaid; his lawyers entangled him in court suits; his assistants wasted expensive supplies and ordered more without any regard for the cost. After opening the top two envelopes on the heap, one a past-due statement from Continental Cork for more than eleven thousand dollars' worth of cork sheets, and the other from the local fish merchant for two pounds of haddock, Edison lifted the mailbag on his back, took it to the stove, and fed the lot to the flames.

Sparky could have written another invitation, of course, or he could have invited his father in person to the puppet show, but something cautioned him that the one and only opportunity had passed, and afterward he never again attempted to penetrate his father's world. He was sent to the St. Frederick's School in upstate New York, and here he was very unhappy. Both the teachers and pupils of the school expected great things from the son of the famous man, particularly as the family resemblance had grown striking by this time. There was Sparky, with Edison's unmistakable face and the beginnings, even, of Edison's protruding stomach and sagging bottom, but Sparky's grades were hopeless and his performance in athletics was hopeless, and he was an easy target for every bully in the school. After it became clear that the school was eating Sparky alive, the headmaster wrote to Edison and suggested that the boy be allowed to leave while there was still something left of him. Following the disaster at St. Frederick's, Sparky became the school sad sack at Hopedale, then at Bemis, Fort Allen, and Sunny River.

Even though Sunny River was known as a refuge for basket cases, Sparky assiduously failed to thrive there, and finally wrote to his father asking him to find a lowly position for him in one of his enterprises. Edison did not reply, but word came to Sparky from one of Edison's managers that employment was waiting for the boy in the battery works at Simsondale. Here Sparky worked for three years, first in the lead room and then in the acid plant. Like many other workers in the factory, he developed a chronic cough from the acid fumes. An acid spill that spattered his face caused concern, for some months, that he might lose the use of his left eye, but ultimately its sight came back. In spite of the dangers and hardships, Sparky said later that the years in the battery plant were the happiest of his life, because he had the fellowship of a group of workers who cared nothing about his parents and accepted him for himself. He lived with a kind family called MacFarland who treated him like one of their own.

Sparky's tranquil days ended when a group of New York sharpies found him in the battery plant and offered him an opportunity to go into business for himself. They wanted him to become president and chairman of the board of Edison's Erotechnic, Incorporated, a firm that would sell a battery-powered vibration device useful for, as they put it, gender enjoyment. The fact that Sparky agreed to go into business with them, even though he had been given only the vaguest idea what the device was or how it was used, proves how much he craved the success that would make his father believe he had become a good person at last.

In the first month of life for Edison's Erotechnic, the partners tapped into what appeared to be a soaring demand, and Sparky moved to New York and became a playboy. He established himself in a Park Avenue suite and bought a fast motorcar, a V-12 Hurricane, to park out front. He frequented the best restaurants and pubs—Jack Joyce's, The Metropole, and Inky's Dink. The most gorgeous women in New York were seen on his arm. He was a houseguest for shooting weekends with Barbara Blenheim's family in Cos Cob, and he went with the Beasleys for a week to Fort Lauderdale after their daughter Bunny came out.

One morning he woke up with a woman in his bed and realized with a start that he had married her during an alcoholic binge the previous afternoon. Her name was Daphne Wingate and she had a fast reputation. She was two years older than Sparky and had been married before—how many times, she never really said. She was a tall, black-haired woman with a stunning figure and an acid sense of humor. The morning Sparky woke up to find her in his bed, he also discovered several other people asleep in his apartment. "Who are these people and what are they doing here?" he asked out loud. No one was willing to give him an answer to that question. Some of them were still there a week later.

The first item of business for Daphne was to get herself a checkbook, and she promptly went to work on Fifth Avenue. She bought Siberian furs, South African diamonds, and a set of living-room furniture from Montevideo made from the bones and skins of forest monkeys. When Sparky wrote a check at the tobacconist's for two pounds of Bugler's Blend, the check bounced.

"Darling," Sparky said to his wife. "I'm afraid this check has come back. I think we're going to have to stop spending so much money."

Daphne walked over to where he stood and brought her knee up sharply into his groin. Sparky staggered backward, gasping for breath. "Sorry, dearest," she said. "That's a little tic I have. It only happens when someone says something cheap and boring to me."

The checks continued to bounce, and before long, Daphne realized that she was going to have to make her move on the old man. "Everyone in New York is saying it's disgraceful that the children of the Greatest Man of his Age have to go around with rags on their backs," she wrote to Edison. "Sparky's Honor does not permit him to mention our Needs to you, but I recognized that you would wish to know of this Danger to your Reputation."

Daphne could hardly have known this before her marriage, but in Edison she had at last met her match. "My son thinks frigging is free," he wrote back. "It is not. Let him go to work

& earn his money like I did if he wants to keep his head dry & his jack-whistle wet."

Daphne persisted for another month at trying to shake Edison down, and even went so far as to engage a lawyer to find out how far Sparky's rights might reach into the old man's pockets. The lawyer did some detective work and reported that Sparky owned nothing in his own name, and even Edison himself was debt-ridden, having at that moment tied up all his assets in a scheme for charging electric vehicles from central power stations. His vision was of an electric sow that would give suck to hundreds of little electric pigs at one time. The lawyer's report convinced Daphne that she had better things to do with her life, and she left Sparky without telling him where she was going.

Sparky's self-esteem now slipped out of sight. His partners in Edison's Erotechnic disappeared and left him with a pantsload of debts. He lost his car and his apartment. He drank all day in bars and slept on the sidewalk at night over hot-air grates. He learned the times that the restaurants set their scraps out in the garbage and fought for these with the other homeless men, the rats, and the gulls. In a thousand boozy daydreams, he rebuilt the puppet theater and staged *The Life of Thomas A. Edison* with his father in attendance, and once or twice he even visualized how his life might have been different if that had ever really happened. This was how Francine had found him.

"I can only ask you not to think badly of me for my appearance," Sparky said when he awoke the next morning. "You find me between opportunities, as it were. Sparky Edison is not really this sad-looking person. If you had found me in the past, I would have been much more cheerful, and I expect to be so again in the future.

"In fact, I woke this morning with a solid idea in my head, the first one I've had there in months. Instead of selling my name to sharpsters, as I have recently done, I'll offer to sell it to my father. He should be glad to get it back, and to give it a proper burial. I will take another name; I haven't decided which one yet. In exchange for the return of my name, I will ask him for the only thing that could ever bring my happiness back. I will ask him for my old position at the battery works, and a chance to live with the MacFarlands again, who treated me so wonderfully when I resided with them years ago."

Sparky accepted a cup of coffee from Francine, and took a sip of it. Presently, his eyes moistened and a tear appeared on his cheek.

"But he won't agree to that, you know. Not even if he had the chance to bury my identity. He refuses to see me, and he says getting my job back is just out. He says he doesn't want anyone working for him with as bad a record as mine."

"As it happens," Little Egypt said, "we, too, have some business to take up with him. Throw in with us, and when the time comes, you may find him more agreeable than you thought."

CHAPTER 25

Wouldn't you know it, Billy the Boozer picked this very moment to launch his offensive. He and the Walrus helped themselves to white uniforms from the kitchen. They convinced themselves they looked like bakers wearing these uniforms. Before leaving the kitchen, they filched a cardboard box and loaded it with a dozen doughnuts.

Their target was the telephone company central office on St. Olaf's Street in Boston. They arrived in front of the building on Boston's public transportation. The trolley driver helped them off the trolley and pointed them toward the front door.

They marched themselves into the building and somehow talked their way past the receptionist and a guard. It is amazing—almost unbelievable—that they made it as far into the technical regions of the building as they did without anyone stopping them or asking them questions. They unloaded their doughnuts on an empty desk and stepped into an area filled with clattering switches.

But here's what did them in. Billy the Boozer hit a door. Yes, the telephone company saved itself not with some wonderful piece of electronic defense equipment invented by themselves or by Thomas Edison, but with a simple wooden door. Someone left it half open, and this is a perfect trap that will always catch a low-vision person. Open doors, closed doors—these are fine for the visually impaired, and can be negotiated with ease. But a half-open door is completely invisible, and Billy hit it squarely with the middle of his forehead. He knocked himself out cold and fell to the floor. The telephone company administrators who came to his aid were at first compassionate and then suspicious. Full of anxiety over his fallen leader, the Walrus caved in like a paper bag and blurted out why they were there. The police were summoned. That same afternoon, Billy and the Walrus were placed in the hands of the Bureau of Investigation.

The activities of the telephone vandals were just then coming under investigation by the General Intelligence Division of the bureau. The chief of this division was J. Edgar Hoover, then only twenty-seven years old. Hoover had what was known then as a baby face—handsome, sleek, and pink in complexion. His charge from the attorney general was to come to a broad understanding of subversive activities in the United States.

Hoover's genius was to recognize that the big picture he was looking for could not be found on police blotters or in court records. He found it instead in the library.

He asked for and received a month's leave from his office, and in that time he read all the important works of Marx, Trotsky, Engels, and Lenin. When he finished the last page of the last book, he looked up at the ceiling. There he saw the revelation that would guide his life and his work for fifty years. It came to him with the force of an avalanche. He saw the true nature of the Communist conspiracy, which was never intended to be a political philosophy, but instead was born as a force of absolute destructiveness, a plot to annihilate everything human, everything that makes life worth living. After the Communist victory, there would be no more Sno-Crest Bread, no baseball, no Coca-Cola. Everything American would be swept away. It came to Hoover in a flash that the brains of the Communists could have been infected by diseases from outer space. Their thinking was not the thinking of human beings, but the thinking of monsters. Their purpose was not only to castrate General Motors and RCA but to put out the eyes of Jesus Christ so that he could never look upon the Americans again.

Until this moment in his life, Hoover had not known why he was living. He had been a happy young man, happy in his private life, happy in his career, but he had not known what piece of work he had been put on earth to do. Now that uncertainty fell away, and in its place burned a fire of love for country which was to control his thoughts and actions for the rest of his days. And the Reds quaked in their boots.

Hoover did not travel to Boston to question the captured telephone vandals himself, but he spent many hours reading and thinking about the transcripts of their interrogation. It became clear to him that the two who had been caught occupied a very lowly level in the Communist organization they belonged to, the Venetian Blind. For some time, Hoover pursued the possibility that the roots of this group extended to Italy. He sent agents to Venice, and this caused persons in the attorney general's office to worry that he was about to stick his nose into certain business arrangements which didn't concern him involving influential Italian-Americans. But young Hoover was not looking for dope and vice and booze; he was looking for information naming the Reds in America, and his agents came back empty-handed.

This was also a time when Tesla suffered a flare-up of his old illness of acute sensitivity. It was a disease that afflicted him all his life, and sometimes it became genuinely incapacitating.

The doctors never knew what caused it. It manifested itself as a heightening of the senses, but the heightening was enormous, painful, and pathological. Tesla said he had first experienced it as a young child in Serbia. Standing in a grassy field, he had become aware of the sounds of the meadow voles moving under the ground. Not only could he hear them, he could feel their vibrations in his shoes. Every sound grew loud and unbearable to him during an attack—even the chirp of a robin exploded in his ears and frightened him in some deep part of his brain.

Not only his ears, but his eyes were affected. If someone struck a match, the sound was like a tree branch tearing away in a storm of wind, but the light was more terrible still. It burst into his eyes like the light from a photographer's flash powder, and left behind an afterimage that changed from red to green to blue before disappearing.

The attacks of Tesla's sensitivity illness left him unable to do anything but lie in bed for three days or more. Even sleep was impossible for him in this condition, since his senses were turned up so high that the slightest stimulation would disturb him. He wore both eyeshades and earplugs to bed, but these were not enough to isolate him from the world, since the faintest vibration coming up through the floor could cause him acute distress. At times like this, he would retire to a special bed he had made for himself, one contained within a darkened alcove in his room at the St. Regis. The mattress of this bed was supported on a small boat floating in a tub of water. The tub itself sat on thick pads of India rubber. Lying on this mattress in the darkness, Tesla was as perfectly protected from invading sights and sounds as he would have been on an asteroid floating through space, but even then, a noise came to his ears with terrible regularity and brilliance. The noise was full of rhythm and overtones, like dance music, but it was not music. It was a sound he could not escape and still live. It was the sound of his own heart.

As Tesla floated, Mourly Vold and the others were forced to wait for him. Mourly Vold grew certain, the more he thought it over, that Tesla held the key to the resolution of their difficulties.

Certainly, he did not hold that key himself. He had seen for some time that if a war were to be fought between his own forces and those of Edison and Hearst, the battlefield must not be the telephone networks. Everything there was simply too delicate. If the battle were fought there, sooner or later, some rash move on the part of one side or the other would be bound to damage the system very badly. In the past, he had been obliged, time and again, to pull his punches to keep from hurting the networks. He must find a way to win victory over Edison and Hearst without using his most powerful weapons, the ones he held over the telephone company.

In this doldrum of uncertainty, he wrote to Mabel. His wish, as he sat down to write, was to tell her everything. He wanted her to know every detail of what had happened since he had left Baddeck. Somewhere in the confusion of things—in Fairchild's rejection of his offer to help; in Hearst's escalation of the hostilities; in the Syracuse Stallion's death—was a pattern that Mabel would recognize, a pattern containing a prediction of events to come. He wanted to tell her how precarious he felt things to be at the moment. At the center of his concerns were his feelings for the telephone company, and he wanted to discuss these with her. He felt so much love for the people of the telephone company and so much anger all at once! They were, after all, the organization that had made the world, but they had made it so miserably! And, if Mr. Fairchild represented them, they were fools—open-minded, even-tempered, and hospitable, but fools all the same.

He could not write this. The reason was fundamental and hopeless. Mabel did not know him as Little Egypt, and she never could. There was no way he could take her into the telephone networks, not now and not ever. He could never reveal himself, as he had done for Dr. Bell and for Francine. Mabel would never have any firsthand knowledge of the greatest and most glorious part of him.

Instead of telling her about the present, he wrote about the future. "I am presently in a kind of difficulty I cannot explain," he wrote, "but if I ever get out of it, I hope to attend a university. I plan to study electrical engineering. I have been thinking, over the past few days, that I have been looking for an education all my life. That is what I came for when I traveled to you in Baddeck, and it is what I am seeking still. I have managed to teach myself something from books and from experience, but lately I have become less and less satisfied with my progress. In fact, some days I am really frightened by my failure to teach myself anything worth knowing at all. In the future, I must go back to school."

Mabel's reply arrived soon. "Your letter was a wonderful treat," she said, "both for its words and its feelings. The letter was like you, and having the postman deliver it was like having you return. Now I read it over and over, and feel your presence each time.

"If you do go to university, you will enjoy the experience, I am sure, but in the long run it will mean more to you than pleasant memories. It will be a kind of license for you, a license to take part in the future. I watched my husband trapped in frustrations all his life. As you know, he had training in oratory and speech, but no education in natural science. I believe that if you obtain an education in science, as you plan, that education will keep you safe from the frustrations that blocked Mr. Bell so often. If you do this, you will, in my heart, be taking him to university with you. That will make me very happy."

As suddenly as it had come, Tesla's sensitivity illness passed. He sat up on his floating mattress, stepped into the tub, and waded to its wall. He dressed himself and left his room. In the corridor of the hotel, he had a peculiar experience which delayed him half an hour. Following this, he walked to Francine's apartment to join his friends for dinner.

"I've seen her again," he said. "I've seen the glowing bird again."

Over the meal of black-eyed peas and ham, he explained.

"There is a phenomenon known to the Serbs as avian luminescence," he said. "The old people say that many species of bird glow, but I myself have only seen it in pigeons.

"The first time I saw the glowing bird, I was only a youngster. This was in the mountains, when I was climbing with my grandfather. We were inspecting his traps, and we stayed too long in the forest. The sun went down. It was winter. We would have perished, but a bird with lighted breast and wings flew over us and showed us our way.

"I saw her again as a young man in Paris. It was my habit to swim each morning in the Seine. I always swam before dawn. One morning, I saw her again, flying high up. She was brighter than the stars, and she moved across the heavens like a meteor. I could barely see the flapping motions of her wings.

"When I came to America, I was afraid I had left her behind. But the day I arrived on the boat, I saw her again. She was flying up, straight up between the piers, and glowing so brightly I had to look away. That's how I knew she had followed me here.

"Now I have seen her again, not an hour ago. She was trapped in the air shaft of the hotel, flying alone. She beat against the windows, first this one and then that one. This was the closest I have seen her. The light was pouring from her body. She looked at me as she hovered and brushed the walls. There was panic in her eye. She knew I would help her, and so I did—I went to the roof and opened the skylight. She rose up, through the opening, and passed only a meter from my face, and rose more and more until she was swallowed by a cloud."

CHAPTER 26

Once Tesla was well again, Sparky's first subversive assignment was to walk into the music stores of New York and find himself a few blind piano tuners. Little Egypt and Humberhill knew they were out there, because, in recent generations, the best and the brightest in schools for the blind had received training in piano tuning. Humberhill himself had taken some of this training, and had shown a modest aptitude for it.

It wasn't long before Sparky hit paydirt. In Lowenstein's Music on Twenty-third Street, he found Gus and Gilly Franklin, a pair of blind twins who had graduated from Perkins four years earlier. Because Gus and Gilly had left Perkins long before the telephone chicanery started there, they had no knowledge of the hidden life available within the telephone. They caught on fast, though, and before long, Little Egypt had introduced them to most of the fraternity all over North America. With their piano tuner's ears, they were amazingly adept at remembering the percussive codes of the in-band switching equipment, and Little Egypt was startled at the rate at which their competence grew under his tutelage. Once again he was reminded to think how true his warning to the phone company had been, that what one curious person can do, another can. Gus and Gilly were very bright, very careful, and before long they became very interested. If they had happened to look in the right place a year earlier, then they, and not he, could have been the first ones to make the all-important discoveries.

Tesla, also, found Gus and Gilly to be a couple of clever birds. Their experience with the technical aspects of musical instruments gave them an intuitive notion of the physics they now had to learn in order to be destructive in delightful ways. Tesla stretched a string between two bedposts and let them pluck it to experiment with changes in the tone caused by changes in the tension on the string. Fine, they said. It's an open, half-wavelength note, and the frequency increases with the square root of the tension. We knew this already. Now Tesla held a long watch chain by one end, and let them feel it as it hung straight down. He twirled the end of the chain in small circular motions parallel to the plane of the floor. At certain frequencies of twirling, and at only those frequencies, he showed them how the watch chain fell into an undulating shape, with a series of regions of great agitation and quiet regions perfectly spaced along its length. He took their hands and guided them close to the whirling chain, so they could feel, as it brushed their skin, the fat places and thin places in the standing-wave pattern.

"The chain appears strong when you pull on it, am I right?" Tesla said to them, demonstrating. "It's not weak; you can't break it. But that's only its obvious nature. You have just seen that it has another nature that is not obvious; one that has a delicacy about it. When I shake just one place on the chain— and you notice the shakes I give it are very small—the whole thing breaks into a glorious dance, and certain parts of it move about in marvelous big leaps. So much motion, and from such a tiny seed of motion!

"The whole physical world has these two natures—the obvious one of static strength and the nonobvious one of dynamic vulnerability. Provided that the seed is of the correct species— that is, the correct frequency—and provided also that it is planted in precisely the right place, the dancing motion will spread in all directions, and reach enormous amplitudes."

"Wait a minute," Gus said. "Are you telling us that you could get something big to shake all over, just by tickling it a little in one spot?"

"That is exactly what I'm telling you."

"Something really big like a bridge or a skyscraper?" Gilly asked.

"Yes," Tesla said. "You're very quick. This is just what I was coming to." He brought out a device that looked like a steel hamburger in a cast-iron bun. "This is a particularly powerful seed of motion," he said. "You could make a skyscraper shake quite horribly with that. It would have to be positioned and tuned just right, of course."

"How about a phonograph factory?" This question came from Sparky, who happened to be listening.

"You could make it shake until the pieces flew apart," Tesla told him.

Over the course of the next week, Sparky led his group of commandos out on a series of missions of extraordinary daring. Working with Gus and Gilly and three other blind piano tuners, Sparky climbed drainpipes, invaded heating ducts, tunneled under fences, and clung beneath moving railroad cars to get himself and his people to places they weren't supposed to be. Frequently they would leave at midnight and not return until the middle of the morning. Sparky's charge was to deliver his associates to the spot and to protect them from harm as they worked. In this way, he functioned like a seeing-eye dog. Each morning when Sparky's Moles—as they now called themselves—returned, they were dirty and weary, and frequently their clothes were wet and torn, but always they were elated. A close camaraderie developed among them, and they became inseparable, whether on duty or off.

In the evenings, there were giant parties. Francine and Little Egypt cooked great meals of pan-fried chicken and biscuits, and everyone ate this and drank bootleg beer in the living room. These parties were attended not only by Sparky's Moles and the local crew, but by certain workers from the telephone company home office as well. While it is not appropriate to reveal names here, it will be sufficient to say that at various times there were as many as a dozen traffic service engineers, route managers, and home office operators breaking corn bread with the deadly gang of vandals assembled under Francine's roof.

The telephone company people even gave the place its name. Because so many of them spent so much time there, it became known as the "Home-Office Annex," or, simply, the "Annex." The custom developed among the telephone company people of arriving with a small gift of equipment under their arms, so that before long, the Annex contained dozens of telephones and pieces of switching apparatus connected in bizarre ways to the telephone cables passing overhead on the roof.

Little Egypt was concerned about the possibility that detectives might follow someone to the Annex, so he instituted an elaborate diversionary route. One first went into a restaurant on the same block. The route then led out a rest-room window, up a fire escape, and across the roofs. Near the end of this path, it was necessary to cross a plank Little Egypt had placed there to form a bridge between two adjacent buildings. The plank was ten feet long, and one had the use of rope handrails running on either side, but crossing it turned out to be a significant test of nerve for the sighted visitors to the Annex. With his complete lack of fear of heights, Little Egypt never understood what bothered the people with normal vision as they inched across this chasm, looking down at the five-story drop to the alley below.

In fact, the correlation between fearlessness and sightlessness was nearly perfect—the Moles and other blind visitors to the Annex scampered across the plank without hesitation, and never mentioned that it caused them any worry at all.

After dinner, there was always music. The Moles were excellent musicians, as were several of the regulars among the telephone company personnel. Gus would play his banjo and Gilly would play his fiddle through hundreds of choruses of Smoky Mountains ballads from their native West Virginia. Francine knew these songs and would often sing with them in a clear and melancholy voice that evoked foggy valleys and mountain wild flowers. In the evenings when Tesla joined them, he would sing Serbian lullabies a cappella or recite the great national poetry of his country—narrative chants with the lilting rhythms of a gavotte.

All of this was made available, through the marvels of electronic communication, to telephone experimenters everywhere. Regulars from the old party line—Julie the waitress, Bertha from Toledo, Beetlejuice, and the others—all dropped in from time to time via the telephones scattered throughout the room. They knew something big was about to happen at last, but they didn't know what it was.

"Sparky told me this afternoon that he doesn't want this ever to end," Francine said. It was late; Sparky and the Moles had already disappeared for their nightly sortie. Humberhill was drying the dishes while Mourly Vold washed.

"I know," Humberhill said. "What do you think of the change in that boy? We've really pulled a talent out of him he never knew he had. The young man's a natural-born subversive. What do you want me to do with this platter?"

"It goes up in the cupboard," Francine said. "I'll take it."

"Yes, indeed," Humberhill continued. "After this is over, we'll have to think twice about letting him loose on society. Maybe we should get the army to drop Sparky and the Moles out of an airplane over Red Russia. Hearst would like that. There'd be nothing left of the place when those boys got finished."

The following evening, they were all Tesla's guests for dinner at his hotel. Tesla had received a royalty check the day before from a French company whose management admired him and continued to pay him small sums each year, despite the fact that the relevant patents had expired.

It was a large dinner party. Besides Sparky and the Moles, the guests included Francine, Mourly Vold, Humberhill, and an electrician and two operators from the home office. One of the operators was Suzanne, the girl who had given Mourly Vold the headset with the bows and earrings on the day of his home office debut.

Tesla had ordered an elaborate meal, including clear green turtle soup au Madeira, sweetbreads braisé, steamed cracked wheat, new cauliflower in cream, roast prime rib in dish gravy, Yorkshire pudding Claudia, punch Cardinal, and for dessert, silver cake with claret sauce. According to Tesla's instructions, the entire meal was prepared by the chef personally and served by the maître d'.

During the meal, Tesla was forever rushing into the kitchen and then returning, for only a moment, to taste some delicacy before it was served; then he would disappear into the kitchen once again. The restaurant staff obviously wished he would stay out of their way, but they were too correctly polite to say so.

After dessert, Sparky offered a long toast in which he said that he was now very happy, and he had never expected to be so happy, certainly not at the time he had first met Dr. Tesla. Sparky remembered that he had seen Tesla working in his father's laboratory as a child, and he had never for a moment thought that the two of them might work together as partners one day. He toasted Tesla, and the Moles, and Little Egypt, and Humberhill, but he reserved a special toast and thanks for Francine, who had literally, he said, picked him up off the street and given him a reason for living. After saying all this, Sparky missed his chair when he sat down. This provided a great deal of mirth for the Moles, who had noiselessly slid his chair out from under him while he was toasting.

"I am happy, too," Tesla said. "I have never before had

such friends, nor have I even missed their friendship, because I didn't know how pleasant friendship could be."

He stopped for a minute, because he didn't know how to say what he was feeling.

"I hope all of you will continue to be here," he said, "that is, will continue to visit me, after . . . when our work is finished."

There was a silence for some minutes.

"When is that going to be?" Suzanne the operator asked.

Several people glanced nervously at one another. The table where Tesla's party sat was off by itself in a corner, far from other restaurant guests. Even so, the serving staff was passing by from time to time, so indiscreet talk would not be safe. Mourly Vold answered Suzanne's question with a single word.

"Soon," he said.

Acting on Little Egypt's instructions, Tesla called the office of Murdoch MacLeod at Hearst's *New York American* and asked the famous reporter to meet him for lunch at Delmonico's. MacLeod had interviewed Tesla several times in the old days, and still took Tesla's intelligence seriously.

Over lunch, Tesla revealed that he had developed a new invention, a derivative of his World System. He said the new invention was a ray which could focus millions of horsepower in a thin beam only a fraction of a millimeter wide. This ray would have a range of several hundred miles, and could cause an internal earthquake within the atoms of any solid object it struck. It could be used as a defensive weapon against hostile aircraft and Zeppelins. From towers placed on the coasts, it could sink ships the moment they appeared on the horizon. A nation that developed it would never have to fear war again.

"Fine," MacLeod said. "Fine. But where's your proof? Show me it works."

"A full-sized prototype would cost many millions," Tesla told him. "Only a government could afford such a development. I am planning to approach the army and the navy to provide the necessary funds." By this time, they had finished their entrées and Tesla was reviewing the menu, selecting a dessert.

MacLeod allowed an uncomfortable look to cross his face. "You mean to tell me," he said, "that this is just an idea on paper? You haven't got anything to show for it?"

"It isn't on paper," Tesla said. "I don't write such things on paper. It's in my head."

Murdoch MacLeod asked for the check even before Tesla's mousse arrived. He stood up. "Do you want to know what I think? I think you brought me here and told me your half-assed idea just to get me to buy you lunch. Well, I'm sorry, but I have better things to do. The next time you feel like mooching a meal, call another reporter."

Even though MacLeod said this, he wrote a story about Tesla's invention, jazzing it up somewhat and calling it a "death ray." MacLeod's editor loved the story and wanted him to do follow-ups, but MacLeod stood his ground. "I've had it," he said. "No more lunches with Tesla for me. He's too sad these days."

A telegram arrived at the Hearst corporate offices. It began, YOU WIN. It went on to say that Little Egypt was prepared to give himself up for prosecution. The condition was that Hearst and Edison must personally accept his surrender. The telegram appointed midnight, two days hence, as the time of the surrender, and Hearst's suite at the Claremont as the place.

"It all depends on their being there," Humberhill said. "What kind of a chance have we got for that?"

"A very good chance, I'd say," Mourly Vold told him. "Both of them are curious as hell about me. They'll show up, all right. Nothing could keep them away."

The following afternoon, the skies darkened, and by nightfall, rain and fog spread over the city. These were the conditions they were waiting for. Little Egypt, Humberhill, Sparky, and Tesla went by taxi to the Claremont, taking two large crates with them. A porter brought the cases in from the street while Tesla went to the registration desk and took a room.

"This has to be the softest rug I ever stepped on," Humberhill said, as he stood beside Tesla at the registration desk. "I'd like to take off my shoes and feel it with my toes."

"Go ahead," Tesla told him.

And so Humberhill sat on the carpet, removed his shoes and socks, and stood up again. "This is fantastic," he said to Sparky. "Like the man says, if you had a million dollars, you'd buy an acre of tits and walk around on them all day."

They went up in the elevator, Humberhill still in his bare feet. When the porters had delivered the crates to the room, Tesla closed the door behind them. Little Egypt opened the crates and began removing equipment. Tesla opened a window and spread birdseed on the sill. Before long, a pigeon appeared, and then another.

"This isn't such a bad neighborhood for birds," Tesla said. "If I could afford the rent, I might want to live here."

"We haven't much time," Little Egypt said. "Could I have your assistance, please?"

Taking a box of equipment with them, they climbed to the top of a stairwell leading to the roof of the hotel. Here they arrived at a locked door. Tesla used a skeleton key of his own design to open the door.

"This is terrible," he said.

"What's the matter?" Humberhill wanted to know.

"Just listen," Tesla said. "Hear that clattering noise? It's the rain on the roof. This building has a metal roof."

"So what?" asked Sparky.

"It means we can't put the field coils on the roof, as we planned," Little Egypt said. "They would be useless because of eddy currents in the metal."

"Exactly," Tesla said.

There followed a pause, during which the rain struck the roof with a heavy sound.

"What else can we do?" Humberhill asked.

"If there were some way to wind the wire around the outside of the hotel, that would work," Tesla said. "There would have to be two separate coils, one near the ceilings and one near the floors of Hearst's rooms. But that would mean someone would have to carry the wire while clinging to the outside of the building. And in the rain, and dark! No one can do that."

"I can do it," Little Egypt said.

"Impossible," Tesla replied. "The roof has an overhang. There's no going over the top; no possibility of using a rope. You would have to come up from below. There are twelve floors between our room and Hearst's suite. That's a vertical climb, all the way, over wet stones. Even the most experienced steeple-jack wouldn't try such a thing."

"Tell me what our alternatives are," Little Egypt said.

"Other than giving up, we haven't any," Tesla replied.

"That's why I have to try it," Little Egypt said.

An hour later, he reached the level of Hearst's suite. He moved across the outside of the building like a sleek, wet squirrel, finding handholds and footholds on the ledges and outcroppings of ornamental stonework. Hundreds of feet below, the sounds of motors and tires on the wet street came up to him. The traffic itself was invisible to him, of course, and he was invisible to it because of the rain and fog.

Hanging at his belt was loop after loop of insulated copper wire. Beginning with a gargoyle on the roof of Hearst's Hapsburg garden, Little Egypt began to coil the wire around the entire perimeter of the building, passing in turn the windows of the library, the south parlor, the kitchen, the servants' quarters, the guest bedrooms, the master bedroom, the north parlor, and back again to the veranda supporting the garden. Each time he passed a window where lights were on, he had to traverse the window ledge hand over hand, hanging by his fingers, with nothing under his feet but dark air.

Once, as his hand slipped in wet pigeon shit on a windowsill, he nearly lost his grip. For many minutes after that, he clung to a frieze of ornamental grapes, his body pressed flat against the stones, his breath coming in startled rushes.

And all this happened in the most remarkable gradient of light—bright below and dark above, so that both the sounds of the city and its lights flowed upward, as from a smooth pipe, into the clouds, while rain drained through the air in the opposite direction. The tops of Little Egypt's naked arms were dark, and therefore part of the void, but the lower surfaces of his arms glowed as brightly as if they bore an electric charge.

Throughout the night, he orbited around and around the building, until he had threaded the wire in two separate coils, as Tesla had specified.

When he finished, it was nearly morning. The rain had ended. The air was clear. A red color appeared on the horizon in the east. His job finished, he picked his way downward over the same handholds he had used on the way up, and entered the room through the open window he had left many hours earlier. Humberhill and Tesla were both asleep, but they had left him one of the three bowls of strawberry rennet custard they had ordered earlier from room service, and he ate this before falling asleep.

That evening at the appointed time, Little Egypt presented himself at the door of Hearst's apartments. A butler let him in and brought him to the north parlor, where Hearst and Edison were expecting him.

Edison had been speaking when Little Egypt entered the room, but stopped abruptly when he saw him. Edison came up and looked him over at close range. He took one of Little Egypt's forearms between his thumb and index finger and gave it a pinch.

"That's the scrawniest fellow I ever saw," he announced,

removing his cigar from his mouth and spitting on the floor.

"Hey, could you take it easy on the floor?" Hearst said. "There's a cuspidor right here."

"I never missed the floor yet," Edison said. "Missed the cuspidor plenty of times."

Hearst was seated on a long couch covered in white silk. "Well," he said. "What have you got to say for yourself?"

"I hadn't planned to talk about myself," Little Egypt said. "People say it isn't polite."

"Haw," Edison said. "That's funny. I must remember that one."

"My question wasn't designed to be personal," Hearst said. "I merely wanted to give you an opportunity for a confession, before I bring the police in. They're waiting in the south parlor."

"Very well," Little Egypt said, placing his carpet bag on the floor and opening it. "My confession is that I have arranged for a powerful ray to be trained on this building. I would like to show you what it can do."

He stood up, holding one of Tesla's tubes in each hand. He lifted the tubes over his head, and suddenly they burst into light.

At the same time, the electric lights in the room flickered and went out, leaving the flamelike shafts in Little Egypt's hands the only illumination. The hair rose from his head and glowed. Hearst's and Edison's hair stood up also. Lightning bolts flashed across the windows.

"That's remarkable," Hearst said. "How does he do that?"

By now, electricity was escaping from the edges of sharp objects. The metal corners of tables and picture frames were glowing and crackling. Tiny lightning bolts began jumping across gaps; a spark jumped from Hearst's ear to the wall. The lightning flashes made sounds like cherry bombs going off.

"My God!" Hearst cried, holding his ear. "That's enough! Turn it off!"

Little Egypt took the bullwhip from his belt and gave it a sharp crack. At this signal, the electric displays were switched off, and the charges began to drain away.

"You say that's enough," he told Hearst, "but that isn't all. The ray is capable of tearing matter apart, as well as causing it to glow, as I showed you just now. You had only twenty seconds of my treatment; if I had let it go on longer, you would have felt the floors shake, and after two minutes, there would be nothing left but a pile of junk.

"At this moment, I have the ray trained on every Hearst property in this city. When I give the word, it will level your newspaper offices, your printing plants, your apartment buildings, and everything else you own. I also have it aimed at Mr. Edison's properties. In fact, they are much simpler to take care of. His phonograph factory and his battery works have so many explosive materials in them that they will go up by themselves after just a little shake."

"What's your price?" Hearst asked.

"Freedom," Little Egypt told him. "And cooperation. And, as you will see in a moment, contrition."

He lit a candle and placed it on a table. "I thought you might like to meet my colleagues," he said. Tesla and Humberhill were now by his side, having let themselves into the darkened apartment with Tesla's skeleton key. Standing behind them, with a bag over his head, was Sparky. At the last moment, Sparky had been so overcome by fear of his father that he had grabbed a paper bag and pulled it over his head.

"You!" Edison said, recognizing Tesla. "The last time I saw you, you were covered with pigeon dung, cadging nickels in front of the public library."

"This document," Little Egypt told them, "is a contract between us. It states that for valuable consideration received, namely my forbearance, you will do a number of things. First, you will desist from harassing our investigations of the telephone system. Second, you will underwrite the costs of improving the telephone networks as we direct. Third, you will establish a museum at Baddeck, Nova Scotia, honoring Alexander Graham Bell and preserving his accomplishments, including the projects he was working on shortly before his death. Lastly, you will give us a certain piece of satisfaction Dr. Tesla feels we should have."

"And what would that be?" Hearst inquired.

"You will kiss our asses."

"No!" Edison said. "No, no, no!"

Hearst signed the document and passed it to Edison. "Sign this, you silly bastard," he said, "and do what they say. These people can ruin us, don't you understand?"

Edison stared at Tesla. "I say your death ray is so much stewed prunes," he said. "And so are you. Always were. Time was when I thought, here's a foreign boy with some sense. Now you go and show me there's no such thing."

He turned to Hearst. "Now that I get a look at Tesla here, I remember when I saw him do this all before. The gas lamps, the sparks, all of it. If there was a vaudeville for quack inventors, he'd be in it. He used to do shows more elaborate than this in his laboratory after dinner. Then he'd pass the hat among his rich pals. I told you, I've seen him do it. There isn't any death ray. If you ask me, there's only a stewed-prune ray, and this fellow has turned it on his own brains."

For a long moment, the candle flickered on and nobody said a thing.

"Well, that's it," Little Egypt said at last. "We have our answer." He withdrew his homemade telephone from beneath his shirt and plugged it into the bullwhip coupler, which he had wrapped around the cord to Hearst's fancy ivory-handled telephone earlier.

"What are you going to do?" Humberhill asked him.

"I'm going to tell the Moles to go ahead," Little Egypt

said. "I'm going to put these two right out of business." With that, he began the tongue-clicking sequence that would connect him to the Annex.

Humberhill had a hasty whispered conversation with Sparky. After this, he pulled Little Egypt aside.

"Hang on a minute," he said. "Sparky tells me there might be people in those buildings, even at this time of night."

"I've thought of that," Little Egypt told him. "The Moles are calling them right now and giving them a warning. They have five minutes to get out. Then we take the buildings down."

Sparky whispered to Humberhill again. Sparky's voice sounded odd, coming from inside the bag.

"Sparky says how can we be sure that they're out?" Humberhill said. "I think that's a good question. We're talking about the real thing here."

Little Egypt faced his friend. His mood freshened into a rage.

"Of course we're talking about the real thing!" he shouted. "It's always been the real thing! Are you telling me you think I've been playing a game? You've just heard from a man who has done his best to destroy Dr. Tesla in every stage of his life. Was that a game or was that real? That same man has hurt his son about as deeply as one human being ever hurts another. Was he just pretending? Was that only a joke? Tell Sparky that all the terrible things his father did to him in his life weren't real! Look at him! He has a bag over his head! He only has to come into the same room with his father and he doesn't want to have a human face anymore! Edison should be on his knees before these two, begging for their forgiveness, but instead— you heard his tough talk just now! He thinks he's still winning! Well, let me tell you, by God, he is *not* winning. He will *not* beat us. His days of grinding people under his heel are *over*!"

Little Egypt's face was blood-red. Humberhill could not see this, of course, but he could hear in his friend's words emotions he had never heard before.

Humberhill deliberately took the time to light a cigar before replying.

"Yes," he said. "Ah, yes. You *have* beaten them. But the thing is to let them know that, in a nice way, without actually tearing them apart."

"I'll tear them apart if I have to! You heard what Edison said. He doesn't believe I can hurt him!"

"I also heard what Hearst said," Humberhill replied. "He just signed your agreement. You have what you wanted from him."

"No, no," Little Egypt said. He was weeping now. "It's too late! Too much has happened. This is the one moment we have to get these cruel bastards good. Tell the Syracuse Stallion it was all a game, and now he's won! Tell Dr. Bell!"

Although he said this, Little Egypt agreed to talk on the telephone with Francine at the Annex, after Humberhill had explained to her what was going on. They spoke together for half an hour, including long silences.

"You can only expect them to stop, not to undo," Francine said.

"What do you mean?"

"I mean they did things," Francine said. "They hurt people. I'll give you that. But you can't expect them to go back and reverse things that happened years in the past.

"What if someone asked you to undo your part in the Syracuse Stallion's life? Could you do that? Would the request be fair? If he had never gotten involved with the telephone, he'd be alive today. Hearst and his bullyboys contributed to what happened there, but so did you. And nothing you could possibly do now, no smashing of buildings or any of the rest of it, could change that. The same thing goes for Tesla's situation, and Sparky's, and Bell's. None of them want you to get revenge for them. They don't need it. Don't take revenge for them. They simply don't need it."

She heard him weeping into the telephone.

"Am I right?" she said.

No answer.

"Are you there?" she asked.

"Yes."

"What are you going to do?"

"I don't know," he said. "Something not as bad. Not the whole thing. I have to go now."

"I love you," she said.

"Well, this is a hell of a time to tell me that."

"You knew it anyway."

"I suppose I did, but you never said it."

"Now I've said it. Are you glad?"

"Yes," he answered. "I'm very glad."

After this, Little Egypt composed himself. He wiped his eyes and asked Hearst for a glass of water. When this arrived, he drank it and announced: "I've decided what to do. For the moment, your newspapers and factories will be spared. I will be satisfied if both of you will agree to be bound by the terms of my contract. I understand, however, that Mr. Edison doubts our capabilities, and is unwilling to meet our terms. Is that correct?"

"Friggin' right," Edison said. "You little crooks can go whistle through your billy-holes."

"Very well," Little Egypt said. "I'm putting the contract here on this table. In a moment, I'll begin another demonstration of our weapon. It will be applied to this building only, and I will leave it on until you indicate your willingness to accept my terms."

Little Egypt gave the signal, and a moment later the floor began to jiggle. A tone with the lowest, darkest quality imaginable flooded the room. Tesla's vibrator had begun its work. The feet of the sofa Hearst sat in tapped against the floor. Vases slid across tables and smashed on the tiles.

"Jesus Christ!" Hearst cried out. "He's doing it!"

By now, pipes were bursting. Water ran down the walls

onto the floor. A large piece of plaster broke free from the ceiling and crashed down. Plaster dust rose in a cloud. A nest of mice had come down with the ceiling—these now ran in all directions. From the kitchen came the sounds of smashing china.

"Where's the paper?" Hearst screamed. "Edison will sign! Just turn it off! Turn it off!"

Little Egypt gave another signal and the terrible vibrations stopped. Throughout the building, people were wailing. Mayor Hylan's police had come out of hiding. Some of them were vomiting on the floor.

Edison emerged from under a pile of plaster. His hair was thick with dust. Hearst pushed him to the table where the contract was. By now, all of the uninvited guests had taken their trousers down and turned about-face. William Randolph Hearst, a man with a modern attitude about honor, went down on his knees and kissed each fanny in order: Little Egypt's and Tesla's looking almost similar in their bony compactness; Humberhill's and Sparky's florid and generous by comparison.

"I'll sign the paper," Edison said. "But I will not kiss Tesla's ass."

"You'll do it," Hearst cried. "You'll do it if I have to pucker your lips with my bare hands and plant them on his cheeks! Do it! Just close your eyes and do it!"

And so that's how it ended. Edison got down on his knees and did the deed all around. It's funny how fair life seems some days.

CHAPTER 27

A month later, Francine and Mourly Vold announced their plans to be married. The wedding was to take place in the old stone church on the town square in Beauty, and the reception would be at the farm. Telephone experimenters from all over the American continent arrived to take part. They made their headquarters in the barn, and were warm and dry there, thanks to the new roof Mourly Vold had put on earlier in the summer. Francine's neighbors sent pies, sweet corn, and watermelon to feed them.

"I like your friends," Francine said. "They're so full of beans."

"They are definitely full of beans," Mourly Vold replied. "I just hope the barn is still standing when they decide to go."

Absolutely everyone came. Beetlejuice, whom no one had ever met outside of the telephone, arrived from New York. The bus driver carried him off the bus and placed him in his wheelchair. For the remainder of the week, the wheelchair never had fewer than three young men hanging from it. With Beetlejuice in command, the wheelchair raced across the barnyard and through the blackberry bushes. Once, it went into the farm pond with three youngsters aboard. After that, it made a terrible squeaking noise until Sparky took the wheels off and repacked the bearings.

Telephone company people arrived to take part also. Bertha came in from Toledo, and Suzanne came from New York.

"Oh, my goodness, you're so tall," Bertha said to Mourly Vold. "I pictured you as just a *little* rascal. But Humberhill is exactly the way I thought he'd be. He's a good eater. I like a good eater."

"He's a *very* good eater," Francine remarked.

Mourly Vold had not heard from his mother in many months, not since his visit to the Murch house. Now he tried to reach her by telephone, but found that her number in Bucks Falls had been disconnected. Mrs. Murch, when he spoke to her, said that his mother had left abruptly without giving a forwarding address.

"That's it," he said to Francine. "She's lost."

"Don't give up as fast as all that," Francine said. "I want her to be invited. You're her only child. I don't think it's fair to cheat her out of our wedding."

Mourly Vold went back to work, calling his mother's neighbors and friends until he was given an address where she could receive a telegram. He paid for all these calls and for the telegram, too, because he said he had turned over a new leaf.

Both Ilse Vold and Mabel Bell made the long journey from Nova Scotia. They shared a room in the farmhouse for two days before the wedding, and became friends. Mourly Vold's three women—his mother, Mabel, and Francine—spent much time together. They walked along the mountain paths and brought back armloads of wild flowers for the many vases throughout the house.

On the evening before the wedding, Mabel Bell presented Mourly Vold and Francine with a gift. It was one of Bell's research notebooks.

"This was the last one he used," she told them. "It has in it the thunderstorm machine you made together."

She opened the book and showed them the relevant pages. There, in Bell's wavering hand, were a series of vague drawings and comments. The sight of Bell's handwriting brought Mourly Vold a flood of emotions.

Bell had represented the sheep house by a rectangle crowned with a triangle, and he had shown the pointed rod Mourly Vold had erected above the roof and the accumulator ball below. Various notes were written to the right and left of the diagram: "Point creates a local electrotensive hollow," and "Give this part room— It bites."

Below the drawing was a shorter sentence on its own, not directly connected with any explanations, and this was what Mabel particularly wanted them to see. Bell had written there, "He thinks like me."

As morning came on the day of the wedding, low clouds crowded out the light until after ten o'clock. Rain had fallen the night before, and the downspouts on the house and barn were still dripping as the wedding party and their guests climbed into the automobiles and carriages that would take them to the church. Mourly Vold, Francine, Mabel, and Ilse rode in a cowled phaeton drawn by a dappled horse. This rig had been loaned by a neighboring farmer. Before they reached the church, the cloud cover lifted and strong shafts of light poked down into the fields and forest all around. Every leaf on every tree had globes of water attached to its points, and these became trick lenses that launched colored light in all directions. Those who had sight were faced with a most difficult task in describing the spectacle to the others.

After the wedding, tables were set up along the south wall of the barn, and here the bride and groom and their guests enjoyed a country luncheon including local ham, fresh sweet corn and tomatoes, river bass, candied yams, homemade pepper relish, cider, and squash pie.

"It was a beautiful wedding," Ilse Vold said. She spoke to Francine, who was seated at her side. "Weddings are always beautiful, and this was an especially lovely one. Marriages can be nice, too, but they aren't for everybody. I think I'll give marriage a miss from now on."

During the course of the meal, she explained this remark,

and filled Francine in on what had been happening to her since her son's visit at the Murch house.

"They were all a bit disagreeable," she said, "but you have to give them credit for being themselves. I was never myself when I was living with them. I hardly recognized my reflection in the mirror.

"I'll tell you what was really difficult. They had a notion about me that I was forced to live up to. I was supposed to be polite and outgoing all the time. They insisted on being the selfish ones. If they had let me behave naturally, I probably would have been much like them. I don't think I could have kept it up forever, being the way they imagined me.

"I say forever, but I'm not sure Mrs. Murch actually intended to have me in her family. Her son was enthusiastic, but, thinking back on it, I don't think the old woman was ever prepared to give her consent. All this finally wore me out, and I broke it off. Good thing, too. That would have been a miserable life. I wonder now why I ever wanted it. The truth is probably that I was afraid of poverty and loneliness."

Ilse left the table for a moment and returned with a package. "This is for both of you," she said, handing the package to Francine.

Francine opened it and withdrew the contents. From the puzzled look on her face, it was clear she didn't know what it was.

"These are stainproof seat covers," Ilse said, "for a car. Now, I know you don't have a car, but perhaps you'll buy one sometime, and then you can use them. I made them out of a kind of oilcloth that doesn't let water through. That's my business now, and I'm doing quite well at it. I started last year, and I'm so busy these days, I have two ladies helping me."

Ilse took a few bites of ham and sipped her cider before continuing.

"I'm doing so well, in fact, that I've bought a house. I've moved out of the one my husband and I rented. It's a lovely little house by the sea. It's out on a point of land, all by itself. There are drawbacks, of course, to being a woman alone in such a place. A lobsterman has taken an interest in me. He spends a good deal of time sitting in his boat, looking in my windows. He's a bald man with an enormous belly. In the mornings, when he hauls his traps, he opens his trousers and pees off the end of his boat. I suppose he thinks I find that irresistible.

"But, all together, I have a very nice life now. I have my work and I have my friends. We belong to a Gaelic singing group. In the spring, we tour all over, giving performances in halls and churches. I have my independence, and that was what I wanted all along, not another marriage, and certainly not another loveless one."

In this opinion, Ilse was far ahead of her time. A little business of one's own; an end forever to the tyranny of the family. Eventually the same thought would light the imaginations of women everywhere, but not yet.

Not for another twenty-five years, and not until another world war had passed, would such ideas find broad acceptance among women in North America. But when that acceptance did come, it would change the relationships between men and women profoundly. It would be so important that it would appear to be a biological mutation, rather than a social one. And Ilse was an early heroine of this transition—a pioneer; one of the first through.

In the years that followed, Hearst and Edison lived up to most aspects of their agreement. Hearst provided the funds for a small laboratory on Long Island where Mourly Vold and Tesla worked together. Their greatest contribution was the multifrequency signaling system, an innovation that changed everything. It listened for constellations of tones—music, actually, coming over the wires—and made long-distance routing connections in a jiffy. The faint high-speed burst of notes you hear in your receiver today when you call from one coast to the other is

Mourly Vold's multifrequency system communicating among its various parts in coded tones.

With Tesla's help, he made it fast and efficient. He also made it secure against tampering—far more secure than the old percussive signaling system had been. There came a moment at the end of months of development when Mourly Vold could have locked the secrets of the coded tones away forever. He chose not to do this. Instead, he put a rational pattern in their design that only a fine intelligence could ever find. He left a puzzle in the organization of the tones, fully aware that a sufficiently great mind might one day solve the puzzle and thereby gain access to the networks. In this way he left to the future an opportunity—not the identical opportunity that had been given to him, but a similar one. He did this out of a sense of fairness to the future.

This work was so successful that the telephone company saw the value of having their own long-range research organization with the freedom to pursue applied problems it considered interesting. Bertram Fairchild offered Mourly Vold and Tesla important positions in this organization, but they declined, since each had other fish to fry. Tesla began a long series of theoretical researches on the relationship between space and time. Mourly Vold went to college.

He studied electrical engineering at the University of Illinois. Among the cornfields, he made mathematics and physics part of his permanent mental equipment. He found it easy to add to his intuition mathematical ways of looking at the world. Francine taught the sons and daughters of corn farmers at a local school. In the evenings, she read to her husband from his textbooks when his poor eyesight would otherwise have stopped his work. In this way, she helped him into his growing delight, his scientific maturity.

During Mourly Vold's graduate studies and afterward, they had children together, first a son and then two daughters.

And while Hearst seemed to have written off the minor

costs of his brush with Little Egypt and never looked back, the event demoralized Thomas Edison more than is generally recognized. In the years immediately after his humiliation, Edison could not bear to view the human posterior in any condition approaching nakedness. Mirrors were eliminated from the bedroom and the bath to prevent him from catching a glimpse of any bared fanny, even his own. At one point, it got so bad that he required the personnel in his laboratory to wear their shop aprons turned around, with the broad part covering their backsides.

Through this period, Edison's deafness worsened. At meetings, he required George Phillipson at his side to tap out Morse code on his knee. The conversation around the table was supposed to wait until Phillipson had gotten the message through. Edison would then nod his head. He said once, in a melancholy moment, that he had not heard a bird sing since he was twelve years old.

Edison struggled to keep on inventing. He worked on an artificial flower to be worn in a man's buttonhole. This flower would receive its scent through a flexible tube from a flask carried in a pocket. He invented a pair of roller skates whose wheels wound up elastic bands suspended from a garter belt. Wearing these, a man who lived at the top of a hill could skate down to the town, carry out his business, then release a catch and be returned up the hill, rolling backward.

He became dismayed by the amazing increase in flatulence which comes with age, and offered a physician a thousand dollars to find a cure that would guarantee he would never fart again.

Some years later, Henry Ford convinced him that there was a fortune to be made in a substitute for natural rubber, and he put his staff to work on getting rubber from goldenrod and other weeds. One morning, Edison was seen to leave his house and walk down the front steps, carrying a bowl of tapioca pudding. He moved slowly toward his laboratory buildings, holding the bowl out ahead of him. A small crowd of laboratory workers watched from the windows. When he had covered a little more than half the ground between his house and the lab, he tripped and fell heavily. Seeing this, several of his senior staff went out to help him.

"Where's that bowl of pudding I had in my hand?" he wanted to know as they were helping him up.

They handed him the bowl, but said the pudding was splattered all over.

"Aw, shit," Edison said. "It had a nice stretchy skin on it. I wanted you to try and get rubber from that. Get busy and find the damned thing!"

But when they found the skin of the pudding, all they were able to extract from it was gravel and dead leaves, no rubber at all.

Meanwhile, Henry Ford's infatuation with Edison and his legend was growing stronger. He conceived of a great tribute to Edison, a reconstruction of the old Menlo Park laboratory in a Museum of American Life he planned to build next door to his estate in Dearborn. He spent many millions to bring this off in time for a great celebration of the fiftieth birthday of the electric light. Not only Edison, but President Hoover, Harvey Firestone, George Eastman, Walter Chrysler, and poor old Madame Curie attended the ceremonies. Edison shuffled over miles of buildings and was shown hundreds of pieces of apparatus he had long ago thrown away. Ford had somehow located and brought here all these broken and discarded light bulbs, burned-out commutators, moldy packages of South American plant materials, and jars of used battery acid. Edison wondered whether they were all genuine. By close examination, he convinced himself that at least some of them were. Stuck to the bottom of a dynamo casting he had thrown away forty-five years ago, he found one of his own cigar butts.

Edison returned to New Jersey ill and tired. He spent the next several weeks in bed. One day, just after noon, his wife looked out the window and saw Henry Ford pushing over an iron boiler that had been sitting there for years among the weeds. Ford and his assistant spent the afternoon gleaning through the scrapyard.

"Mr. Ford has become quite a nuisance," she said to Edison. "I wish you'd tell him to go away."

In Baddeck, the Alexander Graham Bell Museum was finally built, not by Hearst and Edison, but by Bell's neighbors. Many of the people who contributed money toward it remembered Bell personally. They dragged the hull of the hydrodrome from the rocky beach where it had sat for years and built the museum around it. You can visit the Bell Museum today. It is as nice as Mourly Vold wanted it to be.

For reasons never explained to anyone, in his later life, Nikola Tesla adopted the Institute of Immigrant Welfare as his forum for scientific reporting. After many years of solitary thought, he addressed this body and told it that Einstein's theory could not possibly be correct. He spoke to the assembled Poles, Croats, Lithuanians, and Armenians, and told them that he had read the scientific literatures of eight countries far back into the past, and found no mention of curved space, no evidence that space and time are joined together. Most of his listeners made their livings with a broom and did not understand what he was saying. Nevertheless, they listened politely because Tesla was a great man of their own blood.

Over the years, reporters from Hearst's papers occasionally tried to get new developments on the story Tesla himself had started, that of his great ray. Tesla refused to answer their questions, except in the most general and ambiguous terms. His answers were dismissals, but somehow they always left room for further speculation. By this time, he had invented his dynamic theory of gravity, and wished to tell the reporters about it, but they were interested in nothing but the ray.

And, of course, this was a time when Tesla's early inventions were transforming the look of the world. His greatest work, the system of polyphase power, originally exploited by Westinghouse, now transported Niagara's energy to New York City and beyond. His alternating-current motors turned the machinery of industry in every country. His gaseous-tube lamps were twisted into letters and mounted on signs, and these were found to catch the eye with the force of a steel trap.

Neon! It changed the look of cities everywhere. Overnight, the streets of Pittsburgh, Chicago, and New York grew glowing hamburgers and palm trees. People went downtown at dusk and waited for the signs to come on. Popeye and Wimpie, EAT, Quaker Oats, Quaker State, ESSO, Horn and Hardart, Joe and Nemo, Coca-Cola, and arrows, thousands of wonderfully glowing arrows! Every year the projects grew grander. In Reno, a gambling establishment created a buckaroo on a leaping horse which would jump into seven different positions before returning to the first. Although no one at the time noticed, this sign was a reinvention of the Edison Kinetoscope. It gave the illusion of motion through the rapid display of a sequence of static images. No projector or screen was required, because the images were twenty feet high.

Young men learned to be neon glassblowers, and created a new itinerant class. The most famous of these was Sparky Edison, now married to Billie Williams, a handsome former barmaid. A master of the art, Sparky designed and built the White Tower sign in Philadelphia, the Cities Service sign in Cleveland, the Blatz sign in Milwaukee, and the great and wonderful Camel sign in New York. Sparky and his wife discovered, as many Americans did at the same time, the aphrodisiac properties of neon light. They lay together in sagging beds in hotel rooms across the country, where the red-and-purple glare from the neon sign outside their window flashed through the curtains, and fucked like bunnies. There was something warming and exciting in the light, something in its rhythm of on-again-off-again, that revealed the eerie beauty of a naked body—its natural electricity. Throughout the Jazz Age, Sparky and his loving wife lived on the American road and bent the tubes that made the country shine.

These and other Tesla inventions were making the modern world the glitzy place it is today, but the inventor himself had fallen back into near-penury.

The newspapers called him the "Pigeon Man of Manhattan," and it is true that with each passing year, he slipped farther out of the realm of human beings into the life of the city flocks. The noise and the dirt of the birds, combined with the tardiness of Tesla's accounts, forced the management of the Hotel St. Regis to ask him to move. Before long he was given the boot from the Hotel Pennsylvania and the Hotel Governor Clinton for the same reasons. He came to rest at the Hotel New Yorker, where he lived until the end of his life.

This occurred in January 1943, during the darkest days of the Second World War. Tesla was now eating very little. Every day, he would break a soda cracker into half a glass of milk, and on this he managed to continue the halfhearted collaboration between his body and his soul.

On the night of his death, Tesla spent several hours gazing out the window, as was his habit. He searched the horizon above the city skyline. What was he looking for—a comet, a star? An airmail flyer passed overhead, his lights appearing to dim now and then as he passed through snow clouds, but Tesla was not looking for an airplane. He was looking for something else, something specific, something he had seen before. Among the distant lights of so many windows, it would be difficult to see. He expected to recognize it as a faint light moving among the stationary ones. He strained to see it, as he had on so many other solitary nights, but it was not there. Under the eyes of his friends, the birds, he put on his silk dressing gown and lay down on his bed.

Twenty stories below, a pigeon searched for food in a gutter. The citizens of New York regarded pigeons as flying rats.

People were disgusted with their filth and their noise. Everywhere, naked electric wires were installed on ledges to drive them away. When the pigeon alighted, an alert New Yorker saw his chance and poured kerosene on the bird. He tossed her a lighted match. The kerosene went up with a whoosh and the bird took off on flaming wings.

At this moment, the pigeons in Tesla's room heard him cough, and he never took another breath. The window was open as usual, and before long his body began to cool. His eyes were open. His lips grew cold. Just then, the burning pigeon landed on the windowsill.

Too late! Too late! Tesla could no longer help! The feathers of her wings and throat were burning brightly. She stood at the window, a bright animal torch, and the curtains curled and flapped around her. Clouds of parasites jumped off her. Before long, the curtains were burning. She fell to the floor and died. The other birds fluttered about the room in alarm. Some of them escaped through the window. The fire department had to break the door down to put out the fire.

J. Edgar Hoover was now running the Federal Bureau of Investigation. The United States was at war with the Nazis. Hoover's mind was on his counterespionage program in South America. His agents had penetrated nests of platinum smugglers in the Choco jungle. They risked their lives wandering the rough coasts looking for the hiding places of Nazi submarines. If caught in Argentina, his agents knew the police would insert the *picaña eléctrica,* the electric spur, into private regions of their bodies.

When Hoover was informed of Tesla's death, he gave orders to have his men remove the safe from Tesla's burned-out room. The safe was brought to Washington in a special plane. Hoover saw that his agents could make use of Tesla's ray invention, if such a thing existed, not only in Argentina, but at home in the United States. With Tesla's ray, the bureau could become a very powerful organization, as powerful as the U.S. Army or Navy. When it came to congressional appropriations,

Hoover told himself, he would no longer have to be satisfied with sucking off a hind teat.

The safe was taken to a remote explosives range. Hoover himself was present in the blockhouse with the ballistics men when the safe was blown. With great anticipation, Hoover rushed out of the blockhouse and approached the smoking safe. He found it filled with birdseed.

Tesla took with him any ideas he might have had for a death ray, and thus it is possible that he deprived the United States of some advantage over its enemies, but Mourly Vold and his colleagues more than made up for this through the steady flow of developments they contributed to the war effort. During the war, Mourly Vold and other members of the gang of vandals—Beetlejuice, Gilly, and Gus, to name a few—joined the great cadre of scientists and engineers who literally manufactured the Allied victory from the improved cathode-ray tubes, solid-state amplifiers, and ultra-high-speed switching circuits they invented. Later, in the great and creamy postwar boom, one or more of the original telephone experimenters served in key positions at Bell Labs, the General Electric Research Labs, and at Westinghouse. Humberhill, never really a technical man, became one of the first in a new job species that came to be called "public relations." He had his office at G.E. in a building not far from the lab where Mourly Vold worked in the Advanced Research Group. He became a regular dinner guest at the small farm owned by Mourly Vold and Francine a short distance from Schenectady.

"The pay is good," he said to them one evening, "but the job puts a strain on my integrity, if you know what I mean. In fact, I spend most of the day lying faster than a dog can trot."

Humberhill was always quite sentimental about the old days. He kept in close touch with the old gang, and often had news of their comings and goings. "That was the finest time of my life," he said once. "I wouldn't mind living it all over again, if someone gave me the chance."

They were sitting in the living room by the fire. Francine was there also, brushing the hair of her younger daughter, Meg. She pulled the brush slowly through the girl's hair in a steady rhythm that relaxed them both. Certain bright filaments of hair loved the brush so much that they lifted up and pointed toward it after every stroke.

When his remark failed to provoke any response from his friend, Humberhill asked, "What about you?"

"Oh . . ." Mourly Vold said. "No. I wouldn't want to live it over again. I spent too much of that time cold and hungry."

"Listen," Humberhill told him. "You may have spent some of that time cold and hungry, but you spent all of that time *great*."

For a complete list of books available from Penguin in the United States, write to Dept. DG, Penguin Books, 299 Murray Hill Parkway, East Rutherford, New Jersey 07073.

For a complete list of books available from Penguin in Canada, write to Penguin Books Canada Limited, 2801 John Street, Markham, Ontario L3R 1B4.